Italian Canadians at Table:
A Narrative Feast in Five Courses

ESSENTIAL ANTHOLOGIES SERIES 3

**Canada Council
for the Arts**　　**Conseil des Arts
du Canada**

Guernica Editions Inc. acknowledges the support of the Canada Council
for the Arts and the Ontario Arts Council. The Ontario Arts Council
is an agency of the Government of Ontario.

We acknowledge the financial support of the Government of Canada
through the Canada Book Fund (CBF) for our publishing activities.

Italian Canadians at Table:
A Narrative Feast in Five Courses

Edited by

LORETTA GATTO-WHITE & DELIA DE SANTIS

GUERNICA

TORONTO • BUFFALO • BERKELEY• LANCASTER (U.K.)
2013

Loretta Gatto-White & Delia De Santis, editors
Michael Mirolla, general editor
David Moratto, book designer
Guernica Editions Inc.
P.O. Box 117, Station P, Toronto (ON), Canada M5S 2S6
2250 Military Road, Tonawanda, N.Y. 14150-6000 U.S.A.

Distributors:
University of Toronto Press Distribution,
5201 Dufferin Street, Toronto (ON), Canada M3H 5T8
Gazelle Book Services, White Cross Mills, High Town, Lancaster LA1 4XS U.K.
Small Press Distribution, 1341 Seventh St., Berkeley, CA 94710-1409 U.S.A.

First edition.
Printed in Canada.

Legal Deposit – Third Quarter
Library of Congress Catalog Card Number: 2012951263
Library and Archives Canada Cataloguing in Publication

Italian Canadians at table : a narrative feast in five courses / editor:
Loretta Gatto-White, Delia De Santis.

(Essential anthologies series ; 3)
Issued also in electronic format.
ISBN 978-1-55071-675-7

1. Canadian literature (English)--Italian Canadian authors. 2. Italian
Canadians--Literary collections. 3. Canadian literature (English)--21st
century. 4. Italian Canadians--Food. 5. Food in literature. I. Gatto-White,
Loretta II. De Santis, Delia, 1943- III. Series: Essential anthologies series
(Toronto, Ont.) ; 3

PS8235.I8I73 2013   C810.8'0851071   C2012-906960-4

*I dedicate this book to the memory of my late beloved husband,
Jim White, whose passion for life, art, good food and all things Italian
inspires me still, and to my late father, Gary Gatto, the best cook
and raconteur in the family. Mi mancate entrambi.*
— LORETTA GATTO-WHITE

*To my late parents, Antonia and Saverio, and to my husband,
Ercole and our loving family.*
— DELIA DE SANTIS

Menu

Fourth Course: Contorno

Fifth Course: Dolce

MENU

Introduction

A bite of Canada's culinary minestra might taste like smoked salmon stuffed perogies, on a bed of curried lentil couscous layered with foie gras quenelle, garnished with a crackling of pemmican prosciutto and a dusting of dulse in a pool of ginger, lemon grass and sake reduction, followed by a molten butter tart a la mode; a feast to which every culture calling Canada home has contributed.

Canada's rich food culture has run the gamut from old world culturally diverse commercial and domestic artisan products available wherever predominantly working-class "ethnic peoples" settled, such as Toronto's Ward, Montreal's "The Main" and Vancouver's Chinatown, to post-war, French-inspired haute cuisine, or as I call it the grand hotel, country club scoff of smugly prosperous1950s Canada.

Prosperity also created the new world fast-food nation purveying a distinctly American cuisine and bastardized old world ethnic dishes where Aunt Jemima and Betty Crocker "duke it out" for shelf space with Mama Bravo and Chef Boyardee. In our twenty-first century, we see a return to old world artisan products and the slow-food cultural values attached to their production, sale and consumption, now ironically the purview of the privileged class.

The progressive acculturation of Italian cuisine into Canada's national culinary identity is a testament to this social phenomenon. At the turn of the century, Toronto's Italian bakeries vied for supremacy, some even resorting to branding their loaves to ensure the customer quality and authenticity,in Muskoka, family-run macaroni factories produced artisan pasta extruded from bronze-dies. Socially ambitious Italian families fed the gentry's hunger for fine European comestibles, opening wholesale and retail gourmet food emporia throughout our urban centres.

Still, Italian cuisine, especially that from the *Mezzogiorno*, the origin of a large share of Canada's Italian émigrés, was disdained by restaurant patrons who regarded French haute cuisine as being truly refined, even though it was usually cooked and served by Italians. The economic turmoil of the Depression devastated many Italian family-owned food businesses which, being reliant on a labyrinthine system of community banks, precursors to credit unions, failed early and hard taking the Italian communities' entrepreneurial house of cards with it. This interruption lasted until "the boys came home" when Italian cuisine was once again relegated to behind the kitchen doors, except for its new canned and frozen incarnations, whose stereotyped public face was represented by Mama Bravo then signora Michelina, et al.

Greasy spoons and restaurant chains served-up giant bowls of gluey, over-cooked spaghetti drowning in an acrid pool of canned tomato sugo graced by polpette as hard as bocce balls and crowned with a sprinkling of ersatz parmesan, washed down with domestic red plonk from gallon jugs, or worse, if it was a festive occasion something sparkling like Spumante Bambino.

The public's concept of sophisticated five star cuisine was still solidly French with few exceptions, until the 1980s when Northern Italian cuisine, by little stretch of the culinary palate, became trendy with its focus on butter, cream, truffles, risotto, polenta and veal, and a notable absence of strong tastes and colours. Its soft and velvety textures were an easy segue from central France to Italy.

But something has happened to our palates, arteries and social aspirations between then and now. We want to eat food that is as sustaining of our bodies as it is of our environment. We want the rustic produce and products directly out of the farmer's field or the artisan's hand, to gather-up our families' generations on Sunday and share boldly coloured and flavourful food from big steaming majolica platters. We'll plant heritage tomatoes amongst the genteel delphiniums in our urban courtyards, challenge city hall for our right to raise chickens and wood-roast peppers in midtown backyards, forage in city parks for spring cicoria, and take courses on how to cure and hang our own Berkshire Pork prosciutto in downtown lofts.

In short, Canadians have begun a risorgimento of homey, predominantly southern Italian cuisine which resonates beyond the domestic kitchen to the gregarious communal restaurant table, the bustling boisterous farmers' markets, the clang and clatter of outdoor cafés, the weekend line-ups at the deli counters of the few remaining mom and pop's Italian grocers where you can run a tab and delivery is free. As the cheekily chauvinistic saying goes: it seems there are only two kinds of people, Italians and those who wish they were. Melanzane, spaghetti, polpette, rapini, oregano, peperoncini, baccalà, tripe, anchovies, bottarga, pecorino Romano, the yin yang of agro-dolce verdure and the deep dark red of Nero d'Avola — bring it on! cries Canada. The cucina casalinga and cucina povera are the new haute cuisines.

There's no poverty of taste, history or tradition in the rich cultural heritage of our Italian Canadian cuisine; its bon gusto and piquancy is served-up in these entertaining narratives. Tutti a tavola a mangiare.

— Loretta Gatto-White

First Course: Antipasto

Plump Eggplant

MARISA DE FRANCESCHI

ONE OF MY relatives once suggested it would be far better if I took up cooking instead of writing. She may have had a point. What sheer, unadulterated pleasure it is to cook up a delightful dinner, to soak up all the oohs and ahhs that come with the territory. Rejections? I hardly get a one. How infinitely more satisfying it can be, at times, to poke the sharp end of a knife into the purple skin of a plump eggplant, to feel that spongy texture, to slice it into thick disks for grilling after brushing them with a bit of olive oil and freshly ground pepper, or to dice for an autumn *peperonata*. How joyous to see the ease with which I can coax the bitter juices out by simply sprinkling the slices or chunks with salt, and letting all stand for a while, draining the unpleasant dark liquid into the sink. How much more difficult to coax words from my pen, to extract the bitter juices from life and drain them away. Instead, I tend to catch and store them, and turn them into stories. Ah, yes, this too can be sheer unadulterated pleasure, except when I unintentionally pour salt into wounds, and bring forth shivers of pain. More often, my poking into life's mysteries is a Herculean feat which brings ill results: rejections, criticism, noses twisted out of joint, hurt egos ... Sometimes applause, as in cooking, but how much more safe is cooking with its predictable results: always applause? I have maimed many with my words, but I have yet to poison or kill anyone with my *ragù* or *pesto* or *gnocchi* or fragrant autumn apple pie. Simple things matter too. They relax the mind.

When that relative advised I give up the pen and take up the cooking utensils, she was certain this was an either or situation; one could not do both. She was wrong, of course. The rituals that sustain the physical body can lie side by the side with the rituals that sustain the mind and spirit. In fact, as my own experience can testify, one must pay attention to all these facets in order to nourish and sustain each. I know what it feels like to be slowly shrivelling, decaying, composting. Or was it desiccating from not being able to fortify and nourish the body, from not being able to swallow and hold anything down? But I'll leave that for a later chapter.

Liliane Welch, the Luxemburg-born, Canadian author with a bit of Italian blood, frequently wrote about the interdependence of the natural world and the fingerprint man has put on it. In one of her books, *Untethered in Paradise,* she constructed essays on some of her favourite artists: Rodin, Cezanne, Chardin, Monet, and more. Her piece on Cezanne entitled "Cezanne's Heroes" struck me as exemplifying the connection I want to make between the simple things of nature and the whole of who we are. At the Museum of Fine Art in Basel, Switzerland, as she viewed *Still Life with Apples and Peaches,* one of more than 170 of Cezanne's still lifes, she talked about the bond between "natural and man-made things." I was particularly captivated by her statement: "It is as though the apples and peaches remembered the sun that ripened them ..." In that essay, she also says she is convinced "the secret heart of things resides in a simple yellow apple which rests on a pile of peaches ..."

Sometimes, I think we become so caught up in our man-made world that we undervalue, underestimate and even scorn the simple things of nature. There was a time when I used to scoff at my grandmother and my aunts' obsession with their gardens, orchards, and animals and their total abstinence from anything to do with the arts! But I learned later that, without taking reasonable care of the body, it becomes impossible to sustain the other.

Man-made masterpieces like Cezanne's and Welch's essays make us stop and think. If, as Welch writes: "All his life Cezanne persevered, painted humble things, and did not listen to his father's admonition: 'My son, think of the future. You die by being a genius, and you eat by having money'," what does it say about the importance of apples and oranges?

I laughed when I read Cezanne's father's words to his son. They sound much like my old relative's admonitions when I failed to take up cooking as a profession. But what can we infer about the fact that this work of art is still around after ninety five years? That Cezanne is still with us? That this is how he chose to reel in a bit of eternity?

In another masterpiece, the movie *Like Water for Chocolate*, we are again exposed to the intricate and intimate connection between food and spirit and art. In a Cinderella type story, Tita's wretched and domineering mother will not allow this younger daughter to marry the man she loves, dictating instead that her older daughter must have him, despite the fact that he too is in love with the younger Tita. As the youngest child, Tita must take care of her mother, and help run the household. This magnificent film pulls together all manner of food and food related symbolism in order to show that the overlooked Tita can indeed entice and hold on to her lover through the preparation of delectable food despite the fact that she and her beloved do not consummate their love sexually. In contrast, the older sister, who becomes the wife, is not able to coerce her husband to love her in spite of the fact that they share the same bed. This spiritual and emotional divide is portrayed with food. Tita's sister, the new bride, is incapable of preparing the delicacies that Tita prepares; she is incapable of being Tita. Food, then, takes on spiritual significance. It represents Tita's nurturing qualities. Food also takes on artistic value since the manner in which Tita presents it to her beloved becomes a visual feast, as they say.

The interdependence of body, soul and spirit is obvious in the film. When any one aspect is suffering, the others follow suit. Ironically, in this film, the wife who does not cook becomes gluttonous and dies as a result of her little sister's culinary talents, finally leaving the husband/lover for Tita. In the dramatic ending, when Tita and her lover finally consummate their love, and all the forces collide, we are shocked at the eruption that ensues. Watching this scene, and the entire film, I once again go back to my premise that, if we hold back on any one of our needs, the whole will suffer the consequences.

In the fall, when there is a bounty for us who live in Essex County, we have traditionally followed the templates of nature. My husband will make wine because the grapes are now available; I will roast red peppers, carefully peel off their thin, charred and now brittle skins, clean out the seeds and freeze the pulp for winter antipasto or an appetizer when I will defrost the peppers and toss them with a bit of my own home grown garlic and parsley and a bit of Italian extra virgin olive oil. Whenever I open one of my frozen packages of red peppers, I will inevitably inhale the fragrant scent of autumn and recall the day I drove to Harrow to purchase my peppers, which I used to pick myself, but arthritis has reared its ugly head. I will recall the day I roasted them on the barbecue, peeled them and stuffed them into plastic bags. I will recall sitting at my picnic table outside in the back yard cleaning and preparing the fragrant peppers while Eddie, my little Jack Russell, looked on, intent on snatching a piece of this food he has never seen since this is his first autumn, and he is still a pup. I will recall the stereophonic symphony the sparrows played for their audience of two: myself and Eddie, hundreds of them twittering in our cedar trees, flitting about the yard, to and from the birdfeeder, so trusting of myself and Eddie. And I will recall how I felt in the fall. At times like this, I feel enveloped in pure joy. It is a feeling of such deep satisfaction that it supersedes any type of sexual enjoyment, for that seems selfish while this seems an act of embracing the entire universe. *Like Water for Chocolate* comes to mind.

I'm sure that my grandmother and my aunts and uncles who farmed and worked the land, who raised chickens, ducks, pigs and cattle must have experienced the same feelings. I used to wonder how anyone could get through life without picking up a book, reading a story, but I suppose they expressed themselves with their gardens and barns, and read the heavens. Whenever I have done hard, physical labour, working myself to a sweat, working until my muscles ached and longed for rest, I also remember the feeling of satisfaction one gets from physical exertion, the sound sleep one sleeps after a long hard day of picking tomatoes, or hoeing weeds in the fields.

But it is no different from the feeling of satisfaction I get when I get up from my writing chair and lift my weary hands from the computer keys or drop my pen after editing or writing out thoughts. The muscles of the body let go and relax as if I've just plucked bushels of peppers from their plants, snapped baskets of Italian beans from their vines.

The first rose of the season always comes to keep me company at my desk as I write. My husband will go out secretly and cut it, place it in a vase and set it beside my computer, something he will do throughout the season. It never fails to bring a smile to my face. I myself never find the time to go out and cut a rose for my work room, but he does. He tries to bring in the most fragrant of our roses: a 'Mister Lincoln' dark red or a 'Tropicana' with hues of red/ orange. When I approach my study, which is often a chaotic mess, much to my dismay, it is the rose I will notice first because it is the rose which will perfume the air and I will be aware of its presence even before I enter the room, the scent preceding the actual sight of the flower. I will inevitably smile. I will smile at my romantic man, but also at the incongruity of things. This beautiful feat of nature, this work of magnificent art which has inspired the likes of now famous artists, is in such contrast to the austere lines of the computer, which are so different from the frilly, delicate beauty of the rose. The twinkling lights of my apparatus, which indicate I am in communication with the world, the hum of the machines, the whirr when I press a button and print out a page jar me. The contrast is inescapable and yet, for me, they are entwined, the one feeding and nurturing the other much like my poking into a plump purple egg-plant and getting it ready for grilling, or my poking into my stories feeling their sponginess and getting them ready for the page.

tomatoes

DOMENICO CAPILONGO

alla maniera di George Elliott Clarke

I GOT PASSIONATE *pomodori freschi* big red fat ass sons-of-bitches tomatoes. round firm mother fuckers perfect for salad. I got tiny testicle cherry tomatoes bouncing up a storm like you wouldn't believe. watermelon sized beefsteak tomatoes ready for a hot veal *sangwich* if you know what I mean. how about some smooth virgin plum *pomodori* to make the best salsa from here to halifax? *caro mio*, you know who started all of this? columbus found *pomodori* for you and me in 1493.

Summer and Figs

JOSEPH RANALLO

IN 1952, WHEN I was eleven, my family emigrated from one of Italy's smallest regions, Molise, to one of Canada's largest, British Columbia. In Molise, I had completed grade five, but because I didn't speak English, when I enrolled in the Rossland elementary school, I was placed in grade four. Such was the E.S.L. strategy of the time. However, soon I became adept at communicating in three distinct languages: the Molisano I spoke at home with my mother; the semiformal Italian I used with the few non-Molisani Italians in Rossland; and the strained, broken English I spoke with my non-Italian friends. I was fully aware that, though I could make myself understood in these three different languages, I was not really fluent in any one of them.

Despite the language barrier, as I grew up, I adapted well to the new culture and I felt proud that my English speaking friends enjoyed my mother's cooking, especially her spaghetti, gnocchi, polenta, baccalà, and home-cured Italian prosciutto, salame, and sausages. Unfortunately, though, I never managed to recover the two-year setback and move up into my peer grade. When I did finish high school, I was already twenty years old. Ironically, next to the teachers and support staff, I was the oldest person in the school, a situation that I bore in mild discomfort, but with good humour.

Before my last year of high school and during my first two years of university, to help to pay for my studies, I spent the summer months working for the Trail-based Inland Gas Company that, among other things, installed the first domestic natural gas services in my spectacular region of the West Kootenays. Each hot new day, the summer students and the seasonal workers who had been hired on a temporary basis showed up, lunch buckets in hand, waiting patiently to be assigned to one of several teams that were charged with the responsibility of installing brand new gas services to the local residences.

The favourite team leader, by far, was a joyful, carefree Calgarian bachelor named Jack. He was a fun-loving, creative welder who was clear with his directives and generally easy to appease. All that he requested from his subordinates was that they did their jobs well, whether it was digging a ditch with a hand shovel, loading and unloading the truck orderly, cleaning the work site before departing, or turning the pipes that he had to join systematically and evenly so that he could showcase his skill as a master welder.

Jack was far from being the typical construction welder. Even to those who hardly knew him, he presented an intriguing blend of vision and ambition. He had applied to teach welding at the Southern Alberta Institute of Technology in Calgary, and by his late twenties, had established a reputation as a promising leader with a future. The workers acknowledged that Jack had a forthright presence about him. He was well informed and well read in literature, politics, and history. He was especially fond of the sensual poetry of D.H. Lawrence, and loved music, especially the popular songs of the day. His appetite for learning was legendary. After the day's work, Jack became a formidable orator in the bar room political debates. For those of us who were summer student relief workers, Jack became the charismatic dream boss. We all wanted to be on his crew.

In late July, quite by accident, Jack invited me to join him for the day. His customary helper, who had already worked with the company for several of the spring months, was needed elsewhere in some other capacity. Jack made sure that I understood clearly this arrangement was only temporary and not a permanent partnership. Nonetheless, I was both delighted and grateful for the invitation.

When we arrived at our destination, we were greeted by a dignified gentleman with a white mustache and wavy silver hair who spoke English with a distinct Italian accent.

"*Da quale parte dell'Italia venite?*" I asked him.

"*Io sono da Grimaldi, in Calabria.*"

For the next few minutes, we exchanged pleasantries in our native dialects. I switched to English when I noticed what I interpreted to be a disapproving look that had crept over Jack's usually jovial face. I suspected that he probably felt uncomfortable being excluded. I feared that, by talking in Italian, I had cut short my work association with Jack. Luckily, I was wrong.

Within minutes, we got started with the work. Jack seemed pleased that I was quite prepared to do the heavy, tedious, and dusty tasks such as digging and drilling into the concrete basement walls with a Hilty. He was also gratified to note that I had brought a lunch bucket. For Jack, this meant that he did not have to bring an additional labourer with him nor would he have to drive me around to find a place to eat. Jack also confided that he was glad that he did not have to eat his lunch alone in the truck.

We worked hard most of the morning. When we stopped for the coffee break, Jack asked: "What's in your bucket that smells so good, mate?", eyeing my crusty bread, golden chicken drumstick roasted in a veneer of tomato and red pepper sauce, shiny black oil-cured olives, and succulent white grapes.

"Does your mother always pack your lunch?"

"Most of the time."

"You're so lucky she does, all I have is a mystery-meat sandwich on pasty white bread I bought at the deli and some of their industrial strength coffee."

Just before lunch, the old Italian gentleman, who had mysteriously vanished for a couple of hours, suddenly reappeared with a tray of freshly cut salame, prosciutto, and hard cheese. On a second plate, he carried a loaf of thickly sliced white Italian homemade bread with a hard, firm crust. The gentleman disappeared momentarily again and returned with a bowl of grapes and a few fresh, purple figs.

"*Fiche!*" I practically shouted. "I have not seen them since I left Italy ten years ago. I love them. My grandfather used to grow them in his orchard. I used to eat them by the handful."

"*Per un giovane come te,*" the old man winked, "*è impossibile mangiar troppo fiche.*"

My face must have turned red at the double entendre. In most regions of Italy, the female form of fico was the most common synonym for the female genitalia. I was glad Jack didn't ask me to translate what the old man had said.

He left again and returned with a half gallon bottle of red Zinfandel wine he had made the previous fall. Although we were forbidden to drink alcohol on the job, in appreciation for the old gentleman's hospitality, Jack decided to make a slight exception this one time. He had heard there were only three things that could offend an Italian man more than insulting his wine: disrespecting his mother, wife, and daughters. Jack declared that it would be most impolite to insult our generous host.

"We will drink only one glass now," Jack said, asking me to translate, "otherwise we won't be able to work sensibly in the heat of the afternoon sun." Jack knew that I was old enough to drink alcohol. I had already told him my age on the way over.

"Then we save the rest for after quitting time," the old gentleman answered in his broken English as he laid out the food on a wooden bench for us to enjoy. "Eat the fig first," he said, winking at me again. "When you are young and single, you never know how long it will be before you are offered another one. They don't grow around here, you know. I was sent these by a relative in the states."

At the end of the day, we cleaned up a bit earlier than the customary four o'clock. When the old gentleman brought out the remainder of the wine and some other cold meats and bread, we moved to the back lawn and sat on his garden chairs. Jack gave me permission to drink one more glass while he drank two. "Both the food and the wine are exquisite," Jack remarked as he thanked the old gentleman. "You Italians are fortunate; you eat food that has been prepared and served to you by loving hands and not someone who is being paid to ask you if there will be fries with your order." The old man smiled and nodded in appreciation, obviously satisfied that his generosity had not passed unnoticed.

On the way back to the office, Jack asked me if I would like to stay on as his helper for the few remaining weeks of the summer. Without hesitation, I responded with an enthusiastic yes. The only condition he lightheartedly imposed on me was a pleasant one. I had to speak Italian to all our Italian clients. "I know that the more Italian you speak," Jack kidded, "the more and better the wine and food will get." To my pleasant surprise, Jack, who seemed wiser than his years, turned out to be right.

That hot summer, we serviced many of the Italian residences in the Trail area. Almost without exception, as soon as I spoke Italian, the food and wine appeared. When it came to drinking wine on the job, Jack made many concessions. He did not want to offend any of our hosts. Most of the time, we were only given cold meats and cheese. On rare occasions, we were treated to entire meals: freshly cooked aromatic pasta and gnocchi dishes that turned concrete dingy, dark basements into fragrant, joyous parlours; pizzas with their pungent blend of baked tomato and cheese; or the different kinds of polenta that reflected the culinary customs brought to Trail from the different regions of Italy. Jack already knew that, with northern Italians, polenta was a real staple of their diet. He joked good naturedly, that he had heard from reliable sources that Cominco Northern Italian workers actually packed it in their lunch buckets.

Whenever we were offered a new food, like lupini or finocchio, Jack asked me to pronounce its Italian name several times. On the way back to the office, he would repeat the word over and over until he got it just right. He even memorized the second verse of Nicola Paone's *Tony the Ice Man*, a lighthearted, popular Italian American tune of the fifties. The section he committed to memory consists exclusively of a litany of anglicized staple Italian foods:

> I see un provolone, un salsiccione, nu pastrami, nu big salame,
> Un capicollo, na meatballa, na scarola, a gorgonzola, la
> mozzarella, la, la, la

In fact, when Jack saw a surname that ended with a vowel on his morning work order, he began singing this verse in anticipation of the reception we would likely get at that house. For him, this verse became a kind of anthem, much like the ones sung at the start of major athletic events.

As we worked in the scorching sun, Jack, acetylene torch in hand, like a latter-day Prometheus bringing fire and warmth to a cold, indifferent humanity, would sometimes lift the goggles off his sparkling, green-blue eyes and talk to me. "Women are like figs," he would say, obviously delighted with his uncanny ability to weld words into metaphors with the same ease and agility that he could weld steel pipes together. "D.H. Lawrence has written a splendid poem about that. You should read it. In their prime, whether golden, purple, or black, on the outside they are firm, symmetrical, and shapely. But on the inside, they are all mysterious and oh so succulent, tantalizing, and sweet."

Practically every day, Jack would surprise me with some other memorable, striking extended metaphor in which at least one of its two elements was an item from the Italian menu we had been offered that particular day. "Black olives," he would say wistfully, "are enchanting. But only because they have been picked by full bodied, alluring dark skinned, southern Italian women in whose tender embraces lay the opiates of oblivion."

Sometimes, the metaphors became quite elusive, complex, philosophical, and personal. Occasionally, they even revealed a slight trace of vulnerability and insecurity that Jack's common, everyday vernacular guardedly camouflaged. "Most women love salame," Jack, who was beginning to entertain thoughts of marriage, would say pensively, "but they can soon tire of the same lacklustre brand. This is why the Italian meat industry wisely offers them an endless variety to choose from: Genoa, Friulano, Prosciutto, and Soppressata, to name only a few. Perhaps if we can present them with this infinite diversity, they might be less inclined to listen to the messages from the little men in the canoes between their thighs urging them to paddle away from the predictability of their matrimonial beds to explore other distant, exotic horizons."

These philosophical chats, on hot summer days, taught me a lesson that I could never have learned even at the most prestigious university. I learned there is something special about the Italian food we prepare and eat, the quasi religious attitude we have towards it, and, most of all, the magical words we choose to describe it. It was this food, given to us sincerely and unconditionally by people whom we hardly knew, which helped me earn Jack's admiration.

I really don't know to what extent these talks about my ancestral cuisine and Jack's passion for language influenced my unlikely determination to enrol in Honour's English in my last three years at the University of Victoria. Through Jack's poetic diction, inspired largely by his love of Italian food and the care and respect we give it, I learned to make my peace with English, the language that initially held me back when I first came to Canada. Now I wanted to embrace it fully. Without forgetting my native tongue, I came to love and respect English, my adopted language, a language that has given immortality to Chaucer, Shakespeare, Keats, Lawrence, and a host of other writers who at some time or other have paid their poetic homage to the joys of food.

And, in his own way, through his subliminal metaphors, Jack also taught me that perhaps, like lovemaking, the sheer enjoyment of good food is the most sensual experience we can engage in. On our tongues, we feel the granules of the ripe fig's seeds; with our eyes, we appreciate the delicate beauty of its near perfect symmetry; through our ears, if we listen closely enough, we hear the juicy gush of the first bite into a ripe fig. Put your nose to a warm ripe fig and inhale its subtle fragrance. When perfectly ripe, the humble fig, offers a sensual palatal delight almost unmatched by any other fruit. As D.H. Lawrence demonstrates, this is the stuff that poetry is made of. And, as poetry nourishes and calms the restless soul, Italian food satisfies the ever- yearning flesh.

An Extra Helping

LORETTA DI VITA

CONSIDERING THAT LANGUAGE originates from a people's life experience, it's no surprise that Italians have so many different terms for expressing generosity. Just like inhabitants of the Arctic have an extensive vocabulary to describe snow, the Italian lexicon is well-stocked with expressions describing a preoccupation with giving — especially as it relates to food. Anyone who knows Italians recognizes their inclination to dig deep into the refrigerator and basement *cantina,* to make sure guests never leave with a rumbling stomach. What predisposes the breed to this bountiful collective trait is more mysterious than the secret to a good *ragù* but, in Italian communities, rapport building has long been based on the gentle gesture of breaking bread.

As a first-generation Italian-Canadian growing up in a tradition-al-Italian household, I experienced first-hand the hospitable nature of my parents and grandparents, when welcoming guests into their homes (and a guest could be anyone from the accountant to the plumber). Anybody crossing their threshold, bearing the most min-imal smidgen of a friendly link, could easily be invited to a little something to nosh on — a *spuntino,* or snack, often ballooning into a midriff-expanding multi-course feast.

Many a non-occasion called for the uncorking of a cherished bottle of wine, and the slicing of some piquant cheese, topped off by a Sambuca-spiked espresso and crunchy hazelnut biscotti (there was always a zip-locked reserve in the freezer). My gracious parents would never breach etiquette and risk *brutta figura, or* lose face, by neglecting to show such basic courtesy toward a "visitor." Declining the decorous duo's urgings was a challenge, to say the least. The most emphatic "no" could easily have been interpreted as a "yes," and any "no-thank-you" was promptly countered with a "no-you-must-I-insist-please." The premise behind their well-intentioned insistence was that guests, minding their p's and q's, might be reluctant to help themselves or take more, fearing to be seen as mooches or, shudder, under-satiated.

The uninitiated reader should know that the give-take dance between the traditional Italian host and guest can be as tricky as the footwork to the Tarantella. Proper hosts understand that it's their responsibility to make the first move, since well-mannered guests would never dig in before the host offers. Even when the host *does* offer, it's expected that one show at least a hint of hesitation before accepting. While most polite exchanges would stop at this point, the Italian host pushes the etiquette envelope and further prompts the guest by saying, "*senza ceremonia*" [without ceremony or formality] — a bon ton term giving license to accept without any restraint. This fussing is often repeated until the guest, reeling in obligation, finally throws in the dinner napkin and accepts whatever's being handed over. All posturing aside, this protocol, as intricate as it is, usually comes with no strings attached and, as if to underline this noteworthy clause, Italian genteel folk will sometimes respond to a guest's "thank you" with "*per carità*" [for charity], implying that the generous act has been carried out without any expectation of repayment or reciprocity.

Colourful stories abound of Italians' over-zealous attempts at encouraging company to eat, and eat, and eat. A friend of mine enjoys recounting that as a youngster he found himself the hapless victim of affectionate torture — as I call it — at the hands of his well-meaning uncle who was hosting a family get-together. Beaming with pride, his zio insisted that he taste a slice — or rather, a chunk — of his legendary home-cured prosciutto. When my friend turned down the desiccated delicacy, his uncle became more persistent. "What are you sick?" he asked, half jokingly. "Why aren't you eating?" Finally, it was the ol' 'When I was your age, I could eat a horse' remark which caused his nephew to cave and chomp on the rubbery bit. After an arduous, unsuccessful mastication session, he escaped to the back porch, when his kindly uncle wasn't looking, and pitched the meaty morsel across the yard — smack dab into the tomato garden.

I could also tell many personal tales attesting to such unbending big-heartedness. My all-time favourite is the one about the octogenarian Italian man seated next to me on a flight to Rome. Over the roar of the plane's engines, I could hardly hear his strained voice, oddly reminiscent of Marlon Brando playing the Godfather. "*Mangia, mangia*," I finally understood. "It's a long way to Rome." No sooner had the aircraft begun its climb, than the generous stranger pulled out some crusty *panini* from his carry-on and pointed one in my direction. "Eat, eat," he insisted, clearly unwilling to entertain any of my polite excuses.

I remember how I'd cringe when my parents encouraged my friends to take another ladleful at the table. Looking back, it seems almost warped that I'd have been so embarrassed by their exemplary manner of sharing. I mean, if generosity is a lofty, noble ideal, which all God-fearing peoples strive for, why did I urgently command: "Stop, don't force them!" whenever my folks pushed my friends to have second servings? I say, with much shame, that their hyper hospitality often caused me, er, shame. Maybe it was the uniqueness of their behaviour that made me want to disappear into thin air. Admittedly, I worked hard at blending in and being like everybody else around me, living in my white-washed, non-ethnic neighbourhood. Oh, how I feared my inherited culture would rear its proud head, exposing me as "different"! Whenever I happened to visit a non-Italian pal's house, I was never, ever, pressed to eat when not so hungry, or take more when reluctant. Interestingly, at the time, I thought this was a good thing.

Now I can't help but wonder where the motivation behind all this bounty came from. I like to believe that, in most cases, it wasn't motivated by the all-too-familiar what's-in-it-for-me factor, or any ulterior motives (although I do remember some of my parents' *paesani* thinking they could influence their underachieving son's teacher to round up his grades to a passing mark by bringing her some fresh farm eggs). Suppressing even the slightest cynicism, I've concluded that the intentions of *generosi* Italians were mostly good,

and that they took great pride in branding themselves as unconditionally generous.

Growing up, I'd hear my relatives say "*favorite*" to visitors, when
offering them some chow, inviting them to partake if they so wished
(heh, little did the unsuspecting know that they'd get an arm twisted if they chose to decline ... but, I digress). The formal expression
was dropped rather rotely, as a token customary utterance — pretty
much the way one would say in English, "help yourself." I wonder if
the usage of this term, which derives from the Italian verb *favor-
ire* — meaning to favour, foster, support, or aid — might not also
have signified that the act of sharing fodder was a natural means
toward relationship building. While my parents, their parents, and
their parents' parents didn't count incoming text messages and
pokes, they surely sought connectedness and revelled in popularity
just like we do. (Is that *soo* wrong?) And what more genuine way was
there to initiate, cultivate and secure an enduring connection than
by generating the feel-goodness arising from the ritual of eating
good food in good company around the same table?

Continuing to scratch further in my search for more rationales
(or rationalizations?) explaining this charitable phenomenon, it's
plausible that the largesse displayed by migrant Italians, particularly
those originating from rural regions, had lots to do with a need to
validate themselves, after a long time of not having had much. By
giving the impression of having access to an unlimited supply of
food — a seemingly unending cornucopia — the implicit message
that they were no longer needy shone crystal clear: Not only was
there enough in the larder, but plenty more grub from where that
came.

Shifting to my reality: I've never been needy, thankfully. And
since I'm not prone to any keeping-up-with-the-Joneses neuroses, I
don't really have much to prove in terms of distinguishing myself
from the haves and the have-nots. So why, then, do I ask my dinner
guests twice — not once — if they'd care for another serving of, say,
risotto alla Milanese? "There's more in the kitchen," I sing song, even
when there's none left — the whole time hoping no one will call my
bluff. I admit that, on more than one occasion, I've nudged (alright,
pestered!) my invitees into scoffing more than they set out to, or ever

thought they were capable of ingesting. And as the hostess-with-the-mostess in the making, I have no qualms at dessert time, carting out two or three cakes, instead of one perfectly good one.

There's only one explanation for my personal preoccupation with wanting to feed (and possibly over-feed others)—and that's: culture. It's become apparent to me that cultural convention is difficult to smudge out, no matter how mighty the eraser. The rush of self-satisfaction that I feel (ta-da!) when presenting an overflowing platter of *antipasti*—meant for twelve to my party of six—riffs the titillation my kin experienced when they spoiled their guests. I'm convinced that I've acquired my long arms, which apparently haven't shrunk much in the process of assimilation, from a long line of compulsive givers. Sure, tradition gets watered down as Diaspora transfers it from its indigenous context to another paradigm, but habits run deep—just like bloodlines—no matter how long after, or how far from their inception.

As much as I try to distance myself from the customs which shadowed me in my formative years, I can't seem to escape them, and, in the right light, they still cast themselves alongside me. And although I take offense to the cheesy Olive-Garden-esque media stereotypes depicting my heritage—the kerchief *nonna* stirring a stove-top caldron, or the grinning, ruddy-faced *nonno* slicing an enormous, flour-dusted loaf of bread held tight under his armpit, beckoning viewers to step into their saccharine cosmos—the sentimental montages do seem a tad too familiar. Waving a white, lace tray doily, I acquiesce to the generosity gene: I'm unbendingly, unshakably and unequivocally of the same ilk. Let's face it—it's all in the hardwiring. In any case, whether my givingness is virtue or foible, I trust you'll forgive me if I should ever invite you to an extra helping—or two. After all, I can't help myself.

The Kitchen Table

CARLINDA D'ALIMONTE

This kitchen table,
draped in oil cloth
of reds and yellows,
is where our lives unfold,

where bags of newly bought groceries
are placed on Saturday mornings,
unpacked by small hungry hands
looking for Cocoa Puffs, marshmallows
and bananas not seen in this house for days,
where important things are prepared
from scratch — pasta, pastries, plans,
where we come together each day
to allay our hunger for food or belonging,
where homework is done after dinner,
where papers are lain, scrutinized,
where guests are seated
coaxed with sweets, lupines, olives, and wine,
where we play our hands of crazy eights and euchre
raising our voices, slapping the table to make a point,
where grandparents sit every night
reading the bible aloud,
where late-night talks in hushed voices
over coffee and biscuits find us
forever giggling.

The Birth and Rebirth of Biscotti

DOSOLINA COTRONEO

O Sole Mio
Che bella cosa è na jurnata 'e sole
n'aria serena doppo na tempesta!
Pe 'll'aria fresca pare già na festa
Che bella cosa na jurnata 'e sole.

Ma n'atu sole,
cchiù bello, oje ne'.
O sole mio sta 'nfronte a te!
O sole, o sole mio
sta 'nfronte a te ... sta 'nfronte a te!
—ENRICO CARUSO

FROM THE TIME I learned how to put one foot in front of the other, I remember the meandering aroma of Ma's almond biscotti bright and early on Saturday mornings, with Enrico Caruso's *O Sole Mio* playing in the background. This was considered her only "day off" from the assembly line at the chocolate factory, where she worked alongside other Italian immigrant women. Saturdays were sacred and reserved for baking, cooking, and cleaning. Sundays were dedicated to St. Anthony's Church, where Ma attended every mass from 8:00 a.m. till noon, followed by confession, her rosary group, and finally a quiet but filling family dinner.

My sisters and I always prayed for Ma and her Italian immigrant co-workers, "the teapots" as we called them since they all had the same build — short and stout. We prayed that they would patiently tolerate another week under the reign of the boss lady or "bossa" as they referred to her, an evil shrew of a woman who, although small in stature, had the voice and build of a man, ruled the assembly line with an iron fist. Indentured servants can only mildly describe the deplorable conditions they silently worked under. They froze in the winter, died of heat in the summer, and at 10:00 a.m. each day, looked forward to their 10 minute bathroom break — all for $1.75 an hour.

Less often than a blue moon let alone the death of a pope, "Bossa" would let the Italian ladies take home a ten pound, two-inch thick block of solid milk chocolate. Besides Christmas, birthdays, and summer holidays, this was one of the highlights of our childhood years. I remember Ma grating that chocolate, and gently spreading it on top of our beloved biscotti, every Saturday morning, with Enrico in the background.

It was those very biscotti that made fitting in next to impossible during many a memorable classroom lunchtime. The non-Italian children would snicker and sneer as the Italian kids would pull out their Nutella, mortadella, or provolone panini. While they unwrapped Oreos, Chips Ahoy, or the dreaded Wagon Wheel, the Italian kids would carefully unwrap their biscotti, and ever-so delicately dunk it into their thermos of hot milk with a shot or two of espresso and a couple of teaspoons of sugar. Trading and sharing was never an option, as we were wise beyond our years to not forego our delicacy for a store-bought cookie and a can of no-name pop.

Fast-forward a few decades, and those same people are standing in line at the local Starbuck's ordering themselves a latte, cappuccino, or frappucino, with a biscotti on the side. Who would have ever believed that our daily breakfast and school snack would be the catalyst in converting the "Cakes" to latte and biscotti, while generating billions of dollars for upscale trendy coffee shops popping up on every corner of the globe?

Over the years, many bold and desperate souls have dared to ask Ma to divulge her biscotti recipe. Her answer: a brief but direct "No!" According to Ma, the recipe has been in her family for generations. Ever fearful of allowing the trappings of old-age to hinder her memory, Ma has a copy tucked away in a safety deposit box at a bank, somewhere in the hills of Calabria. I only hope Pop remembers where the key is.

According to village lore, a beautiful young woman with a tiny waist but ample bosom, milky and creamy porcelain skin concocted the first batch of biscotti the people of the tiny, remote, and rural Calabrian village of La Petra Mala (the Bad Rock) had ever tasted. Word of Filomena's sweet and crunchy, yet delicate and light confections spread like fresh gossip throughout the village of only 89 and, in no time, the virginal young woman had many a suitor knocking on her father's door.

Ma still cries when she gets to this part. It was only three days before his initiation into the priesthood when young Gentile Garbato fell under the spell of Filomena's tempting tasty treats. After only one bite, Father Marcello nodded in agreement, sputtering out the words, "il cuore vuole quello che il cuore vuole," (the heart wants what the heart wants.) And just like that, and a dozen of Filomena's biscotti, Father Marcello led the matrimonial procession through the village streets merely three days later, barely enough time for poor Gentile Garbato's mother, Sarta, to sew her only son a decent suit.

The Garbatos went on to create a biscotti empire, at least by Petra Mala standards. One that even the ever-feared mafia could not sink their teeth into. In fact, it's been said that, to preserve the family's reputation for freshness and secrecy, Gentile and Filomena's two daughters, Mendola and Nocilla, would wake in the middle of the night to shuck the hazelnuts and walnuts for the sought-after biscotti their parents would prepare in a wood-burning oven before sunrise.

Details of how the recipe ended up in Ma's family, when she had absolutely no relation to Filomena or Gentile, besides a once or twice-removed cousin on her great-grandfather's side, remain sketchy to this day. Although none of that matters provided that Ma continues to bake us her almond biscotti until the day she feels her daughters and granddaughters are ready to carry the torch.

Do I frequent the local cafes and trendy corner coffee shops where ordering a coffee and a biscotti sounds like a hip new language? I hesitate to say "yes." I admit theirs cannot hold a candle to Ma's decadent honey almond, hazelnut chocolate, amaretto almond, or apricot almond, but I do enjoy the camaraderie, fellowship and a read through the daily papers. Does Ma approve of her daughter's participating in such activity? Absolutely not. In her words, "no like" and "I no believe" basically explain how she feels about the biscotti and the hideously outrageous prices of their coffees.

I try not to laugh as I patiently stand in line behind those hipsters and take pleasure in hearing them ever-so carefully and proudly order up their frothy lattes, cappuccinos, or Americanos, feeling almost fluent in our mother-tongue — doppio lungo, grande, and venti.

Watching the young barista feverishly prepare my tall decaf-Americano with steamed milk, accompanied by Enrico in the background, I cannot help but crack a smile as I think back to my little red thermos filled with half espresso, half hot milk, two shots of sugar, and occasionally one raw beaten egg, (l'ouvo sbatutto). Ma would toss in a honey almond or hazelnut chocolate biscotti or two, and there was my childhood breakfast of champions.

Coffee Envy

LORETTA DI VITA

WITH THE SAME wistfulness that Seinfeld's TV buddy, George Costanza, longed to be a war history buff, I wish I were a bonafide coffee drinker. You see I'm not like most people who can simply slip into a Starbucks whenever needing a boost, pull out their club cards and order their preferred foamy concoctions. I suffer from coffee envy. On the rare occasion that I've been in a coffee house, I feel so underground, so out of place, that I might as well be patronizing an opium den.

There's good reason I can't hava any java. Let's start with some background. When my mother was born, my grandmother lived without her husband in his miniscule Italian home village, only a pizza toss away from her own. But in those post-war days, geographical distance was a gazillion times wider than it is now, so she was practically considered a foreigner. She lived alone not because she was a widow or *tsk-tsk* a divorcée, but since her husband had emigrated to Canada to lay down roots so that my grandmother and mother could later follow. During my grandfather's lengthy absence, my *nonna* was suspiciously tracked by the townsfolk like any outsider would be. One slip, one indulgence too many, one extra self-allotted luxury and she'd be chastised for having too much fun while her hubby was not there or, worse than that, questioned about the fiscal provenance of such extravagance. Wishing to deflect criticism and keep her reputation intact, she opted out of public displays of merriment, allowing herself and my mother some treats only when they'd travel to the nearest big city, where people didn't know them, or care.

One of the pleasures my grandmother rebuffed was coffee. Drinking the hot brew in solitaire, outside of the acceptable zone of mixed company, was seen by the respectable water-fetching gals hovering by the town well as a man's perk. My grandmother was much too feminine and reserved to engage in such manly nonsense; and my mother, following in her mother's dainty footsteps, never acquired the habit of coffee drinking. Hence, in proper lineage decorum neither have I.

So now you have the history and emotional baggage brewing behind my coffee abstinence. Blame it on habit, conditioning, role modelling, and even evolution — generations before me of caffeine avoidance make it physically (and psychologically?) difficult for me to tolerate the amber nectar. Call me coffee intolerant. I've tried to drink the wake-y juice on rare occasion (under peer pressure). But every time I do, my heart, which normally *thump-thumps* in a predictably controlled manner, percolates its way into triple and quadruple flips and repeat performances on top of that — a veritable cardiovascular Cirque du Soleil act.

Like all the coffee lovers across the globe, I would love to cradle a cuppa joe and feel its comforting warmth whenever my hands need warming up, find solace in its velvety taste when my soul needs stroking, and get an eye-opening buzz when my eyes would rather shut closed. But, I can't: The after-jitters aren't worth the momentary delight. I've tried faking it — going through the motions trying to fit in by downing a mug of decaffeinated coffee, only to be made to feel like a socially backward bumpkin or a plain ol' watered-down bore by die-hard coffee connoisseurs. Decaf? Have you no imagination? Why settle for the faux stuff when you can have the stimulatingly real thing?

I recall once enjoying a lovely meal with my Euro-sophisticate friends in a fancy-shmancy fusion restaurant. When the waiter nodded to each diner, inviting coffee orders, the requests grew more and more elaborate — Doppio Macchiato, Upside Down Double Blended, Triple Mocha Iced, Yuayang — the selections were as stylishly varied as my glamorous posse. "Make mine a regular decaf," I said when my turn came, hoping not to bring dinner conversation to a coffee-bean grinding halt. Well, not only did my bland choice suspend table chatter; it seized it, choked it and threw it against the wall. The ensuing silence was thick enough to slice the most robust coffee bean in half. Finally it was the waiter who spoke. Flapping his white-gloved hand in the air, he snootily asked: *Mademoiselle, but why doo u ate zee life?*

I don't hate life. In fact, I cling to it, like coffee grounds to a paper filter. But I have resigned myself to forever being a café by-stander, watching insiders with envy — all the while wishing I, too, were a coffee drinker.

Giant Rabbits and the Best Way to Barbeque

LORETTA GATTO-WHITE

IN THE SIXTIES, my father built our cottage next to his brothers' and sister's on a large tract of land in Muskoka, outside of Huntsville; their propinquity ensured a practical and cultural 'comfort zone' not only within our extended family, but to the Italian community of Huntsville as well.

Mention Muskoka, and what leaps to mind is ruinously expensive lake front properties, and glossy features in *Canadian House and Home* of fabulous cottages artfully staged, framing their well-heeled, urban owners. But, there is another face to Muskoka. Italian immigration of the last century extended beyond Ontario's urban centres as the men followed the railway north, many ending-up working in Huntsville's tannery and playing in its ironically named Anglo-Canadian Leather Company Band. Eventually, some opened their own enterprises such as a macaroni factory, catering mainly to the needs of this community. Their cultural presence is all but invisible in Huntsville now, surviving in the few remaining lyrical patronymics such as Pesando, Strano and Terziano.

These were our family's *compares* and *comares*, treated with the deference one shows to aunts and uncles. Each cottage season they came bearing trays of fluffy gnocchi, rabbits, and steaks of venison and moose, which were exchanged in our informal economy of hospitality with bags of panini, olive oil, salume and cheeses all brought from the city, and of course, my father's wine. They would stay to catch-up on town gossip, play cut-throat games of bocce, then sit around the over-sized picnic table my father made to eat peppery capicollo, sweet wood-roasted peppers, tart pickled eggplant and salty black infornata olives washed down with fiery grappa. My father produced this deceptively innocent-looking liquor from the must left by the grape pressings, which were then distilled in a homemade contraption involving a kettle, fine copper pipe and endless patience.

The centre of our social and culinary lives was the outdoor brick barbeque built by one of my father's friends, Rino, a convivial bricklayer of boundless energy and goodwill. It was the focus of our family's meals and gatherings and stood for twenty-five years on our tract of the Gatto family's campo before needing repair.

Our cottage summers were spent grilling all manner of beasts and vegetables 'sulla legna', that is over the glowing coals of a hardwood fire. The tannins and sugars in the wood imparted a smoky-sweet aroma and flavour; the slow cooking produced an incredible succulence over which formed a delicious amber crust which needed no condiment. My favourite was rabbit bathed in white wine, olive oil, a bit of garlic and a brush of rosemary. The autumn roasting of bushels of sweet red peppers, to be preserved later in olive oil, garlic and basil, was the bitter-sweet dénouement to yet another cottage-closing season.

This is where, every summer, as children, my three sisters and I and our numerous cousins safely ran amok from cottage to cottage begging treats and slugging back Freshie, building forts and chasing jack rabbits into the musty, insect-infested hinterland that was the woods between and around our cottages. Except when we weren't crashing into the rollers on Kinsmen's beach, cannon-balling from the floating docks, or scavenging for pop bottles to redeem for penny candy at Mrs. May's snack bar.

In the evening, after dinner, which quelled the queasiness brought-on by too much sun, sweets and excitement, we were bathed from a basin, the scorch of our sunburns soothed by applications of Noxzema, generous dollops scooped with the first and second fingers from a beautifully heavy, intensely lapis-blue jar I loved to hold; our oozing mosquito-bites doused with my father's wine vinegar, administered from an old wicker-clad Chianti bottle, reserved for the purpose. This stinging balm did the trick but left us reeking of Carignano, still the uva of choice for legions of wizened, southern Italian winemakers.

Sometimes my uncle Graddy would pile us and one aged female Boxer, named Sam, into his wood-panelled station-wagon for a trip to the Tastee Freeze which purveyed soft ice cream the texture of molten latex: we loved it. Then, on to the town's dump to contemplate the sad, nocturnal foraging of its resident black bears. Afterwards, snuggled in soft flannel 'jammies' we'd roast gooey marshmallows over the crackling flames of the barbeque, listen in the distance for the faint howl of wolves and stare into the flames as if soothsayers, conjuring imaginary beasts and ghostly spirits, frightening each other as much as ourselves.

As the flames turned to glowing embers, our high spirits finally mollified, we were distributed amongst our respective parents and delivered to the treacherous kingdom of slumber which was the thick-black shadow-land of our crowded cottage bedrooms where black bears lurked in the wardrobe, hungry wolves smacked their lips in the darkened corners and giant rabbits leered from beneath our beds.

Grocery Stories

JIM ZUCCHERO

I OFTEN FIND myself reminiscing about food and family and the connections between them, especially when I'm hanging out at the cottage. Maybe, because the days seem longer and less rushed here, it's conducive to day-dreaming and remembrance of things past.

When I mix up a batch of pancakes at the cottage, I use an ages old recipe that was developed by my maternal grandmother when she made pancakes for us from scratch at her cottage in Gravenhurst, Ontario. On those fresh summer mornings when I was a kid, I can remember waking up to the wonderful smell of bacon and her famous pancakes sizzling on a hot griddle (which I still have). We would stumble out of bed mid-morning after a late night of cards around the kitchen table. Gram would complain that we wasted the best part of the day. But the taste of those pancakes smothered in maple syrup with crispy bacon is the taste I always associate with the summers of my youth.

Now, when I make her recipe, I like to toss in a few wild berries we've collected during our morning walk. Sometimes it's those tiny little wild strawberries that grow in patches, the teensy red berries close to the ground, so hard to spot. But they're worth the trouble because the flavour is so amazing, so concentrated in this miniature, undomesticated version ... so wild! Or sometimes it's wild raspberries; they're more plentiful, but equally hard to harvest from thick, thorny bushes by the side of the road. Sometimes we mix both kinds of berries in the batter for a real taste treat. I'm just about to toss the berries into the batch I'm making today when the phone rings. It's our nephew Charlie, calling from his home in Florida. He's calling to check the recipe for Gram's pancakes. He wants to mix up a batch from scratch. What are the odds? We chat for a while, then check the ingredients for the batter. We reminisce about happy cottage times spent together over the past few years, lazy mornings with pancake breakfasts. We wonder if we'll get to see each other this summer. Kids have summer jobs now and it's getting more difficult to coordinate our visits. We try to set a plan to get together, to make pancakes, to go swimming, but I wonder if we'll be able to make it happen. It's getting late in the summer and school will be starting again soon.

⬿ My four siblings and I grew up in an Italian grocery store in Toronto — the one at 22 Vaughan Road — though we did not live there. Our store was located at the corner of Vaughan Road and Hocken Avenue. It was a red brick building, two storeys, with two small apartments above. It opened in 1919 under my paternal grandfather's prideful eye, after he had saved up enough money from his years of peddling fruit door to door with a horse and buggy to finally buy a piece of property. Recently, I was given the deed that he signed when he took possession of the property and I can well imagine how pleased and proud he must have been on that day. When he died, in 1954, the business passed to my father, Charlie, and his sister, Lena — who never married. She and my great uncle Phil (my grandfather's brother) lived in the apartment behind the store for as long as I could remember. Our store operated as a small family-run business on that corner for all of my youth. It kept us very busy and provided our livelihood, but more than that, it provided a way of life, many useful lessons, and a lifetime of memories.

Although, over the many years it was open, the store had various incarnations, I remember it best at the end, as a thriving family business that sold only fresh fruits, vegetables, and flowers. During some of the early years it had also been a corner grocery store in the more traditional sense, one that stocked everything from soup to nuts. But in the 1970s the big grocery chains were expanding and things were changing for the little guys. How many boxes of Kellogg's Corn Flakes or jars of Heinz baby food could you hope to sell at twice the price of the big superstores? They were cutting the heart out of local grocers with their volume buying and loss leaders. It was a tough game. So, in a bold move, in 1972, when Loblaw and Dominion were making it very hard for small family grocers to compete, my father made the courageous decision to convert our store back to its original incarnation, as Zucchero's Fancy Fruits — a store that sold only fresh produce of the finest quality. He was in his glory, doing what he loved to do: buying the best fresh produce he could find, and selling it to folks who appreciated fine food.

❧ I can still clearly remember the physical layout of the store: the back room, the yard, the basement, the shed, the big walk-in coolers — such a nice place to linger on hot, humid days.

In the springtime we stocked box plants and lined them all up by variety — petunias here, geraniums there — all the way down the side of the building. The days seemed endless in the spring during planting season. We would buy the plants at the market before the sun was up, load them up, truck them home, unload, set up, and then the regular day would begin — the shopping hours. Then after the close there was the watering and tidying up. It was often late at night when we finally locked up and headed for home. Dead tired, feet aching from a 14- or 16-hour day, we would tumble into bed and catch a few hours of sleep before the alarm sounded at 5:00 or 5:30 a.m. and it was time to get up and do it all over again.

Sometimes, now, I imagine working like that. Day after day, year after year ... and I think: it's no wonder my Dad didn't live to see 60 — he worked himself to death. But he loved every day of it. At least that was the impression I had, and everyone else too, I think. I realized later, more so than I did at the time, just how much pleasure and pride he took from his work: providing fresh fruits and vegetables to his customers, everyday, for so many years. He loved being there, in the store, being part of that neighbourhood, with the German caterers named Hans and Claus next door, and the West Indian barber shop two doors down.

To be fair, it did "tick him off" when some guys would steal a peach, or snatch a handful of cherries from the pile outside, on their way to the barber shop. But he rarely said anything. The odd time he'd say: "Hey, I paid for that ..." and the culprit would slink away, sheepishly, or promise to pay next time. Mostly, he just shrugged and turned a blind eye, pretending not to notice. Some fruit got stolen, and some was given away. Making fresh fruit available to folks in any way just made him happy, I guess. He loved to serve, and he was always looking for ways to spread the joy.

Our store was located not far from the centre of the city and it attracted gourmands from the toney districts nearby: Rosedale, Forest Hill and Wychwood Park. I can remember being quite struck by the sight of Mrs. Morrow's enormous, curvy, black Bentley parked at the curb, her chauffeur, Cooper, waiting patiently by the car door while she shopped at Zucchero's. She would stand in the centre of the store, survey the produce and simply indicate what she would like and how much. Uncle Phil usually served Mrs. M. and they both enjoyed these exchanges: "Yes, Phil, I would like a honey-dew melon please, one that I can serve on Thursday evening." And the reply: "Yes, Mrs. Morrow." Then, the laying on of hands would begin. No tapping, thumping, squeezing or sniffing took place. It was pure feel. He just laid his hands on the skin and felt the melon. He was looking for a particular texture, a certain waxiness, and he knew when it was just right. No one could pick a melon like Uncle Phil. The next week Mrs. M. would return and rave about the honeydew. Her guests were so impressed. Uncle Phil would smile and silently beam. He took great pride in this special skill, and he enjoyed hearing about the occasion as much as if he'd been there to enjoy the melon himself.

Mrs. M was just one of many memorable patrons of Zucchero's. Some nights our neighbour Mr. Bennett, a short stout Scot who still spoke in a thick brogue, would arrive home from the pub before we were done closing. He would emerge from the back of a cab "three sheets to the wind," as they say. He would struggle out of the taxi and begin to sing like a bird, or whistle loudly as he navigated his way into the store to crack a joke with Uncle Phil. Then he would linger, light up a smoke, and tell tall tales, shifting from one foot to the other, trying to keep an even keel, until Mrs. Bennett heard the ruckus and came along to rescue him and usher him home. It was only two doors down, but I often wondered how she ever got him up those stairs.

Then there was the radio producer from the CBC, Mr. Reeves, who was also a marathon runner. He bought exotic tropical fruits— kiwi, papaya and mangos—which he would puree into a frothy solution to fuel his training sessions for the Boston marathon. We were fascinated by the stories he told when he returned from the great race. There were classical musicians, a married couple who played in the Toronto Symphony Orchestra—she was a harpist and he a trumpeter. Sam, of Sam the Record Man, was a regular. I remember the day he brought us a copy of the Beatles' *White* album, passed it to my dad and said: "Here, Charlie, the kids might like this." We even counted Marshall McLuhan among our customers from Wychwood Park. Attention shoppers! Media guru in aisle two, by the McIntosh apples! I had no idea at the time who he was, just another man in a trench coat with a tweed cap. Little did I know that years later, at university, I would puzzle over his cryptic, visionary writings, and eventually even get to teach his theories about media and culture. He came in and bought his apples, packed them up and took them home, just like lots of other folks. That was part of the beauty of it: everyone came in for one reason—to buy wonderful fresh fruit.

Mr. Gilchrest would come to the store on Saturday mornings in his gold Cadillac that made me think of Elvis—though he himself was nothing like Elvis. Mr. G. was a very dignified elderly gentleman. (I think he was in the fine ladies' wear business.) He would buy 6 baskets of Ivanchuk peaches at a time, and I would place them carefully onto the floor behind the front seat of his car. "I'm going up to the cottage," he would explain, "and I'd like to make some gifts to some folks up there." Sometimes he did the same thing with cherries, six baskets at a time! And he'd slip me a buck or two for loading them into his car. I remember stacking stands high with those 6 quart wooden baskets of peaches. The end of every basket was stamped in red ink: J. Ivanchuk & Sons, Beamsville, Ontario. Ivanchuk peaches were packed quite distinctively; one or two peaches in each basket still had the green leaves attached at the stem, fresh and shiny. It was a unique and enticing visual trademark that hinted at the excellence and flavour of the fruit. It was the very finest fruit from the Niagara escarpment. Every peach was as big as a softball and sweeter than sugar. Those peaches practically sold themselves.

Even now, when I think of peaches I can't help but also think of peach fuzz. There were days in the summer when I stacked so many peaches into neat pyramids on the stands that the peach fuzz would get onto my hands. Then it would mysteriously attach itself to any part of my skin that I touched inadvertently. Then it would start to itch. And it wouldn't stop. Every place I touched itched, and it got into your head too, so that you itched even in places you knew you hadn't touched.

Those were long days. And the peaches weren't the worst of it. The hot peppers were pure murder. I learned about hot peppers the hard way. We had a garbage shed down the street, by the lane that ran behind the store. We would pile up wire bound crates filled with the trimmings from the vegetables out in the shed. There they would sit until the pig farmer came around in his old truck to collect them as feed for his pigs.

Sometimes, when things were slow, we would hang out down the lane, by the shed, killing time, goofing off. We noticed, one day, that the hot peppers that were out in the garbage made quite a popping sound when you smashed them full force on the concrete floor of the shed. But if you handled them, cleaning up, and then happened to touch, say, your eye ... well, big trouble, lad. I spent one afternoon in great misery, lying down in the backroom with a cold, wet cloth draped over my eyes, but it did very little to alleviate the build up of heat and the burning sensation that ravaged my eyeballs. I was certain Hell had no fire so torrid. And a valuable lesson was learned that day about the raw, consuming power of *capsicum*.

I learned a great many of life's valuable lessons in the store; fortunately, most of them were far less painful than my pepper episode. From the time I was old enough to push a broom, and collect a pay envelope at the end of the day with a couple of quarters in it, I always knew I could earn a few bucks if I was willing to work for it. Eventually, I graduated from sweeper to stock boy, then to driver, and later up to buyer. I learned much of what I needed to learn to get on in life working with my father in the store: be honest, be courteous and happy, take pride in what you do, and try to enjoy every day. Simple lessons to live by, and they have served me well.

On Friday nights, because the store stayed open late, we would take turns spelling each other off and go in to the kitchen for dinner. Some weeks we would pick up a bucket of Kentucky Fried Chicken and a big box of fries; other times we would send out for fish and chips. Mr. Joe, the hired man who trimmed the vegetables and took care of stock, would have dinner with us. We sometimes found his table manners a little rough, but he was a hard-working man. Most Friday nights we started to close around 9 o'clock. In the summertime, when there were large displays of fruit and vegetables outside that had to be hauled away and stored in coolers overnight, closing could take an hour or more.

Every Saturday evening we would load the truck with whatever produce was left on the stands that might not be at its best by Monday morning. We delivered it to the Sisters of St. Peter Claver, an order of nuns who had a motherhouse nearby, a few blocks away. They were always so grateful; they showered us with blessings as we carried the boxes of produce into their kitchen, enough to last the week. My father was always vigilant about what could pass; the rule was: Don't put anything in their delivery that you wouldn't eat yourself.

Back in those days, the store was closed on Sundays, a welcome day of rest for us. The real deal for a meal at the store was on those special occasions—a birthday, or a holiday when we would have turkey dinner with all the trimmings, candied yams, baby beans, breaded cauliflower (too many vegetables to count) bottles of homemade wine, pies, coffee, and, of course, those fancy Italian pastries that nobody needed, and nobody could resist. Uncle Phil would make a special trip up to St. Clair Avenue, to La Sem Bakery for the freshest, creamiest cannoli in town, the perfect end to a perfect meal.

After those long, drawn out Sunday dinners, the conversation among the adults drifted on and on. Eventually the kids would slip away from the table to watch TV in the next room, where we would change the channel from *Lawrence Welk* to *Lost in Space*. If their attention drifted far enough and they really lost track of us, or if there was nothing on TV to hold our interest, sometimes we would wander into the store to amuse ourselves. It was like a different place when you knew the door was locked, all the lights were off, and it was dark but for the shadowy light from the street lamps outside and a dull glow emanating from a florescent light in a cooler.

We would team up and have races with the shopping carts, switching up the driver/passenger arrangement for each round, setting out the course up and down the few narrow aisles. We knew exactly where the candies were: one box of Kraft Caramels, and another of Neilson Jersey Milk Chocolates, tucked in right beside the cash register at the check out, so Uncle Phil could treat the kids on their way out. We made regular pit stops there, for fuel. It was only a question of how long before our grand prix races ended with a spectacular crash and someone's mangled fingers or a bloody nose brought our shenanigans to an end for the evening. Then we were reduced to watching the streetcar rumble by in the rain, feeling the floor of the store vibrate slightly as it passed.

Sometimes, on warm Sunday evenings in the summertime, we would get together for a barbecue in the small yard behind the store — "out back," as we called it. There would be thick juicy steaks, done on the grill, and sausage from Pasquale's (it had to have fennel seed!), fresh salads, corn on the cob, peaches and watermelon. In the late summer we would admire Uncle Phil's garden, his pots of basil, each one as big around as a bushel, the ripening red tomatoes, as big as your fist, and especially his prized "gougoutsa" — very long, thin, vegetable marrow. The curious squash grew from thick vines strung overhead, suspended on trellises he made from thin slats of wood recycled from vegetable crates. There were times his vegetable marrow would grow to four or five feet in length, with weird twists and bends, or into strange, exotic shapes. We would place one or two of the best ones in the store window when we closed up for a holiday weekend, just for decoration. There was always a great deal of attention paid to how the store looked from outside, whether we were open or not; everything had to be just so. You sold fruit based first on how it looked — its visual appeal. Then you might get to "taste and try, before you buy ..." I can vividly remember the care and pride we took in setting up displays of fresh produce, placing ripe, red tomatoes stem up, in rows, 'til they formed a perfect pyramid. Apples. Oranges. Pears. Same thing — every one was placed meticulously.

❧ At times I wonder how this stock pile of memories and experiences from my youth, centred on fresh fruits and vegetables and flowers — the daily experience of retail sales, the work ethic that was taken for granted — figures into my present experience of food. In some ways I am very far removed from that experience now, sitting behind a desk all day. But every now and then I have flashbacks. Like when I take a bucket of kitchen waste out to the compost heap at the far end of our backyard, and that slightly sour smell hits me, and I think of the garbage shed at the store. Or when I'm chopping a red cayenne pepper to put in my pot of chili and I feel the pepper's heat entering my fingertips. Or when I'm sitting at my desk at lunchtime, too busy to break for lunch, and I lift a ripe red strawberry toward my mouth, and pause to smell it. Suddenly, in an instant, I am transported by the pungent aroma of that fresh berry to the back room at the store, where I packed thousands of quarts of strawberries before bringing them out to the stand and setting them out for customers. These vivid memories seem to have a will of their own. The effect is lasting, and it comes along at the strangest times.

Like last summer, I travelled to Turkey to visit a friend. On Tuesday morning we went to the farmer's market in the centre of Antalya, just a few blocks from his apartment. As we wandered up and down the aisles, passing the stalls, admiring the great mountains of fresh produce — ripe red tomatoes, fresh figs and grapes — I couldn't help thinking back to my earlier days at our store. To see, smell and taste such beautiful fruits and vegetables, displayed so attractively and with such pride ... to see the young kids, setting up the displays, taking direction from their elders ... it took me right back to the experience of my own youth and the corner store at 22 Vaughan Road.

~ When my grandfather died in 1954 the store passed to my father and his sister. They ran the store as a small family business until we closed the front door for the last time in December 1978. When it closed it was the oldest family-run grocery store in Toronto; it had been operating on the same corner for 59 years. Just as it was a big part of the neighbourhood, it was a big part of my youth. I'm often reminded of the important lessons I first learned growing up in a fruit store; lessons about the beauty and the pleasure of fine food — especially the sensual delights of enjoying wonderful fresh produce; lessons about the value of an honest day's work, courtesy and service to others. My father always encouraged us to stay in school and get a good education, "so you won't have to work as hard as I do to make a living." Well, I guess it worked, but I'm not at all sure we are entirely the better for it. We are all university graduates, all gainfully employed, none in the fruit business. But I'm not sure any of us derives greater satisfaction from our work on a daily basis than my father did when he ran that corner fruit store for all those years. It was a landmark in the neighbourhood for generations. It was a big part of his life, and mine. Now it's a thing of the past. But the memories, and the lessons, will last forever.

~ Tonight, I lingered out on the deck overlooking the lake, watching the sky light up in a blaze of colour that was constantly changing, like a kaleidoscope. It went from bright orange to pink and finally to mauve before the light eventually faded to a shadowy grey, a precursor of the inky blackness that would follow in a few hours' time. But at one point I thought: it's "sky-blue-pink" — my dad's favourite colour! (He would have liked it here ... but I wonder if he ever could have relaxed here. He was so used to staying busy.) After dinner I dipped a slice of a ripe peach into my glass of wine, then swallowed it in one gulp. I thought of Uncle Phil. He used to do that.

It's autumn and our family has gathered at the cottage for Thanksgiving weekend — at least those of us who could make it this year. We've taken a nice walk on a fine, sunny fall day, and we've foraged and gathered some of nature's bounty to add to our turkey dinner. Apples from old pioneer trees that are bent and misshapen but laden with fruit — old varieties we don't know the names of anymore. Some are small, crimson, hard and quite tart; others are big, pale green, with softer flesh, sweeter. Combined in a pie they create a taste sensation unlike any other. We have also found fabulous mushrooms. They are quite plentiful at this time of year, growing thick in some patches of moss, alongside the path, in rocks and dirt, or on broken limbs and stumps.

We have identified a few varieties now that we can harvest and safely consume — known to be edible, easily identified, and even successfully tested by the brave among us. *Lactarius deliciosus* are, indeed, delicious; they have broad tops of pale pink, deep gills, and bleed a bright orange milky liquid when sliced. And we have found lots of *coprinus comatus*, commonly known as Shaggy Mane. They have to be picked young, before they begin to fringe on the edges and throw off their black ink. But they are firm, woodsy and buttery when they're young. I clean bits of moss and leaves from some while my mother looks on: "Your grandfather would be proud of you!" she says.

My maternal grandfather started the Maple Leaf Mushroom Company. He grew, packed and sold fresh button mushrooms, from a farm in the east end of Toronto, what is now part of Scarborough. I can remember in the spring, before we planted the garden at home, making trips to the farm to pick up manure from the steaming mushroom beds to mix into our flower beds. No wonder our pots of basil grew so well — they were stoked with some serious fertilizer.

The roots of the food connection run deep on both sides in my family. Now, I am a little farther removed from those roots, and sometimes a little sadder for it. But when I stop to consider it, I can easily understand why food is such a passion in my life and such a force in our family — it's bred in the bone.

muskoka pasta

DOMENICO CAPILONGO

the backseat a rotini of laughter
as we cut through the parmigiano snow
carving deeper into the winter afternoon
the tortellini moon creeping in the rearview

the power's out in the hotel
we stumble through the cannelloni hallway
like overcooked linguine

the four of us cuddle in the ravioli bed
in lasagna layers of pyjamas
telling stories of minestrone superheroes
until the gnocchi light bulbs pop back on

al dente

DOMENICO CAPILONGO

THE PERFECT MOMENT. not the overcooked soggy feeling in the back of your throat when you don't know what to say like on the first date when I told you that I don't believe in marriage. the perfect light. the sun sitting just right. just so. holding them for the first time. the hospital room spinning. the firmness of that moment. the words forming nicely in your mouth like they were meant to be there. like now. years later when I tell you that you heard me all wrong. I know you don't believe me.

"Pasta is magic, the rest is life"

LORETTA GATTO-WHITE

CONSIDER THIS, THAT from an anonymous act of prestidigitation a pedestrian mound of flour and a trickle of water were transformed into pasta in all its emblematic shapes and nomenclature. This casual act of invention makes the phenomenon that was the Renaissance seem a comparative failure of the imagination, based as its very name asserts, on earlier cultural innovations. Whereas the delightful creation which holds the Italian body together and its soul eternally in thrall, has no primo genitor, it is, like God, its own sufficient cause rising spontaneously it seems, from a magic mountain of flour.

What mystery lay within that golden coil, what secret alchemy woven in each supple strand? Well, Federico Fellini nearly got it right in his characteristically enigmatic declaration: "Life is a combination of magic and pasta." We expect a deeper sentiment from the son of a Barilla pasta salesman. "Pasta is magic, the rest is life," seems more sensible. Doubters may ponder the magnificence that is 'La Loren,' an Italian icon as famous as Michelangelo's David and just as majestically statuesque, who freely admits her debt to the national dish: "Everything you see, I owe to spaghetti" and possibly a little more besides.

One only need survey the 310 kinds of pasta in Oretta Zanini De Vita's *Encyclopaedia of Pasta* to realize that its potent magic resides in its ability to inspire the imagination and motivate the nimble fingers of its anonymous, mostly female creators. Mona Talbott, executive chef of the American Academy in Rome, accounts for the impractical labour lavished on creating these fanciful shapes as a "way of self-expression for women to show their creativity and imagination with little or no resources." Or vent their frustrations, exacting a small revenge. As Brunelleschi raised his famous dome over Florence's Santa Maria del Fiore, a glory to the patriarchal church, an aggrieved Florentine housewife indulged in culinary alchemy, creating a new gnocco of ricotta and spinach for a greedy prelate, baptizing her creation with no small vindication, *strozzapreti* (choke the priest).

Perhaps while a young Leonardo lay atop an Umbrian hill and dreamed of flying like Icarus to the sun, but with better results, in a dark, dank scullery prettily shaped farfalle, painstakingly formed as butterflies with carefully crimped edges, pleated and pinched in the centre, floated effortlessly on the cloudy froth atop a pot of boiling water.

While the sinuous Gothic curves of Botticelli's modest Venus entrance us even today, the heart-warming satisfaction one gets from Bologna's famous tortellini in brodo, its seductive shape inspired by Venus' navel, is more contenting and accessible.

Where the formal varieties of this very plastic substance are astounding, the arched stone loggias, marble columns and pediments of the High Renaissance are rigidly regular; the former is pliable and yields to the artists' imagination, the latter is impassive and only grudgingly conforms. If the architecture of Tuscany was fashioned from pasta it might look like the mad and delightful structures of Gaudi's Catalonia.

However, the names and varieties of pasta are equally attributable to creative genius as they are to competitive regionalism or *campanilissimo*, both renowned features of the Italian national character. An exasperated Garibaldi in the quest to unite his fractious countrymen, declared upon liberating Naples in 1860: "It will be maccheroni, I swear to you, that will unify Italy." A prescient insight indeed. Ms. Zanini De Vita encountered this ages old problem in researching her encyclopaedia. Within one town in Lazio, for example, there were several different names for the same pasta, some differences found as close as one neighbourhood block to another. Her conclusion? That the unification of Italy by Garibaldi was a big mistake; instead in her view, it should have been formed as Switzerland was, a confederation of connected states. Oh dear, bankers and cuckoo clocks; where, we ask, is the fun or magic in that?

The magic of pasta resides in its 'anima,' the white core of the pasta which ever so gently, resists the eaters' teeth; too hard, its spirit lies unawakened; too soft it is dead. Al dente it is, as the golden-locked Lucrezia Borgia might've said, "Just right." Italians like their food, as well as their conquests, to resist a little before yielding.

In Boccaccio's *Decameron*, a gullible painter is regaled by a tale of the land of Bengodi, where on a golden mountain of Parmesan cheese, its denizens spend all the day making maccheroni and ravioli, to be boiled in a sea of capon broth, then ladled-out freely in as large a quantity as the swiftest and greediest can consume. Oh! to be by the capon-broth sea in Bengodi, sliding giddily through slippery tubes of maccheroni or dreamily floating supine upon a plump pillow of ravioli; what playful bliss.

I defy anyone to eat a bowl of pasta in anger; it can't be done. One can certainly picture gnawing, stabbing and cutting one's way, preoccupied by fury, through a porterhouse steak, chicken leg or pork chop, but fury is unimaginable in the gentle dexterity and concentration one needs to encourage slippery strands of tagliatelle around the fork, balancing it delicately to keep them in place on their journey to the patient, waiting mouth. These actions require concentration, and more to the point, do not require the use of any sharp weapon; pasta is a most calming, civilized and peaceful food. It is perhaps no accident then, that it was Italy, in the 11th century that introduced the table fork to the rest of Europe. This civilized utensil was lost on the British though, as they felt it was too effete, preferring to eat with their hands and from their knives until the 18th century.

Its soporific effect is part of its magic too, as anyone who has enjoyed making and consuming a bowl of 'spaghetti a mezzanotte' can attest. It was my unfailing ritual upon arriving home after two pasta-less weeks in the Caribbean to make my way to the larder always stocked with extra-virgin olive oil, black infornata olives, anchovies, peperoncini, spaghetti and a bottle of Chianti, the essentials for the classic, simple feast of aglio e olio.

Over my shoulder, from my position at the stove, I ask my husband, ensconced at the kitchen table, preoccupied with his own homecoming ritual of sorting through the mundane reality that is our weeks-old stack of mail: "Do you want some pasta?" to which he reliably mumbles: "Um, no, thanks." Ignoring his typical reply, I set a bowl at each of our places, pour the wine, and we begin to eat. We sigh and let the oily, golden strands of pasta wend their languorous way down to that final place that is Elysium. This warm, visceral feeling of contentment urges us upstairs to our own familiar bed, to peaceful dreams of Bengodi where we are magically, finally, home.

Spaghetti a mezzanotte;
A symphonic recipe

Whoosh! goes a torrent of cold water into the capacious pot,
Ping! A small handful of *sale grosso* in the bottom
then Click!-Click! on with the heat beneath the pasta pot
and the shallow pan for the sauce.
A few glug-glugs of oil in the pan
followed by a silent sprinkle of hot pepper flakes,
then the sizzle of chopped garlic,
Plonk! in with a scattering of pitted olives,
then the final scraping of the wooden spatula stirring-in a
few anchovies.

Second Course: Primo

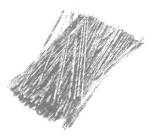

This is Sunday Lunch

ANGELA LONG

LUNCHES ARE quiet at Via Scapardini 9. Father. Mother. Son. And me, the fiancée from Canada. We eat in the kitchen with the ticking of the clock, sometimes an Italian soap opera. We all have our places around the table. Mine is beside the radiator with my back to the television. I face an armoire bursting with all manner of pot and platter, and kitchen appliances stored in their original boxes. I face my future mother-in-law.

I've learned many things at my place beside the radiator. I've learned that no matter how full I am I should always ask for seconds. If I don't, they'll arrive on my plate anyway and everyone is much happier if I ask for them first. "A good appetite!" the father will exclaim and beam in the direction of his son. I've learned that bread sits directly on the tablecloth, that fruit is presented chilled and covered with droplets, that grapes are to be broken off in bunches, and oranges peeled with a knife. I've learned that cheese from Sicily, the region my fiancé's family is originally from, is always best. "Sometimes Sardegna," the father may say if he's feeling gracious.

I've learned that, even though I don't normally drink coffee, I should drink one when all is said and done. I should down the thick, black espresso served in a tiny cup like a shooter. "It helps digestion," the mother proclaims, stacking the cups the moment the last dregs are drunk. It's time to do the dishes. This is my cue to select a tea towel from the drawer. "No, not that one," the mother will inevitably say as she fills the sink with soapy water. There are certain towels, I've learned, for certain tasks. Although, in my opinion, they all look exactly the same.

While I wait with the proper towel in hand and a mind buzzing with caffeine, the father prepares the leftovers for distribution to Briccola, the family dog, and the flock of chickens. Nothing is wasted at Via Scapardini 9. Every fruit peel is minutely diced. Every cheese rind slivered. The father sits at the table while doing all this, big hands grasping a tiny pen-knife reserved just for this task. Leftover pasta is thrown into Briccola's saucepan, topped with all the scrapings from our plates, and sprinkled with fresh parmesan grated from a block half the size of my head.

When the father is finished, his son removes the tablecloth and carries it to the garden to shake out the crumbs. If I still don't have a dish to dry, I go out too. I turn my face towards a sun that always seems to be shining in this country. I watch my fiancé, knowing this has been his chore for thirty-one years. The tablecloth flies into the air and snaps expertly. Crumbs settle gently on basil and arugula. He looks at me while folding the cloth into a perfect square. If no one is around, I clasp his hands where the corners meet and kiss him.

This is Sunday Lunch. It took me awhile not to feel nervous every time my fiancé and I rounded the bend of our street, Via Cairoli, and faced the statue of the Madonna rising into the blue sky. Her white marble form rising from the pinnacle of a pink-stuccoed church marks the entranceway to Via Scapardini. On a really clear day, the Alps backdrop her outstretched arms. Every time I round that bend I'm reminded of two things: first, that Italy is beautiful; and second, that I am not Italian. I am a *straniera*, a stranger, a foreigner in the polite sense of the word.

This fact becomes evident every Sunday Lunch. I don't speak more than a few hundred words of the language, and these are mostly limited to what I see on my plate. I don't wear pointy boots with heels. I don't know the names of the characters on *Vivere*.

My fiancé assures me that none of this is important; his parents don't care about such things. But I know he's just being polite. Of course they care; they're Italian. To make matters worse, they're Sicilian. They're from an island where traditionally *la famiglia* is something worth killing for. And my fiancé is their youngest. The one they've been so patient with. The one they let study jazz in Boston, work as a musician on cruise ships, volunteer at a Buddhist retreat centre in India. He's their last chance for a four-hundred guest wedding. For grandchildren.

I've caught his mother examining my boots on the mat at the front door, scraping the toe with her pinkie nail to test if they're real leather. She has pulled me aside examining the frayed stitching of a shirt collar, insisting I change while she mended it. She clucks when I walk barefoot through the garden. She sighs when I let Briccola jump onto my lap, speckling my jeans with tiny paw-prints.

I know they wonder why their son would ever choose to bring home a pale-faced, scrawny, strawberry blonde with no fashion sense who has never eaten a fresh artichoke before. Sometimes, I wonder exactly the same thing. The longer I live in this place, I too wish I was more Italian. Who wouldn't? They live amidst carved cornices, soaring archways, and white marble staircases. They grow things like persimmons and passion fruit. They greet one another with kisses on both cheeks and words that sound like libretti. Mothers push baby strollers wearing stiletto heels. Every afternoon they close everything down for three hours to eat a four-course lunch and take naps. And every week, after Sunday Lunch, families walk arm-in-arm through the piazza beneath frescoes painted during the Renaissance.

But I've learned that my fiancé's family doesn't go to the piazza. We sit back down at our places around the table and do what I dread most — talk. They ask questions. My fiancé translates: How many brothers do you have? What do they do? What does your father do? What does your family grow in their garden? My fiancé tries to find the words for nuclear power plant and car manufacturing industry. Retired school principal and mega-box chain store. "They don't have a garden?" the father asks, puzzled, looking at my fiancé. I nod, as saddened as he by this discovery. Soon they begin to look at me with pity rather than dismay. We down another round of espressos. We crack open walnuts and pop them into out mouths.

After a few weeks, when my vocabulary begins to expand beyond the borders of my plate, I ask them a question: Why did they leave Sicily? I've noticed that although they've lived in the North for almost thirty years, far from African breezes and lemon trees, Sicily is still home. Via Scapardini 9 is filled with all things Sicilian: sheep's ricotta, cannoli biscuits, olive oil, pistachios, a thick sweet wine reserved for special occasions. The wine is kept on a side rack in the fridge. It's unlabelled.

"Don't drink it," my fiancé warned the first time a small glass of it was presented to me on All Saints' Day. But, of course I'd learned it was best to accept whatever was placed in front of me. "Salute!" I said and took a sip. It tasted heavenly. "Ambrosia of the gods," I attempted to say while they all looked at me confused. "It's really strong," my fiancé warned again as I took another sip. And it was. It made my head buzz in a way espresso could never dream of. The father smiled. I smiled back. We understood one another then. I understood I was tasting where he came from. The essence of the place. The sweetness of sun, sea, wind, soil. I tasted what ran through his veins, what the North could never replace.

"Why did you leave?" I ask again. The mother opens up the drawer where the tea towels are kept and unfolds a square of white linen printed with a map of Sicily, the kind of tea towel tourists buy as keepsakes. It's illustrated with orange blossoms, dancing peasant girls, Grecian urns. She points to a dot nestled in green hills, a centimetre away from the Mediterranean Sea. "Boom!" she says. "Boom!" she says again. "There was an earthquake," my fiancé translates. "They lost everything. They had to move North where there was work."

The mother rushes into the dining room and returns with a vase that before I moved to Italy I would have considered tacky. It's curvy and ornate, hand-painted with the scene of a cypress and a white-washed villa. The sky is pink. The glaze, a pearly opalescence. The mother holds the vase aloft by its golden handles. "Real gold," she proclaims and the father nods his head. "It's all that survived," she says. I look at the vase as the light shifts and everything—sky, cypress, villa—begins to shimmer. I look at all those years preserved beneath the glaze.

"Take it," the mother says placing the vase in front of me and for the first time I refuse something I'm offered at Via Scapardini 9. "Take it," she says again, looking at me, not at my clothing or shoes or hairstyle. And I look at her too. Something in her eyes tells me I've been wrong all this time—I've been family from the moment I took my seat beside the radiator even though I'm a *straniera*. I've been family not because I'm engaged to her son, but because this is Italy. This is Sunday Lunch. "Thank you," I say touching the golden handles.

It's time to pack. Time to return to Canada. Amongst the socks and sweaters, I lay blocks of pecorino, dried porcini, and hand-sewn bags filled with *Carnaroli*. "Our luggage will be over the limit," my fiancé warns. But I don't listen. I reach for the capers packed in rock salt, the boxes of *Pizzoccheri*.

Finally, I reach for the vase on the highest of the kitchen shelves. I hesitate. Could it survive the voyage? The golden handles shimmer in the May light. In the light of Italy. Soon there will be no more white villas or cypresses. Soon it will be just the two of us for Sunday Lunch. "Should we leave it behind?" I ask.

"My mother will understand." My fiancé places the vase to the side, along with the terra-cotta pots of basil and parsley. He doesn't hesitate. He smiles at me with the smile of a people who've spent generations leaving things behind. Of knowing what really matters once you reach your final destination.

And what really matters is Sunday Lunch. We unpack our bags. My fiancé slits open a bag of *Carnaroli*. "I will make you risotto," he offers.

We eat in the kitchen with the crackling of the woodstove. Outside, birds chirp, the ocean crashes. We live over ten-thousand kilometres away on a remote archipelago on British Columbia's northwest coast now. But this is Sunday Lunch. We pass around the parmesan. We clink glasses. For hours we sit and eat, watching the light change, adding logs to the fire. I watch my fiancé peel an apple in one long ribbon. With a small knife reserved just for this task, he dices it for the neighbour's chickens. He looks out the window, across the Pacific.

Learning to Cook
with Dante and my Suocera:
A Fond Memory

CAROLINE MORGAN DI GIOVANNI

IN THE SUMMER of 1972 I was a new bride, living in Toronto in a house shared with my in-laws. Between May and August my life had changed in every way that counts. In May, I had completed the requirements for a Master's degree in Drama from Tufts University in Medford, Massachusetts. Two years of dedicated stage work and theatre scholarship culminated in a final production of my thesis play, including a music score. Graduation was set for June, exactly two weeks before my wedding to Alberto Di Giovanni.

That was the next life-changing event for that summer. Alberto and I had been friends since our undergraduate days at St. Michael's College, University of Toronto. We met because I joined the Italian Club at U of T in an effort to expand my comprehension of the Italian course I took in First Year. Alberto was dynamic, funny, and involved in activities all over campus. I liked him, but I had to turn him down the first time he proposed. It was way too soon! I was only 20! Besides, I advised him from the start: "You have to find a nice Italian girl." After all, I was an American student, born and raised in Pennsylvania. I was in Toronto because my beloved uncle, a priest and scholar, taught Medieval Canon Law at the Pontifical Institute for Mediaeval Studies, located at St. Michael's College, and he convinced my parents that this was the college for me.

Time went by, and Alberto was very persistent. He followed me to Boston for yet another attempt to persuade me to marry him. After six years, how could I resist? I said yes and we set the date for July 1, 1972. Our wedding in a Philadelphia suburb was a very sweet family affair. My uncle performed the ceremony. My parents hosted the wedding guests in a reception in our family home. My new in-laws came down for the wedding, and spent the sunny afternoon chatting with Fr. Joe. He had been ordained in Rome, and thereafter spent several years doing scholarly research in the Vatican Library. His Italian was excellent, allowing for some knowledgeable discussions of wine regions, good food, and Italian history. The day after our first reception we got off the plane in Toronto and I was whisked away to La Luna Ballroom, where my new sister-in-law Maria had prepared the second reception. Ecco! I was introduced to 350 guests, most of them relatives or paesani from Roccamorice, Abruzzo. This was my first Italian wedding. I had a ball!

So there I was, a newly wed bride sharing a house with my aging in-laws, awaiting my landed immigrant status before searching for work, trying to get a grip on the Italian community culture I had just entered into. My two years of university Italian classes had not prepared me for the day-to-day exchanges in a household. Where, in the *Divina Commedia* did Dante talk about finding a good dry cleaner? What were the words for building a bookshelf? Most importantly, how could I learn to cook in an Abruzzese kitchen?

Fortunately, my suocera, the formidable Anna Di Giovanni, had more wisdom in her face and hands than any professor I ever studied under. We got to know each other in the long hours while Alberto was at work. Neither was fluent in the language of the other, but we were both women determined to succeed. She had raised 10 children in wartime and post-war Italy, in a small village high in the Maiella. Her courage had been tested many times. It was obvious that she had gained strength with every encounter. Everyone respected her. She had earned the sobriquet of "la Czara." Yet for all that, her heart was as big as the world. Her family meant everything to her, and by extension, all children she encountered had a deep attraction for her twinkling eyes. She watched the news on TV, making sharp observations about the characters who stepped across the screen. Trudeau was a hero; other politicians came across as "*mezzo uomini*," undistinguished schemers.

I got to know Anna best when we worked in the kitchen together. I knew nothing at all about making pasta. For me, spaghetti came in a box, stiff noodles that you poured into boiling water and cooked until they were soft. What a revelation to have a lesson that began with the selection of farina best for making pasta. The big wooden table was cleared and cleaned; the flour was sifted into a pyramid in the centre. Salt was added, not measured with a teaspoon but by daily practice. Then into the centre of this pile of flour the eggs were broken and dropped, the number of eggs determined by the number of people expected for dinner that day. My lesson proceeded with a minimum of words, but my teacher knew that the best way to learn is to do. I was the one to crack the eggs. My hands were shown how to mix the eggs gradually into the flour. We added some spoonfuls of vegetable oil. At that time Toronto did not have a culinary snobbery about virgin olive oil, so the humble Unico brand was just about the only choice. It worked, as long as the cook knew the labour of kneading and incorporating, folding and flattening the pasta. When the dough looked ready and felt right, it was time to get out *la macchina*.

Now I discovered a kitchen aid totally unknown to me a few months before, when I was researching a paper about Eighteenth Century English theatre practices. The pasta maker in Anna's kitchen had been in use since their arrival in Canada 15 years before. This marvellous invention was attached by a clamp to the end of the table, the handle was inserted, and the rollers inspected to ensure the proper width. Then plenty of sifted flour was used to keep the pasta from sticking to the rollers. The dough was cut into strips and inserted through the rollers carefully, making sure the long sheet that emerged met the consistency required for the type of noodles on the menu that day. Slowly, piece by piece, the dough was squeezed through the rollers, and the long strips that came out were spread across the table. Finally it was time to put the cutting blades in place on *la machina*. What type did we want to make that day: spaghetti? spaghettini? linguini? For my first lesson we choose linguini, not too narrow to confuse the novice, familiar to the family members coming over for dinner. We found the size we wanted and clicked the blades into place.

Once again the long strips of pasta were patiently fed into the rollers. Turning the handle was a tedious job, as Anna knew very well. She had a way of lightening the boredom by happy bits of gossip and conversation. In those first weeks I hardly followed a word. This was not Florentine Italian, not even the language of current Italian cinema. This was pure Roccolana dialect, the talk of her town, and I didn't have a clue. What I could understand, plain and clear, was the kindness of this woman to take me into her family, *straniera* that I was, simply because her son loved me. Anna loved me, too. I learned from her much more than making pasta, that first summer in her kitchen in Downsview.

My Authentic Italian Cooking Experience: in Edmonton

DEBBY WALDMAN

OF ALL THE things I looked forward to when my family and I travelled to Italy a few years ago, nothing excited me as much as the chance to learn authentic Italian cooking from an authentic Italian cook. In fact, when I looked for lodging in Tuscany, I considered only places that offered cooking classes. It meant that we had to stay in the Italian version of Podunk (or, as we say in Yiddish, Yechupetsville), miles from the highway and at the top of a winding road that was so narrow I could stand in the middle and touch the trees on either side. But I figured the culinary payoff would be worth the inconvenience.

Except that there was no culinary payoff. After we checked in and I went to the office to set up a lesson schedule, I was informed that the owner wasn't offering classes that week. I never did find out why but, as a result, my Italian cooking experience consisted of boiling dried pasta from the local grocery store, and watching my husband and a friend grill a frozen pizza on the barbecue in our backyard.

The most important cooking lesson I learned: always make sure that your kitchen has an oven before you buy a frozen pizza at the grocery store.

I also learned an important lesson in culinary humility: you don't necessarily have to travel thousands of kilometres to the source to learn the secrets of ethnic cooking. As it turned out, the best Italian cook I know was a 10-minute ride from my house in Edmonton.

Antoinette was born and raised in Toronto by parents who emigrated from Italy in 1960. They named her Antonietta, but because only they could pronounce it properly, she eventually opted for Antoinette. In 2000, she moved to Edmonton, where her husband became the assistant general manager of the Edmonton Oilers hockey team. I met her through a mutual friend in Toronto, who rightly figured that the two of us would hit it off.

During the seven years that Antoinette lived in Edmonton, her mother came to visit once, during tomato canning season. I never saw Antoinette during that time: it seemed that canning was some sort of secret Italian ritual passed down from mother to daughter. I could only imagine the two of them, holed up in the kitchen crushing bushels of tomatoes, cooking them, putting them into jars with just the right amount of basil, and storing them in the basement so that Antoinette could make spaghetti sauce all winter long.

That sauce is the best I've ever tasted. Because it's not cluttered with unnecessary extras — not so much as an onion or a mushroom — all you taste is the deeply satisfying richness of slow-cooked tomatoes with just the right amount of salt and pepper to bring out their best. It's not quite runny, but neither is it like that inert store-bought stuff that doesn't so much pour as plop out of a jar. I swear it has medicinal properties, but Antoinette insists it's the veal bone she puts in for flavour. Whatever the secret, after I tasted that sauce, nothing else compared.

It never occurred to me to ask her to teach me to make it. I assumed that, if the canning process was such a secret, then the sauce-making was on par with a holy Masonic ritual. Besides, Antoinette lived so close that all I had to do when I wanted magical sauce was drop a broad hint and I'd be invited over for a meal. Inevitably she'd send me home with the leftovers, which I hid from my family.

And then one day, I was listening to the radio and I heard that Antoinette's husband was being touted as the possible new general manager of the NHL's Columbus Blue Jackets. I called her immediately, hoping it wasn't true, but knowing deep down it probably was.

By the end of the summer, she was gone, and with her my ready supply of magical sauce. The last night that my kids and I ate at Antoinette's, she sent me home with two containers, which I put into the freezer and parcelled out as if it were the last bottle of wine from Mr. Rothschild's pre-war collection. It lasted until early fall.

After that I went into withdrawal. At least once a month I experienced such cravings that eventually I realized I had no choice: I overcame my fear of Masonic rituals and called Antoinette to grovel for the recipe. As it turned out, I didn't have to. She was more than happy to tell me what to do: sauté onions and a veal bone, add crushed tomatoes, parsley, salt and pepper, simmer and serve.

I did everything she said, but my sauce didn't come close to tasting like hers, even after I drove all over town to find a veal bone. It wasn't bad, but it tasted like every other sauce I'd made: dull and ordinary, like canned tomatoes crushed in a food processor with some condiments tossed in for good measure. I resigned myself to accepting that if I wanted Antoinette-quality sauce again I'd have to fly to Columbus, which was about as likely as my returning to Tuscany.

With a hockey husband and three children in elementary school, Antoinette didn't come back to Edmonton often. The first time she returned, we had slightly less than an hour together, and I had to share her with a friend. We met in a coffee shop. The friend and I lamented the loss of the sauce. The next time Antoinette visited I was out of town. A year and a half passed before we could see each other again, face-to-face. This time she had almost an entire half an afternoon.

"Come to my house!" I begged when she called to plan her trip. "You can show me how to make the sauce."

"Really?" she said. "You want me to come over and make spaghetti sauce?"

"Yes! Please!"

Antoinette gave me a grocery list: canned tomatoes (I bought a 2.84 litre can of La Pavoncella with basil leaves, as she recommended), a bunch of parsley, garlic, an onion, sunflower oil, salt, pepper and a veal bone.

When she arrived at my house a few weeks later, the first thing she did after exchanging hellos was to pour about a half-inch-deep pool of sunflower oil into my stock pot, far more than I'd used when I'd attempted to replicate the sauce on my own. Was she going to cook the tomatoes or drown them? I contemplated mentioning fats and cholesterol, but then I remembered all that I'd been missing, and I kept my mouth shut and watched.

Next she sliced up a fist-sized onion, very thinly, and when the oil had heated she dropped in the onion slices with the veal bone. Within minutes the entire house smelled like fried onions, a comforting scent that took me back to childhood Friday afternoons when my mother prepared Shabbas dinner. I felt positively swoony. Also hungry.

While the onions and the veal were sizzling, Antoinette pulverized the tomatoes in a blender with the garlic and parsley. I could actually smell the parsley, which only reinforced my suspicion that fresh makes a difference. Because we had so many tomatoes, we had to do two batches. We put in two cloves of garlic and half the parsley with each.

After the onion had browned, Antoinette removed the slices with a fork and put them into a bowl, another step I'd neglected. She left the veal bone in the pot and poured the pulverized tomatoes on top. While she was doing that, I lost all self-control and began eating the onions, one by one out of the bowl.

"That's what Scott does," Antoinette said, laughing.

I pictured her husband, the tall, handsome former hockey player, snacking on onions while his wife made dinner. I was tickled. I was always the clumsiest kid in gym class, picked last for every team. Nobody had ever compared me to a professional hockey player before (and doubtless never will again).

Antoinette poured about two tablespoons of salt into the pot, along with what appeared to be an equally horrific amount of pepper: it looked to me as if she was coating the top of the sauce.

"What are you doing?" I asked.

"Don't worry," she assured me, and she was right. It was as if the salt acted as a volume control, turning up the aroma until you could no longer smell onions, only flavourful tomatoes simmered with just the right amount of accoutrements to turn them into something magic. It was surprisingly comforting, conjuring up memories of the early days of my friendship with Antoinette. Back then our kids were little and we'd spend hours together at her house, the kids playing downstairs or in the TV room, us in her sunny kitchen drinking tea and sharing stories. And always there was pasta and homemade sauce, and I took for granted that Antoinette would be around forever.

When she left my house that day, I had five containers of sauce. I used it sparingly, so I didn't have to replenish it for several months. I felt confident that I could recreate the magic on my own. I was wrong. My initial attempts weren't exactly dismal failures, but they sure didn't taste like anything that had been graced by Antoinette's participation. Sometimes I put in too much pepper, other times not enough salt. A few times I couldn't find a veal bone so I went without. That was a mistake.

The best batch I've made so far was also the smallest. I used a combination of plum tomatoes from my garden, a 796 mL can of crushed tomatoes from my pantry, and a veal bone. Because I had fewer tomatoes, the veal flavour was more intense. That supports Antoinette's theory that there's no magic, only veal. (It also suggests that if I use more tomatoes, I need more veal.)

Still, I'm not quite ready to abandon the idea that there's magic in the sauce. I think it comes from being prepared by a natural, someone who learned at her mother's side and doesn't need to bother with a recipe and measuring utensils. From that perspective, I'm at an obvious disadvantage. But at least I now have some skills to make a close approximation, something to tide me over until the next time Antoinette comes to town.

My Mother's Tomato Sauce

VENERA FAZIO

Sunday mornings my mother
fingers inflamed from pickle factory brine
meditatively sculpted meatballs:
tender veal bought the day before
from a butcher a five-mile-bus ride
finely minced garlic
crisp parsley
onion
freshly grated breadcrumbs and parmesan cheese
eggs.

The meatballs slow-danced with
fennel sausages and pork ribs in
pulp squeezed from garden tomatoes.

At noon she served penne
the colour of family blood.
Instead of tasting love
I savoured mouthfuls of teenage bile
complained of monotony
same meal each week.

My children long for Nonna's pasta.
My imitation is mediocre.
I should have learned my mother's gift
of transforming tomato sauce
into ancestral legend.

Crostoli, Intrigoni, Bugie

GENNI GUNN

THE AROMA OF deep-fried delicacies wafts through the open window of my mother's kitchen, releases memories of *home*. It's July 1992, and my aunt Ninetta's arrival from Verona has precipitated a family reunion, though my mother, uncle, nephew and I form a tiny splinter group in Vancouver. Inside, my mother and aunt are laughing; I rap on the kitchen window to get their attention, while *La Traviata* blisters from the speakers in the living room.

This is zia Ninetta's first trip to Canada, and my mother is anxious to exchange the hospitality she enjoyed when she visited my aunt in Italy. In the past month, she has painted the guest room, sewn a new bedspread and cushion covers, driven to Bosa on Victoria Avenue to buy *taralli*, Italian olives, *panettone,* figs, mascarpone, mozzarella, and enough flour to bake for eternity. This, from an artist mother disinterested in cooking when we were small, but who, as the years pass, experiments endlessly to rediscover recipes her mother made, resulting in strange, savoury delicacies, vaguely familiar, as if in our collective memory, there exists a familial palate.

Married to brothers, my mother and zia Ninetta spent their twenties and early thirties in Trieste and Udine together, their history intertwined. They were accomplices against my grandparents, who had hoped my father would marry someone "more suited to him," meaning a fellow student he met in Tuscany when he was sixteen, and with whom his sister had developed a friendship, although my father had not encouraged the relationship, nor corresponded with the young woman in the intervening years. I suspect my grandparents objected to my mother's crimson lips, her outspoken demeanour, and her larger-than-life personality. In zia Ninetta, my mother found a kindred soul, a free-spirit from Verona, who loved fashion and parties. They formed an allegiance.

My memories of zia Ninetta are forged from black-and-white photographs in family albums. Within the white deckled edges of the small snapshots, zia Ninetta smiles into the camera, her arm around my mother, and beside them, my father and uncle, looking handsome and dangerous. They all resembled movie stars — the men in glistening hair, white shirts and dark sunglasses, the two women in stylish sweaters, midi-skirts and platform shoes in front of the Uffizi Gallery in Florence; in striped bathing suits in Rimini; in sundresses and sunhats in outdoor cafés in Venice — celebrities in my eyes, the women carefree and casually bold, decades before the women's movements of the 60s and 70s.

This is the mother I never knew, the mother I imagined as a gypsy, freed from the manacles of culture, of her parents' disapproval. A gypsy with golden bangles, tiered skirts and anklets, whose small brass bells announced her presence. A gypsy, and not my widow mother, who awakened alone to a frigid Canadian morning in 1972, my father in a morgue downtown.

How different our lives turn out, despite all we envision, our vision marred by the unexpected — a speeding car, an undelivered letter, a heart attack in the afternoon.

Today, Ninetta is the widow who greets me at the door. She is a formidable presence, a handsome woman, with large blue eyes, and hair combed into a bun. She wears a turquoise shirt-dress, and translucent pearls at the neck. We embrace, then she holds me at arm's length, trying to recognize me, though she hasn't seen me since I was a toddler. "You look like your father," she says, fingers on my cheek. "The Donati fair, fair skin."

"Come in, come in," my mother says, clearly relieved, pulling me into the kitchen. Always glamorous, she is impeccably dressed in a white silk shirt tucked into natural linen pants, her chestnut hair cascading in soft waves around her face. "We're going to make *crostoli*."

Her voice lilts in lively, spirited tones, fuelled, I'm certain, by competition. Because they originate from different regions in Italy, my mother and zia Ninetta make different *crostoli*, and my mother will manage to turn the baking into a competition, and her version of *crostoli* the best.

Like most national delicacies, *crostoli* change name and recipe by region or town, as if to embody the personalities of its inhabitants. In Genova, Torino and Imperia, they are called *bugie*—lies; in Toscana, they are *crogetti*, or *cenci*—rags; in Sulmona and centro Abruzzo, they are *cioffe*; in Sicilia, Campania, Lazio, Sardegna, Umbria, Puglia, Calabria, and Milano they are *chiacchiere*—gossip; in Reggio Emilia they become *intrigoni*—intrigues; while in Parma, Modena, Bologna, and Romagna they are *sfrappole*, or *rosoni*—rosettes. The names of these delicacies are as numerous as the towns and people who make them, supplementing and altering the recipes to suit their tastes: *galàni, sfrappe, sprelle, lasagne, lattughe, pampuglie, stracci, manzole, fiocchetti,* and so on. Interesting to note that while some of the Italian names are flippant—"lies, intrigues, gossip"—the English name for these is an earnest "angel wings," the cannibalistic suggestion notwithstanding.

"*Vieni, vieni,*" zia Ninetta says, her hand on my elbow, leading me into the kitchen. "We're just setting up."

I breathe in, imagining the fragrance of dough deep-frying in our first Canadian home in Kitimat, where a week before Christmas, my mother covered kitchen counters, dining room table, and two card tables with clean tablecloths and a variety of small implements: a fluted pastry wheel, a knife, a small bowl of water, as well as several large platters, neatly stacked. My father would reach into the uppermost shelves of the pantry, and retrieve the pasta machine in its original packaging. Despite the box's curled and droopy edges, the machine inside was like a shiny new car, chrome-plated, and heavy with our memories. My father would secure the machine to the edge of the counter with a C-clamp, then slide the handle into its slot. We all washed our hands, pushed up the sleeves of our sweaters, tied on aprons, and began our yearly ritual—in this, we were always united.

The opera crescendos at the party scene where Alfredo sings *Libiamo, Libiamo*, the famous drinking song. As soon as Violetta begins her part—*Tra voi / tra voi saprò dividere / il tempo mio giocondo*—my mother, zia Ninetta and I spontaneously begin to sing along, gesticulating as if we were welcoming guests to a 19C ball, our hands flitting imaginary fans in front of our faces — *Tutto è follia nel mondo / Ciò che non è piacer. All in the world is folly / if it is not pleasure.* My mother has a rich soprano, while zia Ninetta's voice is husky — a sound I associate with *Friulan*, the language of Friuli — its warm contralto, a memory of my father, who taught us Friulan songs with the most unlikely romantic plots — a moon/love thrown into the river and retrieved by a net of stars/kisses. In music, too, we were always united.

"Actually," zia Ninetta says, when we've stopped whirling about, and are back to opening bags of flour, and unfolding tablecloths and dish towels, "at home, we only make *crostoli* during Carnival."

In Italy, these treats are most commonly made and eaten during the two weeks before Lent, when in the Christian tradition, fasting and sacrifice begins and extends for forty days, until Easter. Carniva — the feast before the famine — originates from the Latin *carne* (meat) — *levare* (lift) meaning to remove meat from one's diet. So this season is a *hello* to sweets and partying, immediately preceding *farewell* to meat.

"Well, we don't believe in all that nonsense," my mother says. "Those old men starving themselves and beating themselves with ropes ..." She shakes her head. "We make *crostoli* whenever we have a festive occasion."

Though isolated from the rest of the family in Italy, we observe our own rituals and traditions, albeit either modified to suit us, or invented here. For example, our birthdays are not complete without a St. Honoré cake from Fratelli Bakery on Commercial Drive; a family reunion definitely requires rice croquettes and *panzerotti*; Christmas would not be Christmas without *crostoli*; and my mother would not be my mother if she couldn't revise traditions at will.

"And today is definitely a festive occasion, Zia, because you're here with us," I say quickly, hoping to dissuade a religious tangent of conversation focussing on fasting and self-denial, two things I am not interested in.

For the next half hour, we set our *crostoli* stage. Everything we touch turns into narrative: kitchen counters, tablecloths, utensils, water, even the opera — and soon we are deep in memory, recounting stories, as if this act of cooking together has forged a passage to the past. Our small disclosures bridge years and countries and disparate lives.

When everything is ready, we begin.

This is how we make *crostoli*: empty onto a counter a large amount of flour mixed with nutmeg and cinnamon; excavate a hole in the centre, creating a lovely white spent volcano. Heat olive oil together with the peel of a lemon. When the peel sizzles, strain it out, and pour the hot oil into the centre of the volcano (which now sputters and spits like a live volcano). Add water to make a manageable dough.

"What are you doing?" zia Ninetta says, frowning while my mother builds her small white mountain.

My mother turns, eyebrows raised. "What do you think?"

The small ensuing pause swells with Violetta's and Alfredo's farewell duet. I sigh, and swallow. I can't listen to *La Traviata* without weeping.

"What about the eggs?" zia Ninetta says.

"We don't put eggs in *crostoli*," my mother says, dismissing her.

Zia Ninetta frowns at me. I shrug. All I have is my mother's word for how to make these delicacies. And she, I assume, has her mother's word. Mirrors facing each other, extending to infinity. I retrieve a small pot from the cupboard, and pour in olive oil. Then I draw a lemon out of the fridge and cut off large chunks of peel, which I drop into the oil.

"You're not going to use oil?" zia Ninetta says, alarmed.

"Of course we are," my mother says briskly. "What else would we use?"

I slide the pot on the stove and turn up the gas.

"Butter," zia Ninetta says. "They're made with butter." She eyes the tables. "And where is the grappa?"

"Grappa?" My mother looks at her watch.

"For the dough," Ninetta says, hand wiping imaginary dust off the counter. "But a glass of wine would be quite welcome later on." She pauses, staring out the window at the flowering mock orange to one side of the deck. From the living room come the plaintive arias of Violetta who, pressured by Alfredo's father, has agreed to forsake

Alfredo, and now makes Germont swear that she will not be forgotten. *Dite alla giovine / si bella e pura ...* "Don't you remember those good times we had in Udine?" zia Ninetta laughs a throaty, ironic laugh.

My mother turns. "You always got away with murder."

A subtle shift, and we slide into dangerous territory, into the remnants of a feud begun years ago: an insinuation that my father's money was used to bail out zio Danilo's foolish spending, without my parents' knowledge. It's one of those topics no one has ever alluded to straight on, but rather that we all agree to pretend we simultaneously know and don't know the details. What is certain is that it caused bad blood between my father and his brother. And when my grandfather died, my father and zio Danilo inherited two houses in Udine, joined by a porte-cochère, which perfectly symbolized their relationship: linked yet separate.

"That's not fair," zia Ninetta says. "I didn't do anything."

"No, you didn't have to. You were born in the right family. An only child."

I continue to stir the oil, listening to *La Traviata*, an opera so familiar, I can recite every line. Violetta Valéry, born into the wrong family, destined to remain a courtesan or ruin a man's reputation. The power of tradition, of prejudice. *Addio, del passato / bei sogni rident / le rose del volto / già son pallenti ...*

"I had nothing to do with that," zia Ninetta says.

"My family was made poor by the war and the sanctions, but we were proud," my mother says, and recounts how she designed and sewed exquisite outfits from blankets and curtains, a-la-Scarlett-O'Hara, outfits that looked expensive. For this, she was castigated by her mother-in-law, who was convinced my mother would ruin her son. "I was the bad one in her eyes," my mother says, "while you were beautifully decked out in furs and dresses Danilo bought quite likely with—"

Zia Ninetta draws in her breath. "I know nothing about that," she says. "You know I don't." Her mouth is set tight.

My mother turns back to her flour, and zia Ninetta continues to wipe a small area of the counter. "How could you *not* know?" my mother says. "Did you not speak to your husband?"

I stare from one to the other — these beautiful, self-possessed women — trying to imagine them in Italy, contrasting and exotic, friends and competitors for my grandparents' love.

> *Love is the heartbeat of the entire universe / mysterious*
> *mysterious lordly / cross / cross delight / cross and delight /*
> *to the heart*

"Our husbands were the ones who got away with murder," zia Ninetta says. "They were charming womanizers."

We are all silent now, while Violetta and Alfredo declare their undying love for each other, their intention to leave Paris, and live happily-ever-after in unmarried bliss, a plot turn that requires a suspension of disbelief, given the era of the opera and the obvious consumption of the heroine. My mother sifts flour through white fingers; zia Ninetta riffles through her purse for a tissue.

"We'd better get working," I say, "or the *crostoli* won't be ready for supper." I pause. "Seeing as you make them in different ways, why don't we try both recipes?"

"We don't have grappa in the house."

"It doesn't have to be grappa," zia Ninetta says. "Spirits. Surely you have some of those?"

My mother frowns at zia Ninetta, trying to decide if this is a dig or not. "We have wine," she says, "and Anisette, Amaretto and Grand Marnier."

"Any of those will do," zia Ninetta says, "but the Anisette would be best, because it's colourless." She rolls up the sleeves of her dress, and ties on the apron my mother offers. Then she washes her hands, and gathers the flour bag.

The competition begins.

Zia Ninetta spills flour into a bowl, cuts in the butter, beats the eggs in a second bowl, then adds all the ingredients but the casting sugar. She folds the dry ingredients into the wet ones until she has a ball of dough, which she encases in saran wrap and puts in the fridge. "There," she says. "Now we have to wait a couple of hours for the liqueur to ferment into the dough." She opens the door, lets in a lozenge of sun. A warm breeze filters in.

My mother raises her eyebrows. "You're joking."

Zia Ninetta shrugs, and moves her hand in a circular motion. "That's what my mother always did," she says. "I think it has something to do with the pastry puffing up better." She unties her apron, slips it off, then wipes her brow with it.

On the deck, a cluster of fig trees form a seductive oasis of shade, an escape.

"Our *crostoli* always puff," my mother says, "and we don't lay them to rest."

"No, we don't like laying things to rest," I say.

My mother laughs. She is a veritable energy, both vivacious and tempestuous.

"All right." Zia Ninetta's voice is both resigned and frustrated. She dons the apron, and slides the dough out of the fridge. "Let's just make them now."

Both of them knead and roll their dough into logs, slice off 2-inch pieces they first flatten with a rolling pin, then hand me to pass through the rollers of the pasta machine. The thinner the dough, the greater the puff—also a human phenomenon.

Zia Ninetta places her pasta sheets on her side of the kitchen, and using the fluted pastry wheel, cuts rectangles, in the centre of which, she makes two cuts.

My mother abides by our tradition and wheels the pastry cutter along the length of her pasta sheets, creating bows, diamonds, and rosettes shaped from long strips of dough, pinched at one-inch intervals, then spiralled together.

"Listen," zia Ninetta says, "I almost hate to mention it, but I think what you're making is not *crostoli* but *cartellate*."

My mother looks at her, amused. "Call them whatever you like," she says. "In our family, we have always called them *crostoli*."

We continue to roll and cut, until every surface in the kitchen and dining room is covered in various fragile shapes, some of which do resemble angel wings. Now comes the deep-frying, a delicate, messy job.

My mother reaches into the pantry, and extracts the *crostoli*-frying pot—the bottom of an old pressure cooker we owned in the early 70s, that my mother has carted house to house ever since. I haul out the tin of olive oil.

"That pot is much too deep," zia Ninetta says, peering into its depths. "Don't you have a frying pan? Really, you only need an inch or so of oil."

"Oh no, no," my mother says, "crostoli are deep-fried. You can't deep-fry in an inch of oil."

"Well, we never deep-fry ours," zia Ninetta says. "They would become too greasy."

"It's the exact opposite!" my mother cries. "When you drop dough into deep hot oil, it sears the outside, and doesn't allow any oil inside." She pauses. "When you fry them in a shallow pan, they absorb the oil."

"Let's eat them raw," I say.

They both turn to me, and I grin. "Just kidding. Seeing as we're making two batches," I say, "why not use two different pans?" And I bend down and pull out my mother's frying pan for zia Ninetta.

They shrug, and fill their crucibles with oil. When the kitchen turns cobalt with smoke, they drop a handful of *crostoli* into the pots, turn them over, and whisk them into the colanders beside them, all in less than a minute. Then they wait for the oil to blue-smoke again. I transfer the drained *crostoli* onto large platters.

"These look just the same to me," I say, holding the two platters side by side.

We all stare at the golden, puffed *crostoli*.

"Close your eyes, both of you," I say. "Let's see if you can tell one from the other."

They close their eyes. I make a lot of noise, to confuse them, then I give my mother one of hers, and zia Ninetta one of hers. They each correctly identify it as their own recipes. "Wait, wait," I say. "Let me give you the other one before you decide." And then I give them each one of their own again.

"The second one is definitely Ninetta's," my mother says. "The eggs give it a slightly different consistency."

"I think now the first one is definitely Verbena's," zia Ninetta says. "A little crunchier."

"You are both absolutely right," I say, tasting one of each myself. "And both are delicious."

A plume of blue air swirls past us. My mother smiles and takes zia Ninetta's arm. "Let's finish so we can pour that glass of wine," she says.

We proceed to the last step, where the two versions diverge. Zia Ninetta dusts her batch with icing sugar, while my mother pours a tub of honey, a couple of spoons of sugar, a little water and a handful of pine nuts into a pot on the stove. When the honey bubbles up the sides of the pot, she submerges the *crostoli*, a few at a time, then quickly drops them into the platter I hold beneath her hand to catch gleaming, steaming, sticky delicacies, pine nuts — like memories — embedded in their hollows.

We now have two platters of *crostoli*, both different and similar. My mother and zia Ninetta exchange recipes. I inhale deeply — a sensory inheritance — the fragrance of our early days here, and I think of the last vestiges of our family in Canada — two nieces, a nephew — who have never made *crostoli* in a hot kitchen with my mother, blue smoke swirling and dissipating in the air.

Excerpt from Made Up of Arias

MICHELLE ALFANO

ONCE, A WEALTHY cousin of my father's was to arrive from Palermo, which is forty miles from my parents' village. This cousin, Cristofero, had made his money exporting some of the crops Sicily was famous for: olives, grapes, *fico d'India* and almonds. He was blonde and blue eyed and, Mama felt, inordinately proud of it. He always just happened to mention that his great grandmother was a Northerner from Venice and not a Sicilian.

"Some German *bastardo* raped his grandmother's grandmother and he thinks he's *speciale*," Mama muttered under her breath. She kept rearranging the kitchen chairs as she spoke to my father who was seated there. Later I learned that she meant the Normans who had conquered Sicily at one time but all European blondes were labelled Germans in our household.

"Be quiet," Papa ordered. "He's coming to stay and he's *famiglia* so enough of that kind of talk. Besides what does it matter what colour his hair is?"

"If *we* wanted yellow hair we could get it from a bottle *too*," she said as she angrily wiped and re-wiped the poor kitchen table. "And that peacock of a wife!"

"*Basta!*" My father said. "*È famiglia.*" He's family.

But this didn't stop my mother from complaining unceasingly even as she prepared for their arrival the next day. She was planning a special meal for Cristofero and Yolanda. She got up extra early to make the tomato sauce. She woke me so that I would watch and learn and then be able to "make it for my husband."

"Oh no, I'm not going to get married," I objected as I dragged a weathered wooden stool near the stove.

"Ah, you say that now — *ma*!"

"No never! And I'll never have to make sauce."

"And why not?" She asked fiercely, pulling the ingredients from the cantina.

"C-c-cause," I stuttered. "Why do I have to learn when I have you?"

"Oh paleeez! Are you to live with me always? *Zittiti* and watch," she said. So I shut up and watched.

She poured a dab of olive oil into a huge pot and fried several diced cloves of garlic until they were browned.

I wanted to ask Mama something that had long been troubling me.

"Mama, why does Cristofero have yellow hair if he is Papa's cousin and we all have dark hair? And why do zia Mariangela and cousin Angela have red hair and freckles?"

Angela and I once found an article about Sicily in *National Geographic*. Angela was waving it around and saying to the rest of the cousins: "What do they think we are? Some special kind of orangutan?" We leafed through the copy and found this caption that seemed to summarize for us the unique situation of Sicily: "Closer to Africa than to Rome" under a map of the island. For Angela, that said it all.

As Mama answered me, she added four bottles of crushed tomatoes that we had prepared and placed in new pop bottles from Diamond Beverages last fall. Then she added two small tins of tomato paste.

"Because we are all children of many different peoples that came to Sicily hundreds and hundreds of years ago."

"What people?"

"Go get your geography book and I'll show you."

I pulled out the black and gold Oxford atlas my father had brought home for me one day. It was printed the year my mother was born in 1935. Its pages were yellowing and turning slightly brittle. Each map was tinted in creamy browns and green for land masses and a pale blue for the oceans and seas. Railway lines were spiky, erratic red lines. The railway line ran along the spine of Italy's boot and continued on to the island of Sicily and ended in Palermo.

In Palermo, I was less than a finger's width from Tunis in North Africa.

Mama pointed to a map of Europe and the Mediterranean with one hand and with the other stirred the pot. After it came to a boil, she added a pinch of baking soda and some pieces of boned beef and let it cook.

"People came from all over Europe like *i Normanni*. From the Mediterranean *i Greci*. And even from northern Africa. *Da Cartagine e dai Saraceni*."

"Where is that?"

"*Nel nord d'Africa ed Arabia*."

"Is that why our cousins say Joey and I have curly hair because our ancestors were African?"

"Yes," she said, in a matter of fact way.

Next she started the *cavatti*, hand made pasta particular to Sicily and created with that peculiar hand gesture I had seen done many times by the women in the family. She mixed six cups of flour, three eggs and a touch of water into a thick mound of dough and kneaded it as if it was one of us being smacked for a misdeed.

"Sicily was invaded by many different people and each gave a small piece of themselves to Sicily. Whether we wanted that piece or not," she added, somewhat sarcastically. "Here you might see a Grecian temple, a castle built by *i Normanni*. A Spanish church and an Arabian mosque could sit side by side. The Greeks brought olives and figs and vines for grapes. From *i Saraceni* in Africa came lemons, dates, cotton and sugar cane."

She pummelled and stretched the dough and then pressed it flat with a rolling pin.

"But what if these people came and did bad things to the people there? That's what Angela said."

"Yes, we know that they did do many horrible things. But you and I are here now. *Mi piace che vedo ora*." I like what I see now.

She broke off a small piece of dough and curled it under her second and third finger in one movement then set the piece aside and continued until she had a mound of fresh pasta. The result was a thick nugget of pasta that resembled a shell. When she was finished, she placed a damp cloth over the pasta to "dry" for a couple of hours.

"That's why Sicilian children are the most beautiful in the world."

"We are?" I found this last part the hardest to swallow.

"Yes, you are. Now look at that — " She held up a *cavatti* in the palm of her hand for me to see. "*Non è bello?*" Isn't it beautiful?

"Yes." I had to agree and I was beginning to see that, in the end, the intermingling of cultures was like the creation of some wonderful new dish, kind of like me.

Privately, Joey and I discussed the coming of this cousin — there could be big money in it for us if we treated this guy right we figured. What could we do to make this dinner remarkable?

"Well, Mama always adds something special to our food," Joey said. "Why don't we do that?"

"Yeah, but where are we going to get bits of stars and moon water and angel feathers?" I wanted to see how far he would go with this.

"Hmmm."

We both thought about this. Joey scratched his head and I rubbed my chin as I had seen Papa do when he puzzled over a leaky faucet or a flat tire. I looked out over the window and saw one of Papa's pigeons sitting on the windowsill. Joey followed my glance. Papa was always bringing home animals. We foolishly thought of them as pets. Our parents, very sensibly, thought of them as food. The lambs and rabbits Papa brought home at Easter we nicknamed and fed and they usually ended up on the dinner table two days later. Joey and I could never quite get over that.

"Well, birds are kinda like angels," I said, pointing to the pigeon and smiling in a way I had before I did something really bad.

"Yeah," he agreed. "They both have feathers."

"And Mama has that pasta that looks like stars." Joey brightened.

"Yeah ... she always says that pasta was made in heaven," I offered hopefully.

"And rain is probably from the moon, I mean, where else does it come from?" Joey said.

"Yeah." I had to agree with this line of reasoning. I feared the logic was faulty yet couldn't detect where or how.

So we went about the house gathering our ingredients. Joey plucked a few gray feathers from the reluctant pigeon that had been named Iago by my mother. All in all, we had more than a dozen pigeons named after operatic lovers and villains. Alfredo and Violetta, Otello and Desdemona, Rinuccio and Lauretta, Aida and Radames, CioCioSan and Pinkerton, Mimi and Rodolfo and, lastly, Iago. The unlucky Iago, the unpaired male, had been the only one Joey could trap and pluck a few feathers from.

"Christ! He bit me!" Joey screeched.

"Well, how'd you feel if I tried to pluck something offa you?" I said. We both giggled as I took a few nips at his bare arm with my fingers.

We placed the feathers in the small, battered pot in the basement with the pieces of our semi-successful raid. It was the pot Mama cooked snails in. Clara wandered in dragging one of her dolls, which was almost her height, by its orange hair. My sister was wearing one of her original outfits: a yellow dress with plaid pants. No matter how hard we tried or how we cajoled her, she would not wear one without the other so Mama and I resigned ourselves to her three-year-old fashion *faux pas*.

"It kinda feels like that scene outta Macbeth," Joey said, shivering slightly.

"Yeah, but I want to be the head witch," I said. "Besides there are three witches and I'm the oldest. I should be the First Witch."

I opened the libretto from Mama's copy of Verdi's *Macbeth* recorded in 1952 at La Scala. Lady Macbeth was, of course, Maria Callas. The box containing the records was a delicate blue with gold lettering and resembled a sacred book in design. I leafed through its pages searching for the scenes with the three witches. Clara shifted uncomfortably. These three-years-olds, I thought, they have no ability to focus!

I read from the opening scene of the three witches in Act One in the libretto where Banco says:

Favellate a me pur,	Speak to me then,
se non v'è scuro	Fantastic creatures,
Creature fantastiche,	if the future is not
il futuro.	unknown to you.

"*Fantastiche!*" repeated Clara. She was now chewing on her doll's hair.

"Not that part! Not the predictions. The scene with the boiling pot," Joey said.

"Here it is!" I said excitedly. The scene I was looking for was the beginning of Act Three, Scene One in the witches' cave. I chanted:

Su via! Sollecite	Let us begin. Hurry
giriam la pentola.	around the pot.
Mesciamvi in circolo	Mix in a circle
possenti intingoli;	the potent brew;
Sirocchie, all'opera!	Sisters to work!
L'acqua gia fuma!	Already it steams!
Crepitae spuma.	Hisses and foams!

"I ain't a sister!" Joey fumed.

"Sssshhh! Hmmm, they used a toad and thorns ... a bat. What's a viper? Blood of an ape, yuck! Don't listen to this part Clara," I warned. She dutifully placed her plump hands over her ears. Then I repeated in a whisper: "*Finger of an infant.*"

"That's disgusting!" Joey said. "Besides those old witches are trying to do *bad* things. We're trying to do *good* things. Let's make up our own."

"I give you fea-ther of an-gels," I intoned solemnly and cackled once for good measure.

Next came the stars of pasta. "Primo or Lancia?" Joey asked as he held up both packages.

"Primo!" Clara blurted out. She liked the colours of the package, she said.

"I give you pieces of staaaars," Joey sang in his best operatic voice and added the *stelle.*

"I give you fruuuuits of the earth," I chanted, throwing in pieces of every kind of fruit we could muster: watermelon, cherries, grapes from the backyard, berries from nearby trees and bushes as well as peaches from our zio's backyard. Clara draped a cherry with two stems over her left ear.

"I give you water from the mooooon," Joey chanted and poured a small bucket full of clean rainwater, trying to remove the small, stray twigs that we saw floating.

We mixed the concoction together and added a few herbs from the garden, homegrown *mente* and *basilico*. Clara sucked her thumb and peered at the pot with her black, almond shaped eyes. She was just glad to be there and not be shooed away. Somehow it didn't look that appetizing as the three of us hovered over the pot, peering in as if to read our fortune.

"Let me do just this one part," I said. I had set up the portable record player and found the part.

E voi, Spiriti	And you, Spirits
negri e candidi,	black and white,
rossi e ceruli	red and blue
Rimescete!	Stir!
Voi che mescere	You who know so well
ben sapete.	how to mix.
Rimescete!	Stir!
Rimescete!	Stir!

"It'll look better when we mix it with the sauce," I assured Joey.

We marched back into the kitchen and placed two chairs next to the stove. Joey lifted the lid and I poured our brew into the bubbling cauldron of tomato sauce. The sauce sputtered a little and speckled my arm with the thick, red drops. Clara was on the lookout for Mama but we could hear her upstairs vacuuming violently in anticipation of our guests who were to arrive in a few hours so we knew we were safe. It was Clara's job to periodically inspect the pot and advise us if bits of our surprise had floated to the top. Then Joey or I would scoop it out and re-stir the sauce.

Mama didn't have to ask twice when she told me to set the table that night in the garden.

Mama had decided that we should eat outside under the grape bower. It was a beautiful evening and the drooping clusters and vines created a lace-like pattern on Mama's best linen tablecloth. There was Mama's slightly tarnished silver, folded cream coloured napkins and elaborate salt and pepper shakers shaped like two bunches of grapes. She brought out her wedding china—ivory coloured plates with a faded red rose in the centre and real gold trim, only slightly dulled over the years. The plates had delicate cracks on them like fine veins that dissolved into the ivory whiteness of the plate. Joey and I had destroyed a good portion of the china but she still had enough for a few place settings. As I set the table I practiced my basketball shot by bouncing grapes off Joey's head as he sat in the garden playing army and cheerfully blowing up tomato plants. He used the grapes as grenades so he was happy. Mama chased us both into the TV room and began finishing up dinner.

An hour later, my father's cousin and his wife arrived. As warned, Cristofero had a large blonde pompadour. I was sure I could smell hair spray and it wasn't coming from her. He was tall, thin and Nordic in appearance, turned out in an elegant dark suit and expensive watch. He had an irritating habit of playing with his moustache as he spoke.

I could tell Mama didn't approve of the wife either, with her clanging jewellery, fake beauty spot and Northern airs. I caught Mama rolling her eyes as she took Yolanda's expensive jacket from Milan and deliberately hung it in the closet next to Papa's work jacket. But Mama was the consummate actress and I knew our guests suspected nothing.

I saw our guests carefully inspect the furniture and chairs as if they were debating whether they should sit down or not. My father gallantly pulled back a chair for Yolanda. Cristofero did the same for Mama. She began to ladle the tomato sauce on to the pasta after I dutifully brought each plate to rest at our guests' place.

"What an unusual sauce," Yolanda began, with some trepidation, as she raised a spoonful to her small nose that suspiciously resembled my Barbie doll's. She wrinkled it delicately. Joey and I stifled a giggle and I carefully started scraping the sauce off the pasta and pushing it to the side of the plate, just ... in ... case. Cristofero placed a large forkful of pasta in his mouth and promptly spit it out.

"*Ma ch'è questo?* " Papa sputtered.

Sauce dribbled down the front of Cristofero's shirt and he dabbed at the bits of sauce and pasta that speckled the ivory tablecloth. As Joey and I glanced around the table we noticed everyone having similar reactions. A line of sweat was forming on Joey's upper lip. He never could take the heat. My mother chewed on her food thoughtfully then unceremoniously spit it out into her napkin. She noticed we weren't eating and stood up and grabbed both of us by one ear each.

"Are you trying to poison us?" she demanded. My father's cousins carefully averted their eyes and placed their forks back on the table.

"*Dimme che hai fatto!*" Tell me what you've done!

Piece by piece the story came out. No one noticed Clara finishing her pasta with relish, oblivious to the turmoil, sauce splattering on to her pink top and round cheeks. Yolanda was holding a napkin to her mouth and trying to prevent herself from gagging, but oh so delicately. Cristofero put his hands in his pockets and started to inspect the garden most carefully. My father said nothing but his face got redder and redder with each ingredient we listed until it looked like his head would explode. Suddenly he got up and turned to my mother.

"You see what your *stupidaggine* have lead to? You fill their heads with silly stories and this is what it comes to!" He turned to his guests and started apologizing as Mama jerked Joey and me away from the table. I stared at Clara. Sure, just because you're four years old doesn't mean you don't know what you're doing, I thought.

She brought us into her bedroom and closed the door. For a brief moment, I thought I could convince Mama that this incident was an act of insurrection against the Norman conqueror, the blonde invader. But from the look on her face I soon gave up that idea. As she turned towards us she said: "If there is to be any poisoning to be done, I will do it. *Capisce?*"

Joey and I looked at each other. "*Si*, Mama."

"I do the cooking from now on — okaaay?"

"*Si*, Mama," we replied again.

"Besides if I wanted to poison that rooster I would have been more careful. Now go outside in the backyard. Don't — touch — anything. *If I hear you breathing*, you're going to get it. I'll bring you something to eat."

She left us. Joey and I stared at each other, amazed that we had escaped. Did I see her winking at us, or was she blinking because she was so angry? She made her way back to the dinner table and Joey and I were never able to figure it out.

Making Olives and Other Family Secrets

DARLENE MADOTT

Olive Oil Properties

Sun, stone, drought, silence and solitude. These are the five ingredients that create the ideal habitat for the olive tree. Their colour defines them. Unripe olives are green. Fully ripe olives are black. The longer the olive is permitted to ferment in its own brine, the less bitter and more intricate its flavour will become.

"You have to crack them open, *devi schiacciarle* — crack them open, so they can absorb the sweetness of life." My aunt Vitinna, from my mother's Sicilian side of the family, was describing how to make olives. But when my Sicilian Aunt Vitinna spoke of cracking the olives open — abusing them so that they could become sweet — I thought instantly of my Calabrian Aunt Florence. Aunt Flo, as I knew her, was one who, like the olives, had been *schiacciata* by life.

Sun

Possessed of a legendary beauty that was quite gone by the time I knew her, she was the first to be married. She had a good many suitors — men who later gave decent lives to their women, but my Aunt Flo gave herself to Ercole. I knew my Uncle Ercole as a rude man who rolled putrid cigars wetly between his lips and buffed his teeth after dinner with a folded serviette. His hands smelled of cigars.

Uncle Ercole had made Aunt Flo pregnant before making her his bride.

That was shocking in those days. Today, it would not be a matter of a wasted life, but in those days, to disgrace family was a choice worse than death.

While her belly swelled, Ercole talked long and leisurely about returning to Italy. For six months, he talked.

Drought

In the meantime, Florence's sister Vittoria grew in her own righteousness. Vittoria accused Florence of spoiling her own prospects of marriage. With her buckteeth and draught-horse figure, Vittoria had never been pretty, or sought-after, or loved. Secretly, she probably preened at her sister's tragedy.

Florence wasn't restrained. Not like her sister Vittoria. She used to talk about Ercole to anyone who would listen to her. She didn't care who knew what kind of a man she had married. Florence lived with Ercole in this chicken coop of a house and sold eggs around the neighbourhood to make herself some pocket money. Ercole never gave her a cent, expecting her father to support his damaged-goods daughter.

Stone

When it came time for Florence to have the baby that had so compromised her, Ercole stood at the door of their bedroom, his face hard as stone, watching the progress of Florence's suffering: "That's the way I like to see you — like that."

My cousin's head was showing, but Florence sat up in the bed on her elbows and heaved her pillow at the door. My cousin Frankie was born in a flurry of feathers.

Florence, astonishingly, was without shame. She simply refused to mourn her life, and perhaps this, more than anything, drove her sister Vittoria closer to her own bitter *osso* (olive pit).

Silence

Now was this next development part of the plan? Is this what people mean when they say we all get back our own?

Vittoria had only one child. A daughter, Gioia. She came to Vittoria and Enrico, almost by surprise, eight years after they married. Now Vittoria, who had always criticized her sister's righteous way of bringing up children, had a chance to rear her own.

Chubby Gioia. At sixteen, she wore bobby socks and full skirts that stopped just short of her dimpled knees, and sweaters buttoned up backwards and pulled down tightly over her enormous breasts. She had an open cheerful face and a boisterous way of laughing that reminded some people of Florence — much to her mother's dismay. In fact, Vittoria was dismayed by most things about her daughter, not least of which were those breasts. Jiggling and irrepressible, no harness of a bra could contain them.

From the silent way my parents dressed for Gioia's wedding, I knew something must be wrong. My older sister had been told and preened with the knowledge. But I was thought to be too young. I only knew our Dad had been asked to give Gioia away, that for some reason, her own father would have nothing to do with the wedding.

"What is it with the women in this family," my father said that day, knotting his tie. "All made of Flo's blood? All soft hearts and hard heads?" Words I did not then understand.

Sun

There is a home movie my father made in the late 1950s at one of Aunt Flo's Christmas Eve dinners. In the kitchen, sweating from hot camera lights and the steam rising from the pasta pot, Flo lifts the pasta for the movie. The meal itself would be served on a plywood table, covered with a white linen tablecloth. Her fallen bra strap dangles on her arm, as she pulls the pasta from the water. Her own daughter, dressed in a fuchsia pink, tight-fitting satin cocktail dress, waves for the camera. Aunt Flo is laughing — irrepressibly. Although this is a silent home movie, you can hear Flo laughing.

On the day our youngest sister was being born, my oldest sister and I went to stay with my Aunt Flo. Our father drove us over early in the morning, just as the sun began to rise. Flo greeted us in the kitchen. She wore a pink floral housedress, the brassiere strap dangling on her arm. Her own children were long grown and gone from the house. We had the whole house to ourselves, and Aunt Flo.

Flo played with my older sister and I. I mean, she *really played with us,* as if there were no difference in our ages or imaginations. From a deep bottom drawer filled with costume jewellery, she pulled out the coloured strands of beads, roped these around our necks, and showed us how to dance "the Charleston."

For lunch, we gorged ourselves on black olives.

When our father came to pick us up, I was being sick on the black olives. "What happened to the money I gave you to make them a proper lunch?" Aunt Flo looked flushed and ashamed. She looked like a child being chastised. I wished so much my father would not be so angry with her. It was my first intuition of an odds between one adult and the rest of the grown-up world.

Solitude

"Don't you know your pain is no different than anyone else's," my sister said to me, the winter of my separation, after I had made my own first mistake with the likes of an Uncle Ercole — a man just as abusive, although he came polished and wearing a business suit. I am told that, when I laughed at the altar (how this man had hated my laugh), the wedding guests had heard my Aunt Flo. "No one wants to hear you, or don't you know yet?"

I wanted to tell my older sister then, as I do now: It is not the pain that defines us, but rather our response to it.

Sun

I will eat olives. I will eat olives as long as I can, as many as I can get. I will eat them to excess, even if eating them should make me sick. I will allow life to crack me open, so that I can absorb the salt, the sweetness of it. I will risk making them, over and over again, just like my mistakes. I will do this in memory of my godmother, my very own Aunt Flo — *è stata schiacciata dalla vita.* Cracked, she had been like the olive, but like the olive cured in salt water, had absorbed all the sweetness of life.

Lezioni and Leftovers

GLENN CARLEY

I GO WITH my wife. We are gently chastised by my father-in-law for not coming more often. Our children have come of age and they roam new fields. We are not sure if we are shepherds anymore, *carabinieri* or ready to move into town with the old to find new songs and dance at the feast in the piazza. I am a father, so I am always the *carabiniere*—what can I say? You will know this hardship if you are lucky.

"She" has come to teach him—to give him another lesson on the computer. He has just returned from the library but there, they speak too fast. He wants to know how to create and store *Word* documents. His hands span the girth of cherry trees. How can this man with the grade five education—this man who builds huts to sleep in, with the husks of corn plants, so far out on the pieces of land that it makes sense to stay out there, to sleep with his woman and awake with the sun—tinkle the keyboard and make poems and discover how to save-to-folder? I take my wife's coat and she and her father depart to the little desk in his room. I hear her ask him to boot up the computer and I smile. It is his first *lezione* and she is teaching him to fish. It is in her blood.

An aroma carries me down a set of stairs to the basement and I stand in the doorway of the "downstairs kitchen." A bare bulb sheds a cozy glow. *La signora* is at work. She is before the gas burning stove, jerry-built into a small corner by the furnace. I know what she is making and I have come to learn. Pots and ladles hang from the rafters. There is a spice rack under the basement window. A clean board has been grafted onto a table. A hint of skepticism scents the air.

I am handed a paisley apron by *La signora* to protect my clothes. She summons me to a large pot on the stove and makes me see that the potatoes are to be boiled whole. It is here that we begin the *lezione* on how to make the gnocchi from scratch and I am happy because she too is making the time to teach me. First, there is the *dimostrazione* and then there is the timeless expectation to do it the same way her mother did it. It is the only way to learn. I tell her she is my *professore* in the cooking *scuola* and, when she laughs, I know I have passed the first test. "You have such passion to learn," she says. "I can't help it," I say. "You can teach a young dog old tricks."

Under careful eyes, the lesson unfolds with a little volcano of potato and the egg in the middle and the kneading and the kneading and the quiet concentration, the rolling and the rolling, the cutting and the gentle press with the tine of the fork to collect the sauce after it is boiled and steamy and ready. I love the steam and I hold it deep in my lungs and it changes me.

When you marry-into, perhaps you are forgiven. If she is happy, they are happy and if they are all happy you are a Man. And because you are their Man, you can be Canadian and change things up, like the butterfly effect. It is permitted. I do the cooking and some of the cleaning. I do not leave these things just to her. They know I do not need to be babied by my wife and made to think I am King, when all along, she is the Soul of our Home. It is the alchemy of the melting pot and they concede the concession. The man can cook, he can clean, he can be tender and love the babies, put dinner on *la tavola*, maybe even run the washer the way he did before he was married.

It could be worse. You must make a life in strange ways in the new world. Yes, it irks the ancient order but it is like the grit of sand in the old ways of their oyster. Pearls are formed by unknown design and let it always be so. Leastways, it is providence and I cannot change the twist and turn of the Mobius Life, nor do I wish to. In this way, I know that I am loved because above all this, turning naturally, is the cycle and spin of seasons and the great predictability of the sun. There is seed, there is planting, there is harvest, there is rest. Repeat to infinity.

When we are done, I see that *La signora* is still busy so I leave the kitchen alcove, walk up the basement stairs and turn right into *la scuola del* computer. My wife looks up and tells her father to show me how to save his *Word* document to a file. So he does. The *lezione* is complete. She is happy and they chat in Italian. If she is happy than I am happy. It is the simple law of love.

I leave them alone to be together and I feel vaguely at loose ends for sometimes I am still a tourist in their culture. Aimlessly, I descend to the downstairs kitchen and I am again ushered into that alcove next to the furnace by the texture and dance of aroma. I offer my services.

Somehow, *La signora* has anticipated the end of the work cycle. The food is ready with a precision that transcends the need of a clock. I sense that, when you live on the land ... when you place your hands deep in it ... when it is under your nails every day that you lived ... when your ear sleeps next to it and hearkens to the rhythms of its breath, the tremulations and cycles, the order and predictability of growth transfer into your Soul and you are given an ancient gift of always knowing when it is time. I am not sure why I know this.

She sends me upstairs with a stainless steel bowl filled with our gnocchi. It is covered but I peek and the *reggiano* has changed form and is melting into the sauce. I dutifully return to the downstairs kitchen chewing a small piece of crusty bread. I am sent up with a shallow bowl of *verdura* and upon careful enquiry, I am corrected. It is not *rapini* that I ascend to the heavens with; it is a medley of green *radicchio*, onion, garlic and oil. I am embarrassed to admit that I did not know *radicchio* came in green but I want to put pepper on it now and begin to eat it now while I let go and float upstairs like a bird of prey on moist currents of steam. It is so dangerous to be alone with the food.

I descend to the kitchen with a handful of dry almonds. This time, upon leaving, I observe the great ratio and proportion of love for I see the sewing machine and the ironing board on the left and the tool bench on the right. They are perfectly balanced like rows of things in a garden of sweet being. I pause for a moment and then scale the two short flights of steps to the upstairs kitchen. I escort a covered pan of veal shoulder and something called *muscolo di vitello* to the table. It is still simmering and I know when I lift the lid, a genie will appear before me and that wishes I didn't even know I had will be granted. I tease *La signora* by telling her that I did not know Italians ate moose. She laughs and interprets my English with the spank of a wooden spoon. I was present when the *Palomino* wine went in and erupted in a sweet sizzle because I need to learn these things, to practice them and then to teach. I place the meat on a trivet which, by chance, is placed next to a nub of *Friulano* cheese, so I cut a slice and return to *La signora*. She tells me "this is all we have, there is nothing more" and I am incredulous for soon I will sit and devour a feast that certain angels serve their friends when they drop by in *paradiso*.

As if on a ladder I ascend with her. She efficiently inspects the upstairs kitchen and sees that the *Alberta Springs* bottle is empty. I am directed to fill it and to call my father-in-law and wife to the meal. The two of them are still chatting in Italian. They are completely content in the great ministry of presence between a father and a daughter who left home to make a life. "Dinner is ready," I call out when I pass by. They both genetically pause and look at me with a kind of foreign amusement. I cross the twilight of the basement linoleum and I wonder why my wife and I do not buy the shiny green olives that come in the big jars. I test the pits with my teeth, turn on the bare bulb and walk into the glow of the cantina.

Rather than let gravity do the work, I take a good pull from the gallon jug, pinch off the end of the tube and let the wine flow into the recycled whiskey bottle, expertly filling it to the brim. You could say that I have done it once or twice, before.

The set table beholds the one o'clock sun as it streams through the window and the sliding door to the kitchen. The still-life is exquisite, there are no shadows and the room is warm and expectant. We are joined *a tavola* by the great saint, *Padre Pio*, a black and white framed photograph of *Castropignano*, *Gesù* on the cross and the long picture of the Last Supper with its lurid blues and reds and the yellow flaming heart on the breast of the Son of God. We clasp hands, bow our heads, the father says the prayer and in a moment, you must listen for it, there is the ting and clatter of everyday living. It is symphonic and it heightens my senses. I pause to hear the ancient order and it must be like corn invisibly growing in the moist breath of sky, so easy to miss. I adore the rhythmic, spiritual presence of masculinity and femininity in the room, and to a casual modern eye, you could say that it locks them in, that they are prisoners of it but to me, they are alive in their light, so much so that I am made more alive; made more masculine in its fullest sense and I know I am slightly rearranged, slightly better now than I was before I arrived and I want to leave that way and sustain it.

We are asked about the children and we tell them tales of busyness and growing up. They tell us familiar tales of how hard it was when they first came and I am so fluent with their stories I can tell them back the next part or a detail they missed from the last time. It is a curious property of language for, if you listen carefully and if you are truly present, you will learn the dialect of their Life and, when you learn that, you will know how to speak love fluently, so much so that the traces of your accent will gradually disappear. I have seen it. They taught me to slow down, to listen, to inspect and to observe, to do things in their order, to let it all unfold and not fight it. They taught me to seek out and discover the Arcana of an ancient life.

"The children used to say that I talk too loud," the old guy smiles. It is after dinner, food no longer busies his tongue and he relaxes, now. He cracks a *pizzelle* in two but refuses the sugary sweetness of the brown almond cookie or the chewy vanilla texture of a homemade *torrone*. He might take a banana later, or a handful of grapes, but he is old now and says she makes too much food. Naturally, I help myself to all three magical tastes but only after the gesture is made thrice, with a vague hint of disappointment if I do not accept. Women speak with their eyes so beautifully.

"They tell me it is because my hearing is going but I tell them, back home, there was no telephone and if you wanted to talk to a guy you had to yell across your field to his field," he instructs with a flourish. "That is how we talked back then ... "

"It is not like that now," I reply to finish his thought and he nods.

At some point, the light subtly changes in the kitchen and my wife and I sense it is time to go. We will climb into the car and pick our way past stop signs for the Highway north. We will go back to the kids and to our life. "She" will take her siesta when we leave, for it is time to rest. I know the *old guy* is eager to be in his room, to turn on the computer and watch the light boot it up so he can practice the day's lesson given to him so happily by his daughter.

We bustle to leave. I transfer our shoes from the side door to the front. The *old guy* takes me back down to the basement, through the twilight and we click on the bare bulb to light the cantina. He decants en empty *Gibson's* bottle of white wine for me, quietly whistling as it fills. He is an expert and does not waste a drop.

"This is to cook with, not to drink," I say in a firm instructive tone.

I see him grin and wave his hand in a small circle and, before I protest, he decants an *Alberta Springs* bottle of *Grenache*.

"This is for your neighbours," he deadpans.

At the front door, they stand and watch us put on our shoes. We rise, hug, share kisses and are told to come again. I am handed a weighty plastic bag by *La signora*. It is the left over *gnocchi*, some *vitello* and a large pickle jar of her sauce. It is the great transfer of love from one home to another, from the old, to the children and in a moment I see magnificence in this casual generosity that comes so easily to them like breathing. I swear an oath to return all the containers and I can see she is pleased.

"That way, we can refill them," I say.

Later, my wife and I arrive back to our Canadian home. It was good to be with them.

We can tell by the shoes that our son is out but Lo, unbelievably so, our daughter is present. We enter the warmth of the house and I place our treasure on the kitchen counter. The *gnocchi* is still warm and I set out a plate, a fork and a napkin. For some reason, I miss my father and I put on some classical music that I grew up with. In a curious twist of Fate, don't ask me why, it is Tchaikovsky's *Capriccio Italien*. The upstairs kitchen is bathed in sound and I am happy. Our daughter comes to the table of her volition. She knows where we have been. I pour a glass of *Grenache*, light the candle and sit alone across from her. We clasp hands and say the Italian prayer and I ask God to watch over *Nonno* and to remember *Nonna* well.

"Mom taught *Nonno* on the computer and I learned a cooking *lezione* today," I tell her wistfully.

"You always learn a lesson when you go down there, Dad," she says as a matter of fact.

I look into her eyes and see the depth of my own.

"Is there any more gnocchi?" she asks.

"Yes, for now," I say and I pass her the bowl.

Cosi Sia

Roast Turkey and Polenta

ANNA FORNARI

MY FATHER IMMIGRATED to Canada's West Coast in 1956 from the Treviso area of the Veneto Region in Northern Italy. It wasn't fate that led my father to Vancouver, but the simple fact that he had an uncle living there who had agreed to sponsor him. He was 19, young and good-looking. Who knows what he expected of his new life? One thing was certain, he was only there to make money; sooner or later he was going to go back home. Or so he thought.

However, fate had other things in store for him and shortly after his arrival he met the woman who was to become his wife. They worked in the same company, she as a secretary and he as a mechanic. My Canadian mother, who came from a British heritage, was enthralled with this different young man. In broken English my father rambled on about his country; how he missed his mother's cooking, his family and friends, his territory, his language. One of the things he mentioned often was *polenta*. So often that, once married, my mother set about learning how to make it. She wanted to surprise him with what she understood to be his favourite dish.

When my father came home from work one evening, he found for his dinner a nice steaming bowl of *polenta*, just *polenta*. He almost hit the roof. He had talked and talked about polenta, but not with fondness as his wife had supposed, but with horror at the memory of eating it for every meal during war time. He couldn't stand the sight of the bland, insipid concoction and definitely preferred bread, which back then was a rare luxury. To make matters worse, mom had served it without "*il tocio*," stewed meat, not knowing that *polenta* is never served on its own. It usually takes the place of bread and is complemented with a flavourful tomato-based meat or rabbit stew. His heart's delight, it seemed, was not a plate of plain polenta.

This story has been re-told countless times bringing a chuckle to those old Italians who know what *polenta* is and how much of it was eaten during the war. Yet, imagining the scene, I cannot erase the vision of the distraught face of a confused young bride trying to please her immigrant husband by unknowingly cooking his least favourite dish and a hungry, tired foreigner coming home to a dinner of just boiled salted cornmeal.

Living so far from home my father would continually praise my nonna's culinary prowess. None could cook better than his mamma. So, it was no easy matter for my mother, a non-Italian, to follow in her footsteps.

On her first trip over to the Italian peninsula, my mom eagerly went armed with notebook and pen, ready to observe and take notes, attentive to all the goings on in the old Italian kitchen. She sat at the long, wooden table beside the woodstove fire asking questions in the little Italian she had painstakingly learned to communicate with her husband's family. The same wooden table that every Sunday saw all the Fornari brothers and sisters, and there were six, with their children in tow, slurping tortellini soup, cutting up pieces of meat for the little ones, laughing and talking and arguing while passing the many succulent dishes from one end of the table to the other.

My nonna always had dozens of pots bubbling on that woodstove. There was always enough tortellini so that one could have it in broth if they so desired, or with a tasty meat ragu, both dishes sprinkled abundantly with — parmesan cheese — strictly freshly grated, of course. There was always roasted meat of some kind, mostly chicken or rabbit raised by my nonno (grandfather) and freshly killed, plucked or skinned for the Sunday meal.

I was often witness to the ritual preparation of the family's fresh meat. I was horrified the first time I saw my nonno hit a large, plump rabbit on the head, string it up by its feet then carefully peel the fur down the legs, bunch it together in his gnarly old hands, then quickly wrench it down the rabbit and off its head in one clean, smooth motion. The fur made a gruesome slurping sound as it came off the still warm body of the dead rabbit. My nonno then proceeded to slit open the stomach and take out the steaming innards. The heady nauseating smell that arose from the intestinal mass caused me to wrinkle my nose in distaste and avert my gaze. I would peek out from behind my hand and watch as he separated a bloody liver, heart and gizzard from the rest. The heart and gizzard would be added to the big pot of fresh boiling broth always bubbling on the stovetop. The liver was saved for a savoury risotto. The rest of the innards were dropped on the ground where the dogs were lying in wait to devour the steaming mass.

Where I came from more often than not rabbits, or "bunnies," were considered pets, but as horrified as I was every time my nonno prepared for the weekly execution; it didn't stop me from rushing out with him to witness the macabre slaughter. Watching intently I wondered if that was how the Indians scalped their enemies in the novels I read passionately lying on my bed in my free time. Nor did it stop me from tucking into the sumptuous meal my nonna prepared and devouring the delicately roasted rabbit or chicken bathed in olive oil, sage and rosemary, just as eagerly as the dogs had slurped up their tasty treats. By this time I had grown used to the customs of my father's homeland and I had decided I wanted to learn all I could in the brief time I spent there those long ago summer months.

From butchering rabbits to dessert making, needless to say there would always be something sweet at the end of the Sunday meal. My aunt Luisa, the youngest of my aunts, was the dessert maker in the family. She would faithfully arrive in a last minute flurry, make room at the large table, whip out a few ingredients from her large bag, stir up a frothy mascarpone cream, at the same time filling the house with the smell of freshly brewed coffee. In no time flat she would assemble a Tiramisù while my mother scribbled away in her notebook, trying her best to create order out of the fast, confusing instructions.

"You take 5 eggs and you separate the yolks from the whites. Then you mix 2 tablespoons, heaping, of sugar, white sugar, per every egg yolk, then you beat it all until it doubles in size, nice and frothy, then you mix in 500 ml of mascarpone … what's mascarpone? Well, this is mascarpone; it's a type of fresh cheese. What? You can't get it in Canada?"

Countless times my mother would adapt recipes Canadian-style so she could replicate them across the ocean. Living in Kitimat, BC, a 19-hour drive from the nearest Italian store in downtown Vancouver, more often than not, Italian ingredients were not to be found. So firmly whipped cream became a substitute for mascarpone, very strongly brewed regular coffee was exchanged for espresso, tea biscuits or sponge cake for ladyfingers.

I learned from my mother that recipes could be adapted based on the ingredients available or to suit the occasion. Those lessons served me well when I eventually married an Italian from the same area my father had come from — the Veneto Region and moved to Volpago del Montello, Treviso, Italy. Then it was I wanting to reproduce my Canadian recipes using Italian ingredients. Chocolate chip cookies, bran muffins, carrot cake, Christmas fruitcake. A lot easier said than done.

It was especially difficult at Christmas when there were no whole turkeys to be had; they were only sold in pieces — a breast or a thigh and leg. A whole turkey was never anywhere to be found. I, who had been brought up on at least two stuffed, roasted turkeys a year, one at Thanksgiving and one at Christmas, could not fathom a country whose traditional Christmas meat course was a plate of mixed boiled meat — including tongue! Lovely as that may be for any other day of the year, it was not what I envisioned as a Christmas meal. So every year I would order a turkey from Claudio, the butcher. And every year he would say: "Signora, you know there are two sizes, the "tachinella" or the bigger ones. They don't slaughter them at the size you want." So I would arrange for him to keep his eyes open for the smallest of the big size as the "tachinella" was about as big as a chicken. Faithfully I would end up with a turkey so enormous I had trouble fitting it into the oven and more than once I had to cut off the pope/parson's nose to make it fit.

That was a standing joke in our house. I can still hear my mother muttering "Pope or Parson, depending on your religion." The one-liner always went over my Catholic father's head, but it never failed to bring a snicker and smile to my Protestant mother's lips.

But even so, with or without the Pope/Parson's nose, it was still a tight squeeze. Now, every year as my butcher hands me my oversized turkey, he tells me it is the smallest one available. I have given up trying to find a decent sized bird, and forget a plump, juicy Butterball. Even after thirty years, I still dream of Butterball turkeys.

Turkey stories abound in the expat community. Over the years I have come to know and befriend many English speaking people living in Italy and we all have similar stories to tell. As we all know, along with the tradition of the stuffed, roast turkey with gravy and cranberry sauce, comes the "carving" ritual. It is essential to carve the turkey following a specific procedure, a procedure that is religiously passed down from father to son in most Anglo Saxon families. Having an Italian father who was not at all interested in cooking, it was my mother who did the carving, gradually passing the technique on to my brother who then became the male expert. In Italy it was I who carved until my son was old enough to learn the technique from my brother. Both are now excellent turkey carvers.

But Italians have absolutely no idea what carving is all about. In fact, years ago a dear Welsh friend, newly married to an Italian, managed to acquire a turkey for her first family Christmas. Everyone oohed and aahed at the perfectly roasted caramel coloured turkey when she proudly brought it out to the table — her very first Christmas roast turkey. She went back to the kitchen to get her carving knives and upon return, lo and behold, her husband had already preceded her by cutting it into four with a pair of poultry shears! He had no idea what he had done so grievous as to cause her to burst into tears in front of all of his relatives.

Along with roast turkey it is also necessary to have all the trimmings. Brussels sprouts are a must. Even if many of us hate them, we serve them and eat them because it is the "tradition". No respectable cook would have Christmas dinner without Brussels sprouts. But try and find them in Italy! Any expat from an Anglo Saxon country living in Italy has tried at some point in his/her life to purchase Brussels sprouts. For many years they were not to be had whatsoever. Now they are available in certain supermarkets, and it becomes a race to see who gets them first. Parsnips? Forget it. Italians turn their noses up at them. I have occasionally found them at the grocer's in nearby (a mere 160 km) Slovenia. One or two of us expats will make this trip two or three times a year. When I tell my mom I go to Slovenia to buy my parsnips she just shakes her head. "Such a common vegetable, how could it not be sold in Italy?" she wonders.

For years every trip back to Canada culminated in returning with a suitcase full of "Canadian" food unavailable in Italy — peanut butter, packets of grape, orange, lemon jelly, soft brown sugar, big, fat chocolate chips, home smoked salmon from Campbell River, tins of smoked oysters and jars of maple syrup. In the good ol' days I could fill two 30 kg. suitcases on an overseas trip. Nowadays, that is an almost forgotten luxury. There was a lot of Canada packed into those suitcases. A lot of home.

It wasn't long after marriage that I realized the roles had been reversed and for a very long time I wondered how it had happened that I had fallen into my father's shoes. I began to remember him telling us never-ending stories about Italy, singing nursery rhymes in the Veneto dialect while bouncing me on his knee. According to him life was better across the Atlantic Ocean. I studied the Italian language as a teenager and fell in love with its romantic musicality. I fantasized about life in Italy, little knowing that one day it would become my country, little knowing that the Italian things my immigrant father ached for in Canada, ironically I would as an immigrant in Italy long for in reverse.

My father had pined after his mother's Italian home cooking and the warm embrace of the family kitchen. I, living in Italy, found myself missing even the simplest, most humble of foods that were daily staples and easily found in my mother's kitchen. Those foods and recipes bring back memories of a warm, happy childhood filled with love. If nothing is more heart warming to my father than the smell of a simmering pot of spaghetti sauce that conjures up memories of his mother and their kitchen, nothing is more heart warming to me than the vision of my mother busily making dinner for us, the warm smell of the cinnamon and nutmeg she used in her apple and pumpkin pies and a roast turkey crackling in the oven, its savoury sage and onion aroma wafting through the kitchen and enveloping the house. The warmth and cosiness was palpable.

As my father, with my mother's help, tried his best to respect his Italian family traditions, I too continue whimsically to respect the mixture our family's traditions have become. Those rituals have become deeply significant. For years they helped my father remember who he is and where he came from. And now they help me remember who I am and where I have come from.

The Turkey War: Part One

JOSEPH PIVATO

SOON AFTER WE were married my wife, Emma, and I realized that we had different approaches to the big Christmas dinner. I was raised in an Italian family and our Christmas dinners usually had two meat dishes and a great variety of cooked vegetables and a salad. The meat dishes could include any two of these: veal, chicken, pork, lamb, beef and fish. We sometimes had vitello alla Valdostana, or osso buco alla Milanese. And there were also cheeses and desserts. Emma's parents were Scandinavian, but they had adopted the American tradition of the turkey with the fixings for Christmas. For the first few years of our marriage we followed this tradition of the Christmas turkey. I noticed that this turkey tradition was creating a good deal of stress in the house every Christmas. After our older children left home to study in Toronto and Montreal, they would come home for Christmas and wanted a peaceful visit with us, their parents and their younger sister, Alexis.

Slowly I began to analyze the stressors associated with the turkey tradition. First, there was the problem of which turkey to buy: fresh or frozen and what size of bird. Second, was the question of which recipe to follow: Emma's mother's recipe, or her grandmother's recipe, or one of the two-dozen other turkey recipes. (At one point Emma was getting monthly turkey recipes in her e-mail from a special turkey site). Third, which type of pan to use. Fourth, the question of the turkey's cooking position: right-side-up or up-side-down. Fifth, when to uncover the turkey and to use aluminium foil, or not. Sixth, how long to cook the turkey without making it too dry. Seventh, how to present the turkey. Eighth, the question of carving the turkey: by hand or with an electric knife. Ninth, the hundred different recipes for stuffing and the arguments for each. Tenth, the different methods of making gravy. Eleventh, the cranberry questions: fresh or frozen, homemade or canned. Twelfth, what cooked vegetables can we prepare with the turkey that won't be over-cooked or burned because we have to focus most of our attention on the bird. Thirteenth, the preparation for the mashed potatoes and their different recipes. Fourteenth, the timing, for all of these cooked dishes had to come together in the right sequence. Fifteenth, if one of these dishes went wrong (or was not in the right sequence), it could ruin the meal.

In Emma's family these questions cause stress building up to Christmas, during all the work making the dinner, during the serving and eating of the dinner and even after dinner. But it did not end there, days later members of her family would phone up for post-mortems on the turkey dinner: How good was it? How did it compare to other turkey dinners? What went wrong? etc. In this way the stress of this event continued. I soon realized that it was ruining Christmas for our family, but especially for Emma who had to do all the work. And at this point Emma and I would get into a Christmas argument about the turkey. This too became a Christmas tradition.

One Christmas our daughter, Juliana and her husband, Marc, video-taped us during one of these turkey arguments. I argued that I never liked turkey and that many Canadians, if they were honest, would admit that turkey can be a rather tasteless meat that depends on the gravy, the salt and the cranberry sauce to taste like anything edible. I argued that I was tired of having the turkey tradition ruining our Christmas holiday, and especially when our children came home to see us and their sister. I argued than in my Italian family Christmas dinners were happy. We did not worry about one big, dumb bird. We ate different things every year and enjoyed the different foods. Emma would argue for the turkey tradition. And we would go back and forth with examples and details.

The following May Emma and I celebrated our 30th wedding anniversary. Well, Juliana and Marc surprised us by coming out unexpectedly from Montreal to Edmonton. But the bigger surprise was that they had turned this video-tape argument into a little film which they entitled, "The Turkey Wars" and had added suspenseful music to the drama. It made us all think.

Since that time we have discussed the turkey problems at Christmas and have decided that we will not have turkey in December. Since that time we have been free to try other dishes at Christmas, including ethnic dishes from different cultures. Emma makes an excellent pollo alla cacciatora which uses rosemary but no tomatoes. Sometimes we have had vitello saltimbocca, or salmone alla griglia, or lasagne al forno. She also makes a very good risotto alla Milanese, or with porcini or with asparagi. Our minestrone is made with Romano beans. I have argued that we also have a Scandinavian dish, baccalà, since the dried cod comes from Scandinavian countries. We are now free of the turkey wars and are enjoying Christmas with our family.

The Pro-Turkey Resistance Movement: Part Two

EMMA PIVATO

I LOVE MY husband and I much appreciate his family and his family's traditions, including their tasty cuisine. However, at some point, after the first blush of love and togetherness, I dimly began to realize that I was being swallowed up and functioning as an adjunct to his life story. I am not particularly a feminist but I did believe it was my sisterly duty to fight back. Unfortunately, I had nothing to fight with but turkey. I suffer from "tall poppy syndrome" within my family sphere so any sign of weakness is pounced on gleefully by certain of the relatives. Yet, a kind of family closeness still exists and Christmas get-togethers have been mandatory—with Christmas expectations of a "proper" Christmas dinner, i.e. a turkey. Hence, I have been caught between the proverbial rock and a hard place. The tension referred to by my dear husband was exacerbated because each year I had to argue strenuously for the lone Christmas turkey—and preparing a dish once a year is not a good way to keep in practice.

I appreciate the way my husband's story ends. But men can be so naïve—believing they have won an argument, finally put an end to a situation, when it has only gone underground. This year it is true that we did not have turkey for Christmas—but I did prepare one two days later, a very successful one, I might add. It consisted of a series of creative compromises and, in one fell stroke, I dealt definitively with husband and extended family alike. The latter went off to one of their members to enjoy a Costco turkey roll, which I subsequently heard—to my great satisfaction—was not all they had hoped for. The former, husband, daughters and most amiable son-in-law who obligingly does not care what he eats, enjoyed what

I considered to be a relatively mundane Christmas dinner. It consisted of Pollo alla Cacciatora and some interesting vegetable dishes. Two days later, without advance warning, preamble or apology, and with the family belatedly invited over, the turkey was presented — but with a difference.

❦ The plot unfolded as follows:

1. The turkey had been quietly lurking in the depths of my freezer for two months and I discreetly removed it and thawed it in our cold room overnight, out of sight.

2. It weighed a mere 10 pounds so, instead of using the super duper electric turkey roaster my brother had gifted me with so I could more perfectly prepare our Christmas feast, I used my late in-laws humble but heavy aluminium chicken roaster. It was of a size that just barely allowed me to wedge the turkey in upside down so it would stay moist but the fit was so tight the breast could not quite reach the bottom and so it retained its shape.

3. I stuffed the turkey with a bunch of marjoram branches and a cut lemon and threw in some poultry seasoning for good measure and sewed it quickly together. The actual dressing I prepared on the top of the stove from a package, discreetly disposing of the wrappings. As an aside I might add that I received compliments on it and did not bother to mention I had done the unmentionable by not making my own.

4. The turkey was so small I was able to easily place it on an oven proof platter and store it tented in the warm oven while I made the gravy in the nice thick roasting pan. I added Knorr chicken soup cube and no other salt. It was well received — more so than usual!

5. At the last moment I retrieved some Lingonberry Sauce from the fridge as a nod to our Scandinavian tradition and as an escape from cooking cranberries from scratch and boiling them over on the stove as is my usual custom.

6. The baby red potatoes served with the turkey I had cooked with rosemary, onion and parsley. They were delicious and I received not one complaint about the lack of mash.

7. Some creative vegetable dishes were also presented to satisfy the more esoteric (snobbish?) members of the group.

8. And lastly the entire turkey process was done discreetly, even furtively, with negligible commentary and fuss. *And* it was declared, by both turkey detractors and supporters alike, as the best turkey yet!

I therefore feel quite confident that the pro-turkey resistance movement will arise stronger than ever for next Christmas. However, just to be on the safe side, I may strive to consolidate my gains this Easter!

Third Course: Secondo

Caravaggio's Light

GLENN CARLEY

HE CALLS ME *Il Buffone* or *Il Vagabondo* because he never knows when I will show up to visit. It could be in the morning, unannounced just after the sun has risen and before the traffic gets too heavy. Maybe it will be snowing, maybe it will be raining, or maybe it will just be nice. We have *espresso* then and *biscotti*. I tell him stories of the modern world and about the comings and goings of his *nipoti*. He perks up then. His mind is primed like the pump and soon, without doubt, he tells me his truths of the Ancient Order. Lo, they sound like psalms but we are not in the cathedral, we are in the Life, like stained glass spirits in the midst of prayer, in a canto of daily rhythms across the cycle of seasons that always return to the sun.

He is *my contadino da Castropignano*. His hands are big. He plants his tales in my mind and hopes I will know what to do during the harvest. Twice, I have heard it said that I am "better than an Italian boy" and it is because *Il Vagabondo* shows up all the time and if he is late, he sends *Il Buffone* ahead of him with the apology. Like I say, you will never know when I will appear. I am offered another *espresso* because I drank the first one too quickly. It was beautiful and so unlike the drive-thru *acqua sporca* I am used to. We laugh. We laugh because we are passing time and all you need to do is to be together. It is so simple to be happy. So I speak to him in the cadence of his stories and when I see him grin, he can see that I listen.

"Once, when I was enchanted, *Il Vagabondo* flew in the spirit, to Florence," I tell him. The *nipoti* were with me and *mia bella moglie, his figlia*. We were en route to the home town. We entered a church. We just walked in. There were people there and we stood beside strangers to admire painting and sculpture and graves. It was hot outside, so hot, but the twilight inside was low and cool and felt moist. At the end of the corridor, we saw a knot of people looking with anticipation and we were drawn to them. The people were peering through the dark, as if through dreams and we stood on the periphery and hoped in the darkness too. I saw a hand go to a little box and heard the wet trickle of a Euro coin. Lo, the alcove was lit and before us, the fertile, oily composition of a Caravaggio painting rose like the dawn. I saw an angel then and she was playing an instrument while Joseph held a book of song. Jesus was nestled in Mary's arm. The angel was inner lit and her interior brightness pushed back shadow and darkness, so much so that I perceived the moist light, felt it glint off my heart and saw it flicker in my wife's eyes. My arms grew wider. I gathered in our children to simply gaze at the tableaux. I tell our daughter that Joseph is immigrating to Egypt, to sojourn there and escape the wrath of Herod who hunts by natural light. "Is he in the painting?" she asks and I tell her no, this family is protected by love. Before we are ready, the light departs and the angel disappears into the shade of thoughts. Some of the crowd disperse, some of them stay, more fill in behind us and we are gently moved to the front. "Daddy, can I have a coin? I want to see it again," she says. So we see it again so we can see it forever and then, the current of adventure sweeps us forward and away and we are back home and full.

My father-in-law is pleased by the tale of enchantment. He subtly repays the high compliment of respect by pouring out the last of his red wine into my Mio glass which I have saved from the old days, when the man used to come around in the truck, pick up the empties and leave strange tastes in bottles. We are men of the ancient order and we don't put *gassosa* in our glass. We only use three grapes: *moscato*, *carignano* and a little *alicante* to make it dark. It never goes wrong. It is always right and strong and induces a nap in my weary *inglese* soul.

Bees cannot sting in the morning when you stand chin high next to cases of grapes on the corner. Yes, can you see? I did not take to the language but I took to the dialect of love. I tell him his tales back, so he can remember. I tell him he boarded the SS Constitution, landed on Ellis Island and took the train to Toronto. I tell him when the war came, it ruined his land and there was no future for the young. I took him once to Hope Street and to Blackthorn where he had a toehold. We have been on CHIN radio but that is a tale left for another day and another glass. I tell him the grapes were better in Molise before the blight. He tells me to go to the cantina, to fetch a new *Alberta Springs* bottle of *vino* and we are *contenti*.

Time passes the way it always does. Tradition is thinned. *My* Italian is growing old. The telephone rings and I am summoned to come down. I am not *Il Vagabondo* this time and I will definitely be *Il Buffone* if I do not respond to the old the way the young must. The young must always respond to the old when the old call. It is the great *segreto* still alive in our Urban World. Trust me on this. Go when they call. Always go when they call and if you do you are enchanted. If you do not you have not learned one thing and you are swept away by the currents of an ersatz life. I do not mean to make you angry. I am not a threat. I am a Canadian, somehow, by an Act of God thrust into the quantum Italian-scape of *la famiglia*. I go willingly and my spirit has been re-arranged for I am an orphan. My mother was German and I am not a *shtupnaegal*. My dead *fadder* before me, had some Irish in his Mobius strip so *O, Take your time goin' but hurry back* when I tell you these things. And I have no credibility for, if the truth be told, at the end of the day, when the old flowers are pinched off and the tools of the *giardino* are put away, I have to admit that I still love potatoes more than pasta. I am sorry, but it is true.

No, this time, I am summoned to go get the wine with him. The press is gone. It is unused and replaced now by new "twenty-three" litre pails of juice ... ten pails *Grenache*, loaded into the van in garbage bags and I miss the sound of the crusher and the stiff ratchet of the bar in the cold, early October garage when the door is down and the bare light from the bulb inside reveals the past. Like an Italian boy, I see so much being lost as your Second Wave dies off and—did you know?—a part of me dies along with them for there are twenty four years of marriage in my voice and in my tales. I have worked alongside your men and your women and I love them, the way they loved me, not so much with the words but through the eyes into my eyes, through the gifts of paradise, through your ministry of presence. I am so sad and so happy. These things ferment in me. I have been grafted by large hands and I took and I took and I grew. Are there enough Euros in my pocket? Will I see the light again? Of course. You cannot be with them and not be inner lit. I tell you the Truth. It is the way it has been told to me.

You have to leave everything and make a life to know. You have to be in spirit-form. You have to be an Italian Canadian but it is just *Il Vagabondo's* guess and nothing more.

So we go to the place where they put wine in pails. I talk to the young Italian at the desk and he is patient and it becomes him. I would eat him alive, if he were a *moderno* and did not respect *my old guy* for I am possessive of my coins. The contagion of the bottom-line has affected these merchants: they no longer offer two free pails when you buy ten, even when you have been coming for years. I playfully cajole the young guy and barter him down to a free pail for my father-in-law and half price on a pail of white wine for me. It is the upscale stuff that "you can cook with or drink." I want it to cook with it and I want to drink it. I want to enhance the recipes that I use to teach my "*half-breed*" son so that he will understand the ancient order of Life. The scent of steamy white wine burning off a sauce pan of *vitello, funghi e cipolle* is the aroma of paradise or thereabouts. I know.

We return to his home and I back the van into the garage at a precise angle. There is a trap door that leads to a forty gallon drum standing proudly in the cold cantina. It reigns over the fifty pound bag of potatoes, the jars of olives, the vat of red wine vinegar, the chick peas and the stacks of sauce in mason jars. My Italian has a *sistemi*, a system and using the natural physics of the land we create the siphon and I pry off the lids and skin my hands in the cold while the juice flows like blood, across the tube and down to depths of love. We fill the barrel. *Dio*, for some reason, after all these years, he still treats me like an outsider and he is too polite to ask me to do the scut work and clean the pails and the tubes and put the plastic rinds of the lids into the garbage — so I outsmart the old *contadino* and do it anyway. His generation always sees when a job needs to be done and they see the next job after the main job is done and they do *that* until it is all done and then, they can rest. You have to speak the dialect to know this. You have to pass time with them. You have to be around to learn the thing. If you are not around you will not learn the ancient ways and, if you do not learn the ancient ways, you will probably be watching a 40" LED television and enjoying your shows. If you are like me, you will monitor your friends on Facebook and then go to bed or, in the southern Ontario dialect: *"Mama jeezus Mia! ttyl."*

The job is done. Everything is clean and put back. The polyethylene sheet is efficiently sealed over the drum and like *Il Vagabondo* if you go down later, you will hear it shiver and swish like the warm fermented language of bees speaking. There is no greater sound. To hear it once is to hear it forever so that even when the garage door is down, you will know that inside, the dark space is inner lit and only waiting to be seen.

The Wine Press

CARMINE STARNINO

Hooped in iron, the staves give it a barrel look.
Three legs planted on a patch of shed. An axle in air,
a piston girding a crank, a drilling-rig and spigot
experimentally wed. The handle needs a two-man,
two-handed clockwise push and what was once
squelchingly tread at crude gallop is now crushed.

It was Gutenberg who studied the way the juice,
phrased past constraint, overwhelmed into bucket;
how the screw held the disk, the dole of strength
behind its squeeze, the steadiness and force of the bite.
Then in 1415 he retrofit the grip for moveable type.
He'd tap each letter ready with mallet, sink the tray
until it clenched paper, then lift it on the wet
whiff of ink, the page printed with the turning-spike's
accuracy of compression. (The font? San serif.)

The Jews hewed theirs from rock. I remember ours
as primal, too, a raised-from-the-elements relic
of realness whose hardwood hydraulics sweetly
reeked from the grapes g-forced for our booze.
Also good, in the end, for a nice batch of ooze.
Its ungentleness something I'd read about in school:
The angel thrust his sickle deep into the earth,
and gathered the vine of the earth, and cast it into
the great winepress of the wrath of God. Not wrath, but more
like blooms pressed between the pages of a book.

Oh, I can say all this to my uncle, but he could give a shit,
can't read, and what he's learned, reaching down
to scoop away the flattened mimeo-blue husks,
is that one thing is always being wrecked to make another.
Medieval mainstay. Vineyard's own avant-garde.
Once I saw one big as a boat in the keel curvature of its half-ton
girth.
How it stood there in high-shouldered farfetchedness!

Nowadays it comes to us smaller: oak crate held
in place with pegs, short slats spaced for seepage.

The Creation of a New Grape

CARMELO MILITANO

YOU ARE THE descendant of the Maldenti clan, the great grandson of Rosalina Maldenti, the daughter of the famous brigand, and her husband Sebastiano Filo, the man who grafted the local "Greco Nero" to a pale purple grape no one had ever seen before.

Sebastiano flirted briefly with the local Calabrian brigands as a young man but his spirit and character did not lend itself to the violence expected of him. He was not a mean calculating man but rather he was pragmatic about the business of working and living. His spirit was closer to that of an ignored poet and he preferred the quiet art of tending vineyards and gardens than the robust, sly, and larger than life existence of an outlaw.

He never drew attention to himself or caused a stir (this was to change) although he was pleased one year when he received a letter from a wealthy landowner congratulating him on his able work in his vineyards. Sebastiano was well known for his ability to tend a vineyard and for his ability to create by grafting a new type of grape, and in turn a new wine. You could say he was an artist, a wine sculptor or painter who in his tending and shaping and layering of a vineyard produced not a painting or a sculpted bronze but something equally beautiful and satisfying: a fine barrel of wine.

Sebastiano married young. He was nineteen and Rosalina, one of three village beauties, was only sixteen. She was Sebastiano's opposite. She stood no more than five feet with thick wavy red-brown hair and intense black eyes. Full bosomed at fifteen, she walked to the fields proud of her thin Minoan waist and ample breasts. It was said her eyes flashed hot like coals when she was angry and shone like sunlight when she laughed. Piety and modesty, virtues valued in saints and the Madonna, found no place in her spirit. It was whispered her flashes of stubborn anger she inherited from her father Carmine Maldenti, the brigand.

I have not forgotten about the wine.

Vineyards in Calabria were set up wherever there was sufficient land to grow grapes and more or less angled with a southern exposure to absorb the strong Mediterranean sun. The land Sebastiano had bought was not a large vigneto, more like a vigna, a small vineyard, and after careful study he decided the slope was gentle enough to begin the arduous task of tilling the soil before the planting, and later grafting could take place.

And so the small useless looking pale purple grape found at the opening of a wide gash of land that sloped downward and opened like a wide fan below a grove of olive trees was grafted in 1888 when Sebastiano Filo was nineteen or twenty (don't forget your great-great grandfather) to the fat purple one called by the locals "Il Greco Nero," The Black Greek, for the jet black colour it turned when pressed. The Greco Nero grape produced a type of strong wine called "Il Ciro" and not all that different from the "Malvasia" grape that had been in the Mediterranean basin for centuries.

The hybrid grape was a light purple skinned grape on the outside and dark on the inside, the reverse of most grapes. The dark interior gleamed with small triangular shards of light, and after two or three glasses of the wine this grape yielded, people erupted into careless dance, disorganized dress (clothes suddenly felt uncomfortable and constricting) and impulsive behaviour.

It took some years but eventually those grapes and the wine they produced pushed us westward and ever westward till finally Sebastiano ended up on the streets of New York with his evening spending money tucked under his tongue. Later he found himself in a whore-house in the city of Buffalo, and much later still he found himself in a train station waving to his brother, heading for Winnipeg in a cheese and whisky smelling third class compartment and wondering what he had done and who was in hot pursuit.

The new wine changed everything but no one knew how. Not even Sebastiano. All Sebastiano could recall sitting in the train's cold compartment was a card game. They had been playing scopa at the Café Savoy at the corner of Franklin and Jefferson not far from the tumble of broken and weary hotels that lined the street. It was a sleepy Sunday afternoon in Buffalo. The winter afternoon light weak and dull. Blue cigarette smoke curled slow and lazy above the card tables.

The men played for a glass of wine at the end of each round and dreamed of the Sunday afternoon pasta dinner they used to eat back home with their families. Sebastiano and his slow-witted partner Filippo, a man freshly arrived from Italy who had yet to find work, had lost five hands in a row. Sebastiano suggested the table change seats to break their losing streak and offered to pay for the wine with some of his own wine hidden in a hip flask. He was trying to avoid paying for anymore wine. He needed to save money to send to his wife Rosalina.

But it all turned out wrong. A fist slammed on the table. Shouts from the other men. Mario the café owner slapped his thighs with horror and anger. Blood everywhere, and in one of the men's shoulders, a knife.

No one in our family was ever sure what actually happened. How did Sebastiano get on the train? Who started the fight? What set them off against each other? How did such a mild man find himself in the middle of a brawl?

The problem, of course, was the wine and wine was connected to the hybrid grape and the grape was connected to the gypsies and the gypsies were connected to the villages of Southern Calabria scattered like salt across the plateaus and high edges of the blue Apennine Mountains and the villages were connected to the Saracen attacks and the Saracen attacks were connected to the original Ancient Greek settlements and so on and so on until Sebastiano arrived at Union Station in Winnipeg at the corner of Broadway and Main on a cold day in February, 1919.

The only thing certain was that the wine made from that grafted orphan grape had changed everything.

Meanwhile, back home in Italy, Rosa's infamous temper grew when she learned Sebastiano was trapped in the middle of a frozen continent and she was going to have to raise two children on her own. Her temper grew even worse when she learned the only way they were going to be united again was if she braved crossing the Atlantic with two young children.

The rest is, as they say, history.

Zuppolone

SONIA DI PLACIDO

It is a foreign tongue
that knows this image —
a village of four centuries ago
eroded mountains connected to alps
donkey wagons making passages
diverging clusters of peasants plowing
fields, picking and counting their scores.
Feudal land brawls and competitions
with bouts of wine and bread
midday — every day.

A large man walks among vineyards,
apple orchards, olive groves
keeping a clay jug on his back
as it carries over 4 litres of
cantina made Molise wine.
Zuppolone, he is called, the man that
can drink more than anyone in the village.
The one who takes his wine and bread loaf
each morning. A jug of clay, as large as a demi-john
now placed in my zio's taverna over two centuries later.

Townsfolk locals name him the bread dipper;
the land-owner who dunks it, il pane, as he
devours this large soup of wine.
He dips his bread into the wine and eats
his hearty lunch making salutations to

God, il corpo — becoming Christ-like,
elated as the sun bears down his back.
A farmer envied who suckles at his loaves of bread
dipped well into, la Zuppa di vino. A jug so large it
surmounts his anima, making him a man of soul;
one tenacious and esteemed.

He becomes the family legacy,
the identification of a bloodline; the clan of
Zuppolone. Two, three then, six generations on.
I am the seventh granddaughter of Zuppolone
from Colle Bove, Torella del Sannio, Molise.
We're a family of winos, even now, with cantinas
brimming larger than most at our civita [hamlet] three
miles from town. Across an ocean, in Canada,
we drink it like a succulent juice that makes our bones
scarlet and keeps our spirits light.

Once Upon a Time in Italy's Fine Cuisine

ALBERTO MARIO DeLOGU

IT WAS A humble and curious Italy, one which adopted tomatoes from America and made them into its national vegetable. It picked basil from Persia and turned it into its favourite herb. It learned the art of sauces from the French, and the art of hand-drawn spaghetti from the Chinese. It stole from the Arabs the art of baking unleavened bread — that pita that would later become our pizza.

It was an Italy that was criss-crossed by peoples and cultures, open to Mediterranean winds and flavours of foods from distant lands. It was an Italy that was still poor and war-torn, but rich in history and art, and grooved by rivers of life and passion.

It was not an arrogant or conceited Italy. Most certainly, it was not the same Italy whose Prime Minister would dare to offend an entire fellow European nation, the Finnish, with a haughty: "The Finnish don't even know what a Prosciutto di Parma is. All they know is cured reindeer meat."

Back then, we Italians were very much aware of our faults and shortcomings. Maybe too much so. And so we were easily charmed and moved by novelties and anything that came from afar, by sea or by land. It was a fertile and healthy curiosity that made us the bright, clever and charming people that we were.

Right: that we were.

Today's Italy is a distant relative of that Italy raised on bread, onions and fantasy. Today's Italy is a curled-up country, which avoids contact with the outside world and dallies with the senile obsession of keeping invaders outside the barbed fence.

One of the clearest symptoms of this decline is the hapless sclerosis of Italian cuisine over the last two decades. The Italians' contemptuous refusal to open up to other foods of the world goes hand in hand with our stubborn belief that we have been anointed as guardians of the Supreme Temple of Good Food.

As the world trades, tastes and experiences, we mobilize in defence of the Sacred Traditions. But what are we exactly talking about, if we were the first pirates? The whole world monkeys our products — supreme flattery! — and what do we do? We clamp down like a clam, and in defence of what? Of animals that we first raided from their birthlands (buffaloes)? Pasta made from Canadian, Ukrainian or Kazakh wheat? Prosciutti and salsicce made from Dutch hogs? Cheese manufactured with Bulgarian or Romanian milk curds?

My line of work often brings me into contact with the Italian food industry, or rather, with the image that it likes to project abroad: trade shows, tastings and promotions. In all honesty, the feeling of déjà-vu is every time more pervasive: same products, same ingredients, same packaging and same labels. Same oil, same sotta-ceti and sottoli, same cheese and same wines. Same brochures, same old claims of "ancient tradition," "signature cuisine," "typicality," "identity," and so forth.

The last flash of Italian genius dates back to the 1980s. Those were the years of fashion designers and of new and engaging graph-ics. We were still home to an electronics (Olivetti) and a textile in-dustry. Then, in the 1990s, we took a long coffee break, and today we find ourselves chasing after the pack leaders. In electronics, in textiles, and — ouch — even in the food industry.

The Chinese have learned to make everything we do, and now they even boast about their "high quality." And with good reason: the Chinese government has just allocated one thousand square kilo-metres (one quarter of Molise) in green and pristine Manchuria to the production of certified organic foods. And many more in years to come. What about us? What are we doing? Try asking an Italian food manufacturer why he is not converting to organic production. I did. He shrugged his shoulders and replied: "Nonsense. My prod-uct is good and healthy as it is."

Amen.

Now try sifting through the ingredients of imported biscuits from Italy. You will always come across an unspecified "vegetable oil." Guess what that stands for? It is vile and unhealthy palm oil, filled with saturated fat, imported from Indonesia and for whose production entire rainforests were razed to the ground. Here in Canada palm oil has been replaced by canola oil, on whose health qualities a thousand doubts still loom, granted, but at least you will find it clearly spelled out on the label. And you are free to buy it or leave it on the shelf.

Go look for an indication of trans fat contents. "What are they?" I got asked by an Italian biscuit manufacturer. My reply was: "They are excellent artery liners. Here in Canada they were declared war on five years ago."

He shrugged.

Marylene Iannantuono is an Italian-Canadian chef, with strong Italian culinary roots. She has just returned from an educational culinary trip on the Peninsula. I interviewed her on her return, with a smile of anticipation on my lips. I asked her to tell me all about the good and delightful things that she had learned over there. She replied: "I learned that Italian cuisine is becoming increasingly boring."

The smile of anticipation clicked off my lips.

She told me about the usual ingredients, the usual dishes, and the usual stolid belief that there is only one way, "the right way" of doing things in the kitchen. She told me about their noses turning up when faced with variations and contaminations. She told me about their categorical refusal to try anything different. She told me about the day she tried her hand on a nice lamb shank in maple syrup reduction (Sweet sauces on meat? Anathema!). Three patrons out of four pushed the plate aside, without so much as a nibble.

Where has our desire to learn gone?

Here in Montreal we have a small chain of lovely artisanal baker-ies. Every day they roll out a variety of precious baked objects made of wheat, barley, spelt, kamut, oats, rye, flax, sesame, walnuts and a hundred more wholesome ingredients. In all kinds of shapes and sizes, all strictly organic. Their spelt focaccias remind me of my old civraxiu bread from Sanluri, or the big sturdy focaccias from Altamura. Good old gum-rubbing bread. Months ago I met one of the owners at a food show and asked him: "Where did you learn?" He replied: "Of all people, you should know! We have learned from the Italians!"

Right. A few decades ago, maybe. I was just about to answer, Please, sir, do not go back for more, or you may find yourself munching that atrocious and papery industrial bread that stuffs supermarket shelves in my hometown.

But all around the Boot, now all intent on banning kebabs and throwing aspiring immigrants back into the sea, the outside world keeps imitating, innovating and improving. As we Italians have always done. As we have been doing in our best years. As Gianni Agnelli said once: "There is a time for strength and a time for vanity." It definitely looks as though we Italians have spent too much time wrapped in vanity.

Meanwhile, in spite of our "ancient traditions," last year the Finns won the New York Pizza Show by defeating two Neapolitans with a rye pizza topped with cured reindeer. Mockingly, albeit appropriately, dubbed "Berlusconi Pizza."

Zucchini and the Contadini: an apocryphal tale?

LORETTA GATTO-WHITE

A HOLY TRINITY of Italian vegetables exists, in the popular imagination at least, as zucchini, tomatoes and eggplant, a membership I challenge on the grounds that zucchini are not quite as popular with *all* Italians as people think.

Zucchini are certainly popular with restaurateurs as they are cheap and generally available year-round — a good filler on antipasto plates, with pasta, as contorno and in minestra, leaving the gullible diner with a false impression of its esteem. My chief objection to zucchini is they are exceedingly bland and soggy, even frying doesn't much improve them and that's saying something, as even a kitchen sponge might be palatable if dipped in batter and fried. I know that, to some Italians, this is blasphemy, but no less true, it's just that few of us will fess-up to it.

And beware the well-meaning, beneficent vegetable gardener with a bumper crop of the stuff. The spectre of our green-thumbed neighbour beaming as he carried the bounty of his giant squash from door to door haunts me still. If you have such a well-meaning, but misguided gardener on your block my advice to you is post a notice of 'Wet Paint' on the front porch, secure your back gate, if you don't have one, get one fast, then hang the ominous 'Beware of Dog,' sign and for goodness sake, lock your car doors! Or you will find they have sprouted, like triffids on your front seat.

My culinary disdain for zucchini does not however, extend to cooking and consuming their blossoms, which I think is the only reason to grow this squash, an attitude which often leaves me on the margins of established "Italian Food Culture" and "Popular Opinion."

So it was with glee that I found the affirmation I sought for my iconoclast position in an anecdote my friend related from her region of Ciociaria in Lazio, which was told to her by her mother, a woman whose veracity in such matters is irreproachable and her talent as a raconteur renowned, never sacrificing a good story for the sake of the truth. The infamous incident took place during the time before the mechanization of farm labour when the Ciociari, tall, strong men from this ancient Samnite settlement, roamed the hills and valleys of nearby Abruzzo sickles in hand, to work as itinerate contadini during the harvest season. And it was just such a season which found Nessuno and his paesani harvesting the durum wheat from a prosperous farmer's field.

Typically, the crew worked for subsistence wages, room and board, the quality of which varied from farm to farm, depending upon the hosts' largesse and means. This particular farm family was well-provided; they had sheep for cheese and meat, chickens for eggs, chubby rabbits for cacciatore, a succulent hog for salumi, as well as an olive grove for oil, a vineyard for wine and a kitchen garden besides their cash crop of wheat. The farmer, his wife and four children were hale, plump and rosy-cheeked, in contrast to the gaunt physiques and sunburnt, leathery countenance of their hired help, who sizing-up the situation anticipated a board of good provender.

Nessuno and his crew began at sunrise scything the wheat when the air was fresh and cool, but by mid-morning they were exhausted, bathed in sweat and reposing shirtless in the shade of an oak. That is where the farmer, eager to check their progress and his wife bearing their merenda, found them. The farmer was still in his blood-spattered apron after a morning spent slaughtering a ewe and a few rabbits. The contadini could barely disguise their thirst and hunger while the farmer prattled on about the good dry weather they were having, their work's progress and the salsiccce and salumi he would make from his fat hog in December.

Finally, after what seemed a starving eternity, the good wife opened her basket and doled-out the eagerly awaited repast. Each of the five famished men received their bowl with a nod of the head and a "grazie" to the wife, and wary of making a *brutta figura* before their host and employer, waited until each paesan had their share before lifting their spoons to dig-in. As difficult as it was to hide their thirst and hunger from their hosts, it was even harder to conceal their disappointment over the meal which consisted of a stew of zucchini, tomatoes, and onions, drizzled with last year's olive oil, accompanied by a wedge of stale bread and a meagre sliver of pecorino; at least the wine was good, a young white, slightly fruity and cool, the colour of fresh straw.

As they handed their empty bowls back to the wife, repeating their thanks, they gave each other a side-long glance of chagrin. After the pair were out of ear-shot, the farmer's declaration that he'd better get on with skinning the rabbits for dinner barely audible over the distance, the men fell to commiserating—"Per la miseria!" cried Battista, "I got better food in the army, at least they didn't think hard-working men live on mushy vegetables and stale bread, the army and the contadini work on their stomachs." "Just so," agreed Renzo, "and remember how much the cheap bastard thought we should have cut by sunset!" "Cut!" spat Fulvio, "I'll cut *his* throat, let him know how my poor stomach feels." "Aah! fa'una patata!" contributed Pazzo, who was always saying cryptic things. Nessuno, who was the acknowledged leader and peace-maker, soothed the anger of his compatriots, reasoning that it was only their first day, and the farmer was already busy slaughtering for the autumn store, surely things would improve by dinner, just imagine the rabbit cacciatore!

Unfortunately, that dinnertime the cacciatore failed to make its way from the men's imaginations to their stomachs, and although they could smell it from their shed, all they could taste was the zucchini and a few beans swimming in a thin, greasy broth.

This went on for two more days, the men's work suffered and the farmer grumbled. Nessuno's crew was suffering *debolezza*, feeling weak, irritable and a little murderous. By Saturday night, after their last bitter biteful of the ubiquitous zucchini, Fulvio could stand it no longer, he leapt from his chair, flung his bowl at the door and pounding his fists on the table bellowed: "Porca vacca! What does she think; we're old men with no teeth in our heads to chew something filling and decent? I'll show her teeth—get a bite of that big fat ass of hers!" The others were too weak and despondent to rejoin with anything more than a nod of assent.

The next day was a Sunday, when the pious farmer and his family answered the distant call to worship of the village church bells. Before departing, he dropped off a cold plate of fried zucchini and potatoes in oil and the rind end of some hard cheese to the contadini, explaining that the family would be gone all day as they were visiting relatives after mass. Suddenly, Nessuno's gaunt face lit-up, his sunken eyes sparkled, and his slack, pallid lips formed a firm rosy grin. His paesani thought hunger had finally driven him mad; they'd seen such things happen in times of famine and it frightened them that they might lose their stalwart leader. But it wasn't the madness of hunger that had wrought this transformation, but the inspiration with which opportunity endows the prepared mind! And Nessuno's mind was well-prepared, having searched ceaselessly since Friday for a solution to their problem.

When all that remained of the family's wagon was a puff of dust in the distance, the men set to work in the zucchini patch. They went along each row very carefully, nudging the freshly sharpened tips of their scythes into the soil near the base of each cursed plant, seeking the sweet spot that yielded a slight crunch and the blessed release of the severed root from the stalk. They worked quickly and with a quiet joy like the penitent feels when relieved of their sin's heavy burden; oh sweet deliverance was finally theirs and they thanked their saviour. All that remained was to carefully smooth the disturbed soil and replace the straw mulch, then they rewarded themselves with a trip to the spring-fed brook that ran below the back field, where they could wash and catch a few brook trout to grill over a small fire and drink their cool, fresh wine.

The next morning found the farmer and his family in their beloved zucchini patch staring in disbelief at the yellowed leaves, drooping stalks, collapsed blossoms and shrivelled fruit of each plant. The contadini, barely hiding their glee behind grimaces which threatened at any moment to break-out into satisfied smirks, commiserated with the farmer. What could have afflicted their zucchini so swiftly and completely? They'd never seen anything like it before, Nessuno shook his head in disgust. "It's root rot," he intoned with the gravity of an undertaker. "That's right," affirmed Battista. "Yep, we seen it in the last two farms we worked, just to the north of here, it must be making its way south along the valley," observed Fulvio. "The only cure is to dig it all up and burn it ... and you won't ever be able to grow zucchini here again!" added Pazzo, who once or twice a year experienced a moment of brilliance.

So, the farmer did as Pazzo prescribed. The contadini dug-up the zucchini patch and burned its remains. The pyre held a peculiar fascination for the men, as from the barn the farmer observed them removing their hats and incanting something in their local dialect very like a prayer, their heaving shoulders, it seemed to him, betraying silent sobs. "Huh, the superstitions of the heathen Ciociari," he thought, shaking his head. "What a strange people they are and look how they love their zucchini!"

Pizze Fritte e Baccalà:
A Narrative of Christmas Foods, Past and Present

LAURA SANCHINI

OUR PLANE BEGINS its slow descent into Montreal. Clouds appear through the small rounded window on my left. Before long we are seemingly engulfed by these fluffy white cumulous pillows of air. I lean back into my narrow seat, sighing happily as I squeeze my husband's hand. "We're almost there!"

Ian sleepily glances up from the book he had been reading, nods his head and replies smiling in broken and heavily accented Italian. "Siamo ... arrivati ... salsicce e formaggio." He's been working on his Italian since we met in an effort to impress my uni-lingual Italian-speaking grandparents. Broken Italian or none at all, they love him. He makes sausages with Nonno and makes handmade cavatelli with Nonna. They speak to each other through food, their very own universal language.

I look out the window and see the island take shape. At first, I can only make out bridges and bright lights, but I slowly begin to see the major landmarks of my hometown: Mount Royal, The Olympic Stadium, and St. Joseph's Oratory. I haven't spent more than a month here in five years. This realization gets me thinking about the idea of "home." We're coming to Montreal for Christmas, my hometown, where I spent twenty-three years before moving to Newfoundland to begin my life as a graduate student. Coming "home" to Montreal always conjures up conflicting emotions for me. In the truest sense of the word, home denotes a sense of belonging, of birthplace, of familial connections. Montreal then, is my home. It's where I was born and where my family lives. It's where my heart and heritage is. It's where I go when I really need good Italian food made by Nonna. It's where I insisted I get married. But my adult life, and my love, is in Newfoundland. I'm but a passing guest in Montreal these days. A heartbreaking realization, but it's true.

Our landing is felt by a large thud as the wheels of the plane connect with the frozen runway. This sudden movement jars me back to reality—I'm home for the holidays with my new husband. In the years we've been together, he hasn't yet experienced a full Italian Christmas with my large (and loud) extended immigrant family.

A few hours later we arrive at my nonni's house. Before the car door closes behind me I can see Nonna and Nonno peeking out their front door. Rushing in, it's a flurry of hugs and tears. "Andiamo a fare colazione," exclaims Nonno, grabbing my hand to lead me into the dining room. Like many Italians of their generation, my grandparents live in the main part of a spacious duplex but insist on spending all of their time in the basement. Their elegant upstairs kitchen is rarely used, the furniture in the living room, much like a Victorian sitting room, is untouched by the years it has seen—untouched and generally unseen by family members and friends. They are kept as pristine showrooms to entertain very important guests, though some would say that virtually no one is important enough to be entertained there.

"Prendiamo un' drink," Nonno says, while I survey the table. Every inch is covered with food. Homemade salami is arranged on a plate with pecorino cheese. Platters of chicken saltimbocca surrounded by rapini and Swiss chard. Bottles of homemade red wine adorn the enormous table. In the centre, acting as centrepiece, is a bottle of homemade, grappa-fortified Limoncello. Nonna promptly pours out multiple shots of the syrupy-sweet yellow liquid for us. Ian glances at his watch and laughs. It's ten in the morning.

Our lunchtime conversation revolves around food and the fact that many men in our family do most of the cooking. This is a topic that comes up often, and usually focuses on the fact that my husband is the chef in our home. I love to cook; I find mincing garlic one of the most calming activities when I'm stressed or nervous. However, Ian definitely has more natural talent in the kitchen than I do. He's more culinarily adventurous and inevitably logs more kitchen time than I. This, in turn, means that my nonna enjoys mocking me that

Ian won't want to be with a woman who doesn't cook. "Aren't you embarrassed that your husband does all the cooking?" It's a question I'm often asked, a gross oversimplification meant to humorously shame me into becoming more domesticated. In my family, being a good Italian wife means feeding (and sometimes over feeding) family and friends. I often tease my husband for being a perfect Italian housewife.

This trip home for Christmas isn't purely recreational for me this year. I'm also conducting research on Christmas food traditions among Italians in Montreal. More specifically, I am examining the Feast of the Seven Fishes on Christmas Eve. Apart from being a foodie, the academic study of food culture is my career. I'm a folklorist, interested in why people eat certain foods and how food traditions reflect identity and ethnicity. It's an odd area of study, and especially difficult to explain to those outside academia. A curiosity for most, people often demand clarification. "You wrote your Master's thesis on tomato canning? Why?"

Why? That's quite the question. Why study food? We all need to eat but, unlike many of our other basic life requirements, we are entirely in control of how we nourish ourselves. We decide when, how, and what we eat. Moreover, food and the consumption of it becomes an identity marker for many of us. You're a picky eater, a vegetarian, a spicy food lover, or a foodie. It's not just what we eat that defines us, it's also what we don't eat; some become vegan to oppose animal cruelty, other go gluten-free to combat a host of health issues. We mark ourselves through food. Further, eating also identifies us culturally and ethnically — this is what I study.

Somehow the days flew by and we find ourselves on December 24th — a day I would traditionally spend making pizze fritte with my nonna and eating as much raw dough as I could get away with. I wake up panicked still not having conducted any research for this article on Christmas food traditions. On top of that, Nonna's got the flu, which means pizze fritte-making will probably have to wait until next year.

After breakfast, Ian and I head to my grandparent's house to check on Nonna where we find my mother looking incredibly frustrated. "Your grandmother insisted on making pizze fritte because you're in town and it's Christmas Eve, even though she has the flu. What are we going to do with her?" I understand my mother's concern; at eighty-five, my nonna isn't young anymore and doesn't have the greatest health, but still I'm incredibly touched by her act of strength and kindness. My nonna is priceless to me. When I was writing about tomato canning and needed more pictures of the canning process, she and Nonno went out and bought ten bushels of tomatoes to can with me even though the tomato crop had failed that year and tomatoes were incredibly expensive. Now she's insisting we keep up our Christmas traditions when she really should be resting. That's the kind of woman she is; it's the kind of woman I hope I'll become. Ian and I walk into the kitchen and can't help being dumbfounded when we notice dozens of uncooked pizze fritte on the table.

"Holy hell, there must be at least one hundred," exclaims Ian, wide eyed, taking in the scene.

As Nonna starts heating up oil for frying, Nonno quietly slips into *la cantina* to retrieve a bottle of wine. He's made wine for as long as I can remember, first using a four-foot grape press and recently with pre-pressed grape juice. The shift from grape press to juice was a difficult one for Nonno and for the family as a whole. He had a mild stroke a few years ago, just days before we were to start making wine. While he was convalescing a few of us got together and helped my nonna press the grapes. I'd recently become interested in pressing the grapes by foot but Nonna refused, which saddened me. When I told Nonno this while visiting him the next day at the hospital, he vowed that if he were alive the following year, he'd let me crush the grapes with my feet.

The next year, true to his word, I did just that, crushing and pressing a small batch of white grapes with my bare feet. This, of course, did not happen until Nonna had carefully scrubbed and sanitized my feet. Soon after, those bottles of wine became known as "Laura's Foot Wine," and naturally, everyone refused to drink it. So it stayed in the cantina for years until Nonno decided to open a bottle when I was moving out to Newfoundland. To everyone's surprise the wine had aged into a golden liquid dream of amber perfection. All those years of undisturbed aging had made it one of the best wines we'd ever had.

After that, it became a tradition to open a bottle whenever I was in town. Since Ian has come into the picture, the tradition has shifted to drinking a bottle whenever Ian comes to town. The first time Ian came to meet my family he was tipsy for the first few days of his visit because everyone kept giving him glassfuls of wine and he was too polite to refuse. It didn't hurt that my family can be incredibly pushy when it comes to food and drink. We drank the last bottle of "foot wine" a few days after our wedding last summer. In July, Ian and I decided to take up winemaking in honour of this family tradition. So now, when we visit Montreal, we not only open a bottle of Nonno's wine, but also one of ours.

Nonno emerges from the cantina with a bottle of wine while Nonna begins frying up the pizze fritte. Once they turn golden brown, she sprinkles them with powdered sugar and tries to hide them from my mom or Nonno, who hover close by, eager to devour as many as possible. Pizze fritte are one of those desserts that are best hot and freshly cooked. To me, they are synonymous with Christmas and my grandparents.

After a mad rush of fieldwork, observing food preparation for various Christmas Eve suppers, I'm back at my parents' getting ready for the Feast of the Seven Fishes. We're expecting a few family members over for dinner any minute. Mom is rushing around trying to get all the last dinner preparations ready. Tonight's seven course fish menu is quite a feast. After the antipasto, there is a starter of clam chowder, then thinly smoked salmon with capers and onions, a pasta dish of fettucine with calamari sauce followed by a trio of baked baccalà, grilled sardines, and scampi then finally, roasted herring. However, during the antipasti, my mom leans forward and explains that this year she's serving things a little differently. After talking with my grandmother about my research on Christmas food traditions, she found that the feast was celebrated quite differently in our village before leaving for Canada. "In what way?" I ask. I'm constantly amazed at how many of our Italian food traditions have really only taken hold in their current form in Canada.

She elaborated: "In Barisciano, in the mountains of Gran Sasso, we couldn't get fresh fish. We were too poor and fresh fish was very rare. There was certainly not enough for a seven fish dinner. So we had to be creative. We'd have beets, cabbage and other root vegetables as substitutes for the fish. Then we'd have some baccalà because it was salted and kept well. That was our feast."

The Feast of the Seven Fishes is something I've always taken for granted. I love how resourceful my grandparents' generation had to be when it came to food in Italy. Instead of abandoning the tradition, they simply modified it to suit the availability of fresh fish in their region, as well as their financial issues as poor subsistence farmers. "Since you're trying to document Italian Christmas traditions, I thought I could make some of the foods they ate in Italy," my mom explained to me as she brought out platters of pickled beets and cabbage.

Everyone sitting at our large dinning room table turned to stare at me, clearly unimpressed that my presence meant they now had to dine on root vegetables. My brother leaned towards my dad, scrunched his face up in disgust and muttered: "Ewwww, thanks a lot. Laura." This prompted me to pile my plate high with beets, even though I absolutely loathe pickled beets. My family always tries too hard to help me with my research and I'm always grateful for their interest in my work, even when it may lead to some awkward situations like forcing people to eat pickled beets and cabbage on Christmas Eve.

Once we'd eaten so much we could hardly breathe, my mom grabbed the leftover scampi and started adding them to Ian's empty plate. "Here Ian, eat. I don't want leftovers." And thus begins a very typical round of mom trying to force feed poor Ian an extra meal. "Have more baccalà! Here's some pasta. Do you want more clam chowder?"

Ian looks at me panic stricken. He still has trouble saying "no" to my mom. It's a very Italian thing, force-feeding guests. I find myself doing that when people come to dinner at our place. Ian pointed it out to me one night after a dinner party, definite proof that I am becoming my mother. I'm choosing to believe it's a show of hospitality instead of overbearing bossiness. It's a way to shower guests with affection, only it's with food.

Silently resigning himself to defeat, Ian eats another meal as my mom brings out dessert—a very un-Italian trifle that my aunt made. It's funny how the Feast of the Seven Fishes has taken on some

Canadian multicultural qualities. We eat trifle, scampi and clam chowder along with baccalà and calamari. I know of other families that have added lobster and sushi to the feast and even with all these new additions, we're all celebrating an Italian tradition. I wonder how it's celebrated in Italy these days.

The next day we open presents around the tree and eat a very light breakfast in anticipation of the repast my nonna is making at her house for the whole family. Walking into Nonna's house on Christmas day is like a warm hug. It smells of garlic, rosemary and comfort. Compared to the frigid Montreal weather outside, the house is irresistible and inviting. The whole family is already gathering around the dinner tables looking at the various platters of antipasti—Nonno's thinly sliced prosciutto is surrounded by sharp pecorino cheese, garlicky Sicilian olives and bocconcini. The champagne is poured and we all gather for Nonno's traditional toast.

"Sixty years ago I arrived in Montreal with ten dollars in my pocket. My wife and children were back in Italy. I worked so hard to send money back until they could join me. They brought with them my younger brother and his fiancé. Now look at us, all thirty of us—celebrating another Christmas together. Happiness and health to us all, *salute*! Now we eat!"

One of my uncles is taping this, which prompts my mom to exclaim: "Is there ever a video of our family when we're not eating? All we do is stuff our faces together." Every time our family gathers we do it around food. We eat together for happy occasions as well as sad ones. Plates of food begin arriving at the tables: Nonna's gnocchi, roasted turkey, peas and prosciutto, and of course, Nonna's famous paprika potatoes. These potatoes—quartered, and drizzled with olive oil, rosemary, garlic and paprika, are roasted to such a crispy perfection that we all fight over them. Oh those potatoes! They are the stuff of legends, and have been present at every family dinner since I can remember. When Ian and I cook potatoes, this is the only way we make them. No sense in messing with perfection. It's amusing that our favourite dish is one that clearly has Eastern European roots (my Hungarian aunt was the first to introduce paprika to Nonna), but it's an incredibly important part of our Italian holiday feast.

The dining room is abuzz with conversation and clinking forks. I hear snippets of Italian and English, sometimes some French is added in for good measure as we sit around and devour Nonna's rich gnocchi, Nonno's salty prosciutto, and savoury paprika potatoes. Our food is a microcosm of immigrant culture in Canada, happily living with a hybrid identity. Our country is often called the great mosaic—a tossed salad of ethnicity and culture. Each ingredient retains its own distinct characteristics while combining to create a larger whole. Food shapes our identity and for us, that's baccalà, pickled beets and those paprika potatoes.

International Cuisine

Marisa De Franceschi

Part I

Polente e Frico
Musèt e Bruàde
Cartùfulas, Craùt e Cúeste di Purcit
Salàm cul Asât, Spec di Sauris, Scuete Affumicade
Radricc cul Ardièll
Lujànie cul vin blanc
Mignéstre di Fasùi, Frìtulis, Fis, Formadi di Malge
Umid
Merlot, Picolit, Tocaj
Còculis, Nolis, Cjestines
Cròstuj
Sgnape di Séspis

Part II

Parmigiano, Prosciutto, Pappardelle
Pizza, Pasta con Ragù, con Sugo di Pomodoro
Pasta e Fagioli, Pasta Puttanesca
Peperonata
Panettone
La Fiorentina
Gorgonzola
Gnocchi di Patate, Gnocchi di Zucca

Basilico, Oregano, Rosmarino
Mozzarella di Bufala, Limoni, Aranci
Stracciatella
Aceto Balsamico
Espresso, Cappuccino
Chianti

Part III

Sweet and Sour Chicken
Eggrolls
Hallacas, Empanadas
Sopa de Mariscos
Gyros, Falafel, Couscous, Tabbouleh
Sushi
Baguettes, Pita
French Onion Soup
Bananas, Papaya, Avocado
Ginger, Garlic
Rice Wine Vinegar

Part IV

Hot Dogs, Hamburgers, Hash Browns
Cheeseburgers, Cheddar Cheese
Bacon and Eggs
Sirloin, T-Bone, Porterhouse, Filet Mignon
French Fries
Pork Chops
Doughnuts, New York Cheesecake, Ice Cream
Ketchup, Mustard, Pickles, Onions
Onion Rings, Poutine
Beer
Potato Chips
Coke, Pepsi, 7-up, Sprite, Vernors, Ginger Ale
Pork Hocks, Black Beans

Apples and Oranges
Whiskey
Beer

❧ A mi plasê dut
Me gusta todo
I love it all

From Tomatoes to Potatoes:
La Bella Marca on Cape Breton Island

GIULIA DE GASPERI[1]

I HAVE JUST hung up the phone, and I feel homesick. My friend Leo told me that last night he and Benito taught their class how to make *salsicce* (sausages). I know what you are all thinking. You are closing your eyes and picturing rolling hills, a scorching sun, a Tuscan villa in the distance, a couple on a Vespa driving to the nearby town for the daily market. In the villa, its driveway lined with majestic cypresses, a cooking class is taking place. All the mysteries and secrets of Italian cooking are being revealed and the students will all go home feeling a bit more like Italian chefs. I am sorry to disappoint you, but if you want to learn how to make *salsicce* from Leo and Benito, you need to picture this instead: a mild summer evening in Dominion, a small town on Cape Breton Island nestled along the rocky coast of the Atlantic Ocean, long-necked windmills in the far distance, the cobbled beach filled with locals and visiting relatives searching the sky impatiently for the fireworks to begin. Who will spot the first one?

But for a lesson on sausage making, you need to turn your back on the beach, climb a short hill and walk up along Mitchell Avenue until you get to the Italian Hall, the tangible symbol of the Italian-Canadian community that settled and prospered here. It is at the Hall where you will taste traditional regional cooking of the Veneto but also experience the synergy between Italian and Canadian cuisines.

Dominion is a small town of approximately 2,000 people situated in Cape Breton Island overlooking the Atlantic Ocean and is only a fifteen-minute drive from Sydney. The first time I visited was in January 2009. It was a dark winter's evening, snow banks lined both sides of the road. Judging the vista from the car window, there wasn't much to see. I was there on the invitation of John and Connie deRoche, from Cape Breton University. Wednesday night was Italian class and, upon arriving, the Italian Hall seemed to beckon me and I immediately wanted to go inside. It seemed empty. I thought that maybe class had been cancelled because of the weather; a big disappointment. But all of a sudden, from a door at the back, Leo appeared, wearing his "Italia" cap. He welcomed us and took us to the kitchen where ten students were waiting, sitting around the table, reading and translating from an old Italian textbook.

The class did not last very long, soon books were closed and their attention turned to me. Leo asked me to talk about myself and explain why I was there. I explained that before moving to Edinburgh, I lived in Nova Scotia and taught Italian language classes at Saint Francis Xavier University, while conducting research towards the completion of my PhD. Among my students were Cape Breton Islanders. It was through them that I found out about the Italians of Cape Breton. Apparently, there was quite a community in Dominion which came from my hometown province of Treviso, in the north east of Italy. I was very intrigued and I decided that I had to go and find out about this community for myself.

Life in Italy at the time of emigration to Dominion was tough. The émigrés were predominantly farmers, and the traditions which marked the agricultural calendar regulated their daily lives. They came from large families, sometimes up to thirty individuals in one household sharing small farm houses where the barn took up much of the available space. The long, dark and cold winter nights were spent in the barns where the livestock kept families and neighbours warm, the only entertainment being the tales told by travelling storytellers. They left an impoverished agricultural system to find economic opportunity in Dominion where they worked in the coal mines, a hard job unfamiliar to most of them, but which they did with pride.

The Italian-Canadian community that was established in Dominion during the 1920s and '30s quickly prospered: private homes were built; backyards were turned into vegetable gardens for which the Italians became well known and admired; small barns with pigs, cows and chickens were erected at the back of the houses. For the luxury items that could not be obtained at home, corner stores soon opened. In 1936 the Dominion Italian Community Club began the construction of the Italian Hall, destined to become the focal point of the local Italian-Canadians and of the community of Dominion at large.

The community kept its ties with the Old Country by preserving many of its traditions and customs, mostly associated with food, which are still practised today and are a great topic of discussion, creating for me, a common ground. The first person I interviewed during my visit was eighty-year-old Gino Scattolon, who now lives in Antigonish. We talked about traditional dishes:

Me: When you killed the pig, did you make something called *muséto* (large boiled pork sausage)?

Gino: [laughing] I guess so, *muséto, mamma mia* ... you are bringing it all up, I am forgetting this stuff, oh yes, we made it, people liked it.

Me: Did you ever make polenta?

Gino: [laughing] Jesus, Mary and Joseph, *Maria Santissima,* polenta?! I love polenta, polenta *in umido* (*umido* means 'moist'; a sauce, the consistency of which is similar to stew); everybody made polenta.

Me: And would you make risotto?

Gino: *Setu* risotto [Do you know risotto]? Oh ... beautiful! My wife makes it too and she makes it real good now. [...] Risotto, *mamma mia*!!! I love it. Roast chicken was big too, your salads, *radici* (radicchio). *Radici,* beautiful ...

He went on to tell me about the time his wife was pregnant — it was a New Year's Eve, and she had a big craving for a bowl of *radici* and he prepared some for her in the traditional manner, dressing them with salt, pepper, vinegar, the way you would usually prepare them. Gino was very enthusiastic and had a great time reminiscing about his favourite foods. His laughter and enthusiasm were contagious. Our conversation brought back a lot of memories about dishes that played an important part in his everyday life in Dominion.

These dishes were found on almost every table in the community, as my conversations with Sheldon and Frank Canova confirmed. I went to Frank's house on my last night in Dominion in the summer of 2009. Frank is the current President of the Dominion Italian

Community Club and welcomed me to his home where his wife Mary, his brother Sheldon and Sheldon's wife Maurina awaited. It was a memorable night. We drank good wine and ate *pane e salàdo* (bread and salame). What struck me most about the evening were the memories invoked of their traditional dishes; above all, they stressed the culinary mentality of their parents and grandparents: nothing would go wasted. I completely related to that because my grandparents and my own parents think exactly the same way. Sheldon told two important anecdotes about this attitude: "An Englishman (anyone who is not Italian) will take a tomato and cut it up and make a flower (garnish) out of it, give it to an Italian and he will have dinner and supper *co l'oglio, l' aséo, una cipolla, un cioco de pan, un gioss de vino e mangiare! Tutti a tavola* (with olive oil, vinegar, an onion, a piece of bread, some wine and let's eat. Everyone at the table.)" The food was meant to give nutrition and energy to face a hard day of work. Nothing was wasted, not even a tomato for garnish. Instead, one single tomato could provide even two meals a day.

The idea of not wasting anything was reiterated when speaking of the traditional killing of the pig. In Italy I collected memories of individuals telling me that even the hoofs of the pig were used. In Dominion the same concept was explained to me by Sheldon: "They use everything except the squeal." From Leo [Gaetan] Carrigan who spent a lot of time in his maternal grandparents' house, I learned that his grandmother did something that was very common in Italy: for breakfast she often ate left over polenta with milk.

The consumption of traditional dishes brought over from the Old World and prepared in almost every household defined the community and its members as Italians. Once the children grew up and became adults and married non-Italian wives, there began a process of transition and accommodation because, as Sheldon and Leo said, one needs to eat what one is used to. In front of these new Italian husbands were put plates of meat and potatoes (staples in Cape Breton cuisine) prepared by their new non-Italian wives. But their growing craving and need for pasta, bread, polenta and risotto was soon felt; grandmothers and mothers were invited into the Cape Breton kitchens to teach the wives how to cook Italian dishes where compromises were found without much drama. Then, the next generation arrived requesting food such as hot dogs and hamburgers making the compromise move a step further. It was funny to hear that the children that left for college or work, once home to visit, asked for those traditional Italian/Trevigian dishes that they had clearly missed while away. To this, I relate completely. I always have a very long list of requests when I go home to visit my own family.

The Italian-Canadian community in Dominion maintained traditions both within their homes and at the Hall. The members would meet, and still do so, to celebrate such festivities as Christmas, New Year's Eve, Easter and weddings. It is a way to socialize and express their '*italianità.*' Famous were the picnics held initially in front of the Italian Hall and subsequently moved to the countryside; the challenge of the greasy pole, the spaghetti suppers.

Luigia [Ravanello] Demeyere, current President of the Ladies' Auxiliary Club that, together with the Dominion Italian Community Club runs the Italian Hall, remembers when all the women gathered in the kitchen to cook together. They made sweets called in the Trevisan dialect *cróstoi* and *frítoe; cróstoi,* or in Italian, *galani*, are thin layers of dough that are deep fried and sprinkled with icing sugar; *frítoe,* in Italian *frittelle,* are balls of dough with raisins, also deep fried and dusted with icing sugar. Both recipes have local and regional variations, typical of Carnevale, but prepared in Dominion during Easter. *Fugàsse* (*focaccia* in Italian), is a sweet light cake with raisins, candied fruit, almonds and tiny clusters of icing sugar on top. Everyone I spoke to about the time they spent at the Hall growing-up remembers hours of happiness when the children played, while the parents got together to cook delicious communal feasts.

However, things have changed with the passing years, diminishing the numbers of the Italian-Canadian membership of both Clubs. Some of the traditional activities are no longer organized, but I still found very active members during my stays in Dominion. Indeed, the Hall hosts events all year round. It was Gino during our first meeting that told me about the "Italian Style Chicken Supper" served at the Hall. Happily, the timing of my visit to Dominion coincided with the serving of one of these suppers, so I decided to go. However, by the time I got there, the tickets were sold out. When I expressed my disappointment, two tickets, one for me and one for my partner, immediately materialized.

The "Italian Style Chicken Supper" is served twice during the seven days at the end of July through to August that is Seaside Daze week, a celebration of the history and heritage of the town of Dominion. The first evening it was served, my partner and I took it easy. We were staying only a few metres from the Hall, so I thought that five minutes before the serving began would be plenty to get there. Boy, was I wrong! The road was lined up with cars as far as the eye could see while the parking lot was so filled that not even a toothpick could have found a spot. I was worried we were too late ... but Leo was waiting for us at the door. He had saved us two seats! The hall was brimming with people; there was music and laughter; it was a good time. At six o' clock the doors of the kitchen opened and members of both Clubs filed out with trays of roast chicken. On every table there were baskets of fresh rolls, bowls of coleslaw, bowls of mashed potatoes and a dessert plate for each person.

Everything is always prepared with fresh and quality ingredients at the Hall. The bar was open for everyone who wanted a glass of wine or a beer or a soft drink. You can have as much roast chicken as you want and they usually come out twice with the trays. The Italian-Canadian community of Dominion has grown in popularity thanks to this chicken supper and there being no empty seats at the Hall on both days leaves no doubts. People come from all over Cape Breton to enjoy this meal that has come to represent the Italians of Dominion. The interesting thing to me is that of all the food that I ate during the meal, the one I thought was truly Italian was the chicken, roasted the way I am used to back home, crispy and crunchy on the outside, tender and juicy on the inside. Every bite was bliss, a journey home and back, filled with flavours of familiar herbs and spices.

To my surprise, however, it is the mashed potatoes that are the signature side dish of this meal. They are not Italian-style mashed potatoes. They are mashed potatoes with special gravy, whose recipe is secret and is passed on from one generation to another, from one person to another and Luigia is now its custodian.

What has happened here is a synergy, a coming together of different eating habits and preferences. When I asked the members of the Clubs to explain to me how this meal came to be, they said that they knew non-Italians would not sit through a lengthy, traditional Italian meal having several courses served at different times. Instead, they decided to have everything on a single dish giving people the chance to have one or more helpings. The mashed potatoes are served with *tócio*, a kind of gravy, that isn't thickened with flour. It is simply the reduced juices from the meat drippings. Mashed potatoes with tócio evolved because Cape Bretoners didn't like the Italian style mashed potatoes which haven't any "gravy" on them. It is a compromise that works as people seem to enjoy it a lot.

This meal can only be found in Dominion, prepared by the members of the Italian-Canadian community. It has never been prepared anywhere else. It belongs to and clearly defines the Hall, where there is much work, co-operation and organization involved in its preparation. I was able to witness every step of it last year when I expressed the desire to help. I was enlisted to peel potatoes and serve two tables during the suppers. Despite the work and being nervous for wanting to do a good job, I was elated. It was a great honour and a great experience. Being in that kitchen, that same kitchen where mothers and grandmothers gathered to reproduce the culinary heritage of their hometowns, where Leo and Benito teach how to make *salsicce*, was a priceless privilege to me.

The Italian-Canadian community of Dominion has shrunk and changed with the passing years. We can't stop time, but we can enjoy what time has created. This community is a symbol of Italian emigration in the world and of its achievements. The "Italian Style Chicken Suppers" have made it even more Italian by creating a dish that everyone, Italian and "English," can enjoy and relate to.

I am going back this summer; to eat, to drink, to reminisce, to stand on the beach on a summer's night, searching the sky for fireworks.

---

1. I dedicate this article to my friends of Dominion that have welcomed me in their lives and always made me feel at home. To them goes my deepest 'thank you'.

The Tortellini Connection

ANNA FOSCHI CIAMPOLINI

"YOU ARE TOUCHING the food with your hands!"

The student had stood up from her desk and addressed me with a stunned look on her face, while the rest of the class remained silent. Surprised by her exclamation, I turned around, letting go of the piece of chicken that I was about to dip in the batter for my cooking demonstration of the classic *fritto misto all'italiana*. As usual, I had taken great care to wash my hands thoroughly in front of the students before starting my Italian Cooking class and that remark annoyed me. I pursed my lips not to shoot back with a tart answer. The one that came to my mind was the retort that my mother had once hurled at my uncle during a family Christmas dinner that has remained legendary. Uncle Ascanio, who was a rather finicky man, had made a face at her pointing out that she was serving him prosciutto slices by touching them with her hands. She angrily replied:

"And with what am I supposed to touch them? With my ass?"

However, when I concluded that such impertinence could cost me my job as an evening class cooking instructor with the Vancouver School Board, I decided to ignore the remark and move on.

I had to fight to get that job. When I started my life as an immigrant in Vancouver in the early 1980s, I looked for work. Scanning the *Vancouver Sun*, I found an advertisement posted by the Vancouver School Board for part-time Continuing Education Instructors to teach a variety of evening courses to adults. The ad specified that applicants could also propose new general interest courses. Although I had no experience as a teacher, I had always entertained the idea to try my hand at it. Therefore I got bold and applied for the position by phone. To my surprise, my contact called me to go in for an interview. I had sketched a proposal for a new course on "XIX Century English Poets in Florence," a title far more ambitious than its contents. But, filled with the enthusiasm of a neophyte and the illusions of a newcomer, I counted on the powers of the land of milk and honey where I now lived to magically transform me into a real expert on the subject.

My interviewer, the Continuing Education Programs Superintendent, looked perplexed from the start. "English poets in Florence, eh?" he said, shuffling some papers on his desk. "I don't think we could find enough students interested in that type of course."

My heart sank.

Then, he said: "You are Italian, aren't you?"

"Yes, I am. I am from Florence."

"Well, if you are Italian you can cook. Can you cook?"

"Yes, I can. I love cooking, but ... ?"

"You see, we have many people asking us to offer Italian cooking classes but so far we haven't found anyone willing to teach them. Professional chefs are too busy; nobody is available, so in short, if you can really cook, the job is yours!"

I couldn't believe it: first interview, first job! I enthusiastically accepted the offer and was about to sign the contract when the Superintendent casually asked: "How long have you been in Canada?"

"Two weeks."

He grabbed the contract from me. "Two weeks? No, this is no good," he said, apologizing. "We don't give jobs to people who've just arrived here!"

"But you promised me the job! I can do it—I assure you I can do it!"

In the end, because practicality won over protocols, he mumbled: "Well, we need someone anyway! Sign your contract. I am sure you'll do well."

That was the start of my seven-year career as an Italian Cooking Instructor at various public schools in the Lower Mainland. The classes were scheduled during evening hours, so that students could attend them after work. They were mature people; most of them were taking these non-credit courses to develop new interests and some were seeking an escape from their boredom or loneliness. Each hoped to learn how to cook a few popular Italian dishes, have some mild fun and, maybe, make some new friends. I was surprised at the number of men who enrolled. Back home, it would have been unthinkable for a man to join a cooking class just for fun. Italian men don't learn how to cook: they know it by divine right. Canadian men, who are more humble, are not too proud to come to school. During the three hours of class time, I managed to demonstrate the preparation of a full three course meal and to distribute the necessary handouts. Many female students were not overly enthusiastic about my gnocchi or pasta recipes: they were convinced that any kind of pasta makes people fat, an allegation that I vigorously refuted. Some ladies commented: "How can you eat so much pasta and be so slim?" I never told them that I was religiously working out at the gym, just because I hated the stereotype of the big Italian mama. I also entertained the students by sharing anecdotes and aspects of Italian lifestyle, trying to make them understand the passionate, sensual feelings that Italians experience preparing and savouring a meal, or describing the sense of complicity and camaraderie of the collective ritual of cooking *spaghetti di mezzanotte* with a group of friends.

Sometimes, my fervour for lesser-known, sophisticated recipes backfired on me. Once, as I was about to demonstrate how to prepare a Florentine pâté, I was caught totally off guard. When I started to display my ingredients on the demo kitchen table, a student stood up with an alarmed expression on his face:

"What is *that?*"

"These are chicken livers," I replied nonchalantly.

The student stormed out of the class, loudly complaining: "And do you expect me to eat chicken livers?"

During another class, I opened a bottle of Barolo and spoke excitedly about the art of pairing the right wine with the right dish and of the enhancing power that a shot of good wine could lend to a quantity of recipes. I did not notice the student sneaking out of the classroom in the middle of my passionate speech, but the next day I got a call from the Superintendent. He demanded an explanation about my brash action of bringing alcohol into the school.

The times they are *a-changin'*, for sure, and maybe nowadays not even bringing a wad of *ganja* would raise such outrage, but so was Vancouver in the '80s, and it had its charms.

When I left Italy, I carried a *passatelli* maker in my suitcase and a copy of *La Scienza in cucina e l'Arte di mangiar bene,* the iconic cookbook written by Pellegrino Artusi in the late XIX century. I also took with me Stella Donati's classic collection of traditional recipes *Cucina Regionale Italiana.* I felt like a missionary ready to spread a culinary gospel in the land of drive-thru diners.

After arriving in Vancouver, I often felt a need to seek comfort in recreating some of the rituals that had been part of the life that I had left behind in Italy. When I taught how to make the pasta dough to my sceptical students, I remembered our last festive family dinner in Florence. For that special occasion, I had kneaded dough for fifty-five hand-made tortellini stuffed with ricotta and spinach. I rolled and twisted each one around my finger, as if they were wedding rings. My little daughter helped me with the same pride that I had felt, as a child, working at my mother's side at the kitchen table so many years before. Although I never surpassed my mother's incredible artistry in the gastronomic arts, I did inherit her passion for cooking. Stifled as she was by the societal constrictions that women had to endure in her time, she directed her energy towards the marvellous creations from her kitchen.

My story, instead, is that of a painful re-birth as an immigrant, struggling with different barriers and trying to negotiate a new identity. Food was my propitiatory offering to the indifferent gods of the new land, my way of communication. I brought *lasagne* and *cozze ripiene* as gifts to friends and acquaintances or as a thank you for some small favours received. I found a soul refuge in the colours, textures, aromas and flavours of familiar dishes. I felt comforted in handling the ingredients, in sticking my hands in the moist, soft meatloaf mixture or working the batter of a homemade pie that I would bake to make our dinner more opulent. I felt a sisterhood with Tita, the protagonist of Laura Esquivel's *Like Water for Chocolate,* transfusing emotions, memories and repressed love in the ancient, simple act of preparing a meal.

I soon found myself overwhelmed by the demands of my multiple jobs, while raising a family and trying, at the same time, to nurture my interest in writing. There were stories that I wanted to write about; I wanted to tell the stories of other immigrants, episodes and fragments of their lives that they told me, sharing their hopes, their suffering, their dreams and the half-fulfilled or broken promises of their journey. I continued to think about these stories and to the similarities with my own immigrant experience; I realized that I needed to create a space for my writing, a creative journey that held an even greater healing power than my food interests. Finally, I decided to stop teaching my cooking courses.

Many things happened since. I haven't made tortellini from scratch in a very long time. The aseptic, store-bought variety that I now buy has no symbolic meaning, elicits no emotions. They do not resemble wedding rings forever binding me to the adoptive land; they are just mass-produced fare churned out by some factory. I am no longer a starry-eyed young immigrant instructor proudly demonstrating traditional recipes and proselytizing. I am now nearing the end of my journey.

As the years went by, I slowly started to lose my emotional connection with food. Although it never completely faded, it became more of a perfunctory function for special occasions or an opportunity to reassure myself that I still could work my magic. I realized then that I had reached another shore, a solitary place in life and time in which I was no longer certain of who I was or from where I really came, a stretch of wind-swept desert in which the life-sustaining, warm, sensuous, reassuring smell of fresh bread kneaded carefully by bare loving hands could no longer reach me.

Arrangiarsi
or
The Zucchini Blossom Blues

CATERINA EDWARDS

MID-SEPTEMBER AND the temperature drops to minus five. When I inspect the garden in the morning, most of the plants are frozen. Dead. The summer has been short, cool, and full of rain. I hoped for a mild, sunny fall, deluding myself that there would still be time for the tomatoes to ripen on the vine and for the zucchini plants to produce both flowers and vegetables. To me, the taste of the zucchini blossoms, dipped in a light flour and club soda batter, fried to a golden brown and sprinkled with sea salt, is subtle, delicate, and the essence of summer.

This year that fleeting pleasure was not to be. This year (and too many other years) our plants produced one zucchini, as long as my little finger, and one pickable flower. It wasn't worth mixing up the batter. The absence of zucchini stretched across the province; radio gardening shows buzzed with frustrated vegetable growers. There were exceptions: down the lane, one backyard sported several plants glowing with yellow blossoms. Each time I passed, I was tempted to reach through the metal wire and pick a few. "They won't miss them," I'd say to my husband. "They're not Italian." But he would shake his head disapprovingly. The proprietors of the envied garden are botanists: I classify them with the Italian-Canadians that keep their fig trees alive by burying them in the winter. With their esoteric arts, they flout the Canadian climate and the integrity of Mediterranean flora.

The city where I live, Edmonton, is on the fifty-third parallel and the most Northern city on the continent. Yet in our house, we try to eat as if we were living in my husband's birthplace, Palermo, which is on the thirty-eighth parallel. Italian cooking has always been about fresh and high-quality ingredients. The first "Italian" book of recipes, the thirteenth-century *Liber de Coquina,* produced in the Angevin court of Naples, begins with a long series of vegetable recipes, including ten different preparations of cauliflower. Conversely, in the rest of Europe during medieval times, such recipes were considered unworthy of written cuisine: meat was the symbol of power; the fruits of the earth were for the poor and the peasants. Theoretically, out here in the west, we should be eating more like the French or English aristocrats and less like those of the Italian states. We should revel in our famous beef and root vegetables and stop longing and searching for fresh tuna, crunchy finocchio, and ripe figs or persimmons. We should, but reason rarely rules our taste buds and stomachs.

When I was growing up in Calgary in the late 50s and early 60s, my mother cooked, as much as possible, in the Italian style. Like other immigrants, she had to compromise, improvise, and persevere. In those days, Italian food was neither fashionable nor entirely respectable. I remember many of our English dinner guests asking in worried voices: "You didn't put garlic in this, did you?" One dear lady refused to try even a bite of spaghetti with tomato sauce, because she found it too *foreign.* Calgary had a small population of Italians, and the necessary ingredients (including some, like red peppers, now widely available in supermarkets) were difficult if not impossible to find. In 1959, a small grocery store called Mario's opened in Bridgeland, which was then the Italian neighbourhood, and Mom was happy to have a source of olive oil, authentic parmesan cheese, and dried pasta. But so much was still missing.

If my mother had stayed in Venezia, she would not have spent so many hours in the kitchen. Her sisters and nieces in Italy bought their bread, pasta fresca, and sweet treats from professionals. Mom baked her own bread, as well as jam pie (*crostata*), apple strudel, almond cake, and hard cornmeal cookies. Describing the typical Canadian cup of coffee as "dirty dishwater," she tried buying green coffee beans and roasting them to the correct level of darkness for the stove-top moka machine, but burnt them so often she gave up. She made her own tagliatelle, ravioli, lasagna sheets, and the even-more-labour-intensive crespelle and potato gnocchi.

Shortcuts, canned and packaged food were for Canadians who, she insisted, were lazy and didn't know how to eat. Most of the produce at the local supermarket, shipped in from California or Florida, was not up to her standard, especially the pale, hard tomatoes. My father planted a large garden: lettuce, carrots, peas and tomatoes. Most years, his zucchini flourished. Still, each August we made a pilgrimage to the Okanagan Valley in search of properly ripened fruits and vegetables.

The distance between Calgary and Penticton is 670 kilometres, but the drive took longer than seven hours. The two lane road, which went up and over the Rocky Mountains, was always clogged with slow moving RVs and massive trucks. Once there we scoured the area, Kelowna to Osoyoos, visiting a circle of farms and fruit stands to ensure we bought only the best.

The way home was particularly unpleasant. The Ford Falcon would be overloaded with cases of tomatoes, peaches, and apples, plus smaller boxes of apricots, peppers, and eggplant. With at least five cases piled on top of each other in the back seat, my sister, Corinna, and I would be squeezed together in the small space left. Since the Falcon didn't have air conditioning, we'd be bathed in sweat and the smell of overripe fruit. (I'd make it worse for myself: I'd try and escape by reading and then I'd be car sick.)

At home, the Herculean labour began. Corinna and I were the kitchen slaves. Everything had to be processed, peeled, boiled, pickled, canned, and/or made into sauce or jam quickly, quickly before fermentation or rot set in. And at the end of each exhausting day, either Corinna or I had to get on our hands and knees and scrub the by-then disgustingly sticky floor.

Unfortunately, my father, who was not Italian, also subscribed to the do-it-yourself ethos and made wine, an illegal act in Alberta at that time. Few Okanagan farmers had vineyards then, so we were spared another trip; he bought grapes shipped in from California. It was Corinna's and my job to take turns in a big wooden barrel, stomping the fruit and releasing the juice. Imagine being enveloped in cold, slimy grape flesh, poked by scratchy stems from sole to mid-calf.

In our adult lives, until now, neither my sister nor I have ever admitted to the humiliation of being grape stompers. But when I was thirteen and she twelve, we were outed by an Italian cartoonist, not long after a group of journalists from his country dined at our house in Calgary. Of course, Dad served his rough, foxy wine, and he must have explained the process. One of the Italians had an enormous camera: he took many pictures of Corinna and me. Two weeks later, in *Corriere Della Sera,* a major Milan newspaper sold all over Italy, a condescending article appeared on the mores of the Italian immigrants of the wild west. It was illustrated by a caricature of us two sisters cheerfully stomping grapes in a giant barrel, emphasized by what were presumably flying juice drops.

Unlike my father's wine, my mother's canned goods were exquisite. As Corinna said recently: "In the cold and dark of winter, opening a mason jar of tomatoes or peaches was like unleashing a beam of sunshine." Yet I will never can a tomato or cook up some jam. I view much of my mother's food processing as unnecessary and time wasting — at least nowadays. Since my childhood years, the attitude to Italian food and drink has changed: today it is celebrated, even fashionable. The Italian Centre Shop in Edmonton carries more than the basics. An enormous number of esoteric ingredients are available, including buffalo milk mozzarella flown in from Campania and canned San Marzano tomatoes, certified to be from a small region around Naples and considered by gourmet chefs to be the best sauce tomatoes in the world.

This relatively recent bounty makes it easier for me to continue to cook in the Italian style. I can't change: it was how I was raised. We continue to have a *primo* and *secondo*: pasta, risotto, and polenta are routine. We obsess about coffee beans and spend too much on espresso and cappuccino machines. When my daughters were babies, I fed them *brodo* and *pastina,* rather than baby food from a jar. (And when the time comes, I expect they too will feed their children as I fed them.)

I make as much as possible from scratch: I turn the tomatoes the garden produces into sauce, the basil into pesto. I preserve by freezing, rather than canning. *Mi arrangio.* (I make do.) Although my compromises and improvisations are different from my mother's, in one significant way I am fighting the same battle. In this Northern climate, I can't depend on a large harvest of tomatoes or healthy basil. I'm learning not to expect zucchini blossoms. But I still hope — dream — that next summer, we'll have a full crop.

Mammola's Slow Food: Sagra dello Stocco

MARIA LUISA IERFINO-ADORNATO

THEY MEANDER TO Mammola, Reggio Calabria from all corners of southern Italy. They are food aficionados in search of the pesce stocco (stockfish) or Holy Grail. Yes, they actually rave about the gastronomic feast known as *Sagra dello Stocco*, which is held every August 9th. In the Piazzetta del Borgo there is folkloric dancing, "balli dei giganti," decorated artisan stands and pesce stocco served in traditional "tegami di terracotta." None of the other *Sagre* or fairs compared to this one, not even those for the venerated smoked ricotta or soppressata Calabrese.

The Sagra dello Stocco festival in my parent's medieval hometown of Mammola has become popular. Located near the legendary strait of Messina near the toe of the Italian boot, this region of Calabria known as Magna Grecia, adjacent to the fabled Aspromonte, is a rustic land along the Ionian Sea replete with picturesque fishing villages and extraordinary beaches. It boasts a subtropical climate that produces an abundance of olives, citrus fruit, prickly pears, figs, chestnuts, almonds, red peppers, Swiss chard, eggplants, fennel, truffles and all the aromatic herbs imaginable. An even greater abundance comes from the sea: swordfish, shrimp, sardines, cod, squid, octopus, oysters and clams.

Pesce stocco was traditionally cooked and served on Good Friday and Christmas Eve. In fact now it is creatively prepared all yearround in delicious combinations: insalata di stocco, bucatini con stocco, frittelle e zeppole di stocco, melanzane ripiene di stocco, frittata di stocco, stocco arrostito and of course, the renowned stocco con patate, olive, pomodoro e peperoncini.

Now what exactly is this sacred food or pesce stocco you may be asking? Well, it is the best super food (and supplement) for our over-all health, being low in calories and high in protein. Cod liver oil is processed from the stock livers and is a rich source of vitamin A, D, E and Omega-3 fatty acids.

Unlike the more popular baccalà, which is a salted cod, pesce stocco is a dried unsalted arctic cod imported from Norway. As per the artisanal tradition in Calabria, it is treated and soaked for days, in the purest and richest mineral waters. The art of methodically processing the stockfish into the highest quality product possible is comparable in many ways to that of producing Parma ham, fine co-gnac or aged pecorino Romano cheese. "Time" is the essence of life and food in this ancient land of artists and artisans.

In fact this attitude that one must take time to prepare food and appreciate its consumption evokes the "slow food" movement found-ed in 1986 by Carlo Petrini in response to the sacrilege of opening a McDonald's near Rome's Spanish Steps. Ronald McDonald has captivated our children like the pied piper of Hamlin. Fast food has revolutionized our society, accelerating the time we spend prepar-ing and enjoying food and diminishing the quality of its substance and experience. We must change our collective tune, declares con-temporary figure, Alice Waters. She and other Slow Food colleagues advocate that all our produce, meat, poultry and fish, should come from farms, ranches and fisheries, which are guided by principles of sustainability.

Spraying crops with pesticides, injecting hormones into live-stock to expedite growth, infesting fish with mercury and over-processing foods, are all actions that defy the principles of slow food, sustainability and good health. The end products lack the es-sential energy or life-giving force, as they are far removed from their natural state. There is sanctity in the land and in the sea that we must respect and preserve, as the decline of our own cod stocks have taught us. We must reclaim and celebrate the genuine "terroir" products, and the in-season, organic foods. Now, la "cucina povera" of our forefathers is ironically the richer one.

Somehow, I don't recall the addiction to "fast food" and to yoyo dieting when I was growing up in Montreal. There were slow cooked family meals and "time" for lots of great face-to-face conversations. What I do remember are all the good times, when we gathered around the dinner table, enjoying the fresh vegetables from the garden that my father proudly produced or the homemade pasta, tomato sauce, pesce stocco and "dolci" such as "nacatole e sammartine" that my mother took the time to lovingly prepare.

We religiously learned all the traditions and the one about Sagra dello Stocco remained alive for me as one of the best examples of community commitment to "slow food" and to quality time with family. But, the most magical culinary tradition of all, I must confess, was when the "Seven Fish" were served for La Vigilia di Natale. Christmas Eve was indeed the perfect time to prepare the pesce stocco or the more popular baccalà in Canada. It was a solemn Roman Catholic observance to fast before the vigil mass was celebrated, hence fish was allowed but meat was not.

Even when, in 1983, the Code of Canon Law eliminated this fast, tradition prevailed for the majority of Italian families. The holiday scene for centuries past in Italy was one of pious Catholics fasting and praying throughout the vigil anticipating the gift-bearing "La Befana's" descent upon them in January; however in Canada the scene today would be depicted as an elaborate gastronomic feast, definitely devoid of any true "fasting," filled with merriment and a loving, but not perfect family, that bonds and exchanges gifts that the youngsters believe Santa Claus brought.

Even though there were usually seven different dishes of fish served for this feast in my family, I am told that in some families the number could be eleven or even thirteen. Typically, tradition calls for seven, probably because the lucky number is symbolic of the seven sacraments or the seven virtues. In some households, including our own, there was an historical aversion to preparing the principal pasta dish with tomato sauce, red evoking the blood of Jesus; instead my mother, would prepare a white wine, garlic, parsley and shrimp sauce for the spaghetti after the antipasto and "fritto misto" were served.

The antipasto consisted of insalata di pesce stocco. This was the modern "essence" of slow food where an entire week was devoted to creating the succulent salad, starting with the actual order and purchase of the dried pesce stocco at the Italian specialty shop, usually found at the Jean-Talon market and priced dearly at about $50 a kilo or higher during the holidays. Mother would then soak the pesce stocco for exactly three days before Christmas Eve, changing the cold water each day. The well-rinsed pesce stocco was slow boiled until done and refrigerated for several hours. Extra virgin olive oil, fresh oregano, two ribs of chopped celery, sliced banana peppers, fresh lemon juice with added zest, a tablespoon of white vinegar and one of white wine, were simply combined and then poured over the delicate pesce stocco. The salad was refreshing, full of excellent nutrients and a much anticipated holiday treat.

The satisfying "fritto misto" or fish fry would follow. This consisted of lightly coated, deep-fried calamari rings and their tender tentacles, savoury smelts and succulent scallops or other favourite fish. A fresh arugula salad and plenty of lemon wedges were the perfect accompaniment. Following the shrimp pasta dish, the grand seafood finale included baked lobster plus giant scampi in garlic, with rapini and exotic mushrooms on the side.

The "Seven Fish" family feast was the "Holy Grail," our own unique, epicurean family interpretation of the "Sagra dello Stocco," highly anticipated and warmly savoured in the very heart of winter in Montreal. Our "dessert" was definitely divine, this last course consisted of midnight mass, which served as a gentle reminder of the sanctity of the feast, the importance of love and the true meaning of tradition in our lives.

Taking Back the Meatball

LORETTA GATTO-WHITE

DO YOU REMEMBER the schoolyard ditty that began ... "On top of spaghetti all covered with cheese, I lost my poor meatball when somebody sneezed. It rolled off the table and onto the floor, and then my poor meatball rolled right out the door."?

Sung to the tune of *On Top of Old Smokey*, it recounted the journey of a hapless meatball, which despite its arduous travails remains intact, obviously possessed of all the tenderness of a bocce ball and fashioned with the same indifferent ingredients and ham-fisted technique that too many of its ilk have suffered in urban greasy spoons, suburban kitchens and canned concoctions across North America for decades. This abuse must stop, if not for ourselves, then at least for our children.

The integrity of the emblematic meal of spaghetti and meatballs has suffered greatly in its journey from Naples to the New World. In its Southern Italian habitat we find it as small tender polpette (meatballs) made of ground beef, pork and veal, surrounded by a modest amount of sweet oregano- scented sugo (tomato sauce) beneath which lay a golden coil of al dente spaghetti, the crowning glory being a benediction of snowy pecorino Romano (sheep's milk cheese), the formaggio of choice in the "mezzogiorno," a cultural demarcation kind of like the Mason-Dixon Line.

Tragically, not long after they stepped-off the boat and into the hungry mouths of North Americans, fame and popularity corrupted spaghetti and meatballs. They fell into the evil clutches of 'Chef' Boy-ar-dee and Michelina, who exploited their simplicity and innocence, making them cheap and cheesy, just like their cousin, the pizza; turned into trash, then spun into gold. It seems the New World opportunities for turning a culinary silk purse into a dietary sow's ear were irresistible.

Fortunately, behind the kitchen doors of successive generations of Italian North Americans, the tradition of Sunday spaghetti and meatballs lived on. Recently, celebrity chefs like Mario Batali have undertaken its rehabilitation by introducing it in their restaurants and cookbooks returning it to its delicate and delicious roots, the way I ate it as a child.

However, the eating of this humble family dish is just part of the pleasure it gave me. Sunday dinners usually consisted of some form of pasta, prepared by my father who is an estimable cook. When meatballs were on the menu, he always enlisted my small, nimble hands to shape them. I loved doing this, as it gave me time alone with my father and forged a bond founded on our mutual love of food and craftsmanship. We approached this enterprise with thought and care; each ball should be slightly smaller than a golf ball, perfectly rounded and compacted just enough to stay together, but not to be hard or dense. Once browned, they were dropped into the fragrant sauce, where they would simmer for several hours.

My sisters and I took every opportunity at this stage to sneak into the kitchen, spear a meatball and nestle it firmly in a hunk of crusty Italian bread, running outside to wolf down our stolen treasure. I recall one Sunday when our gluttony overtook caution. Seated around the dinner table, staring at our nearly empty bowls, it became apparent that there was a dearth of meatballs, followed by a plethora of silence, and four lowered heads exchanging sidelong guilty glances.

Now, it's time to take back the integrity of this meal, the ritual of its preparation and the communion of its enjoyment; in short in rehabilitating the humble meatball we are also reviving the conviviality of the Sunday family dinner.

Sunday Meatballs and Spaghetti

Enlisting the help of either much older or younger hands will turn the task into a rewarding experience.

Always use good quality ingredients;

Make your meat balls of equal amounts of ground chuck, veal and pork,

Bind with some egg, milk- soaked, torn-up stale bread squeezed dry and a little ricotta, they will be soft and moist.

Work in a little chopped fresh Italian parsley and finely chopped onion and garlic.

Season with salt and pepper

For the sugo eschew tomato paste and use only pureed sweet canned plum tomatoes, a little chopped garlic, a splash of red wine vinegar and a touch of Greek oregano, the sauce will be fragrant and irresistible.

Use imported spaghetti cooked for the recommended time in plenty of boiling salted water (no oil!).

Finish with freshly grated Pecorino Romano cheese from Italy and the pasta will be perfect.

Last, let me advise you that while the polpette bob merrily about in the bubbling sugo, assemble your family somewhere, say in the backyard, where you can keep an eye on them and perhaps enjoy a lively game of bocce.

Buon Appetito!

Fourth Course:
Contorno

A Colour Called Family

JOSEPH ANTHONY FARINA

the world was black and white
when we immigrated here
black boat to black train.
the canadian landscape in winter
was all black trees and white snow

under a black night and white moon
mamma, papa and i walked blocks
to a paisano's to watch *i love lucy*
and *lawrence welk* on a black and white tv
we wondered at commercials
we did not understand, hawking
white cigarettes and black cars.

nuns in black and white taught me
on blackboards with white chalk.
priests in black and white saved our souls
from the black of hell for the white of heaven
black and white smoke permeated
my neighbourhood, from the foundry stacks
where papa worked.

colour appeared when we gathered
for an evening meal
of white pasta and red sauce
ruby wine and green salad.

Polenta and *Frico*

ANNA PIA DELUCA

MY STORY BEGINS with my mother's noteworthy preparation of *polenta* and *frico,* which was quite a feat in our early days as immigrants to Canada, since Friulian *sòrc* (maize) and mixed aged and fresh Montasio cheese were hard to come by. Having to buy Canadian cornmeal, which was much too finely ground thus mushy and tasteless when cooked, was a cultural shock for my mother who had visions of a coarse and consistent *polenta* that would retain its spherical shape when dropped onto a simple round wooden cutting board with oblong handles.

The dishes that revolved around our Friulian table in Canada had an aura of ancient customs and beliefs, of familiar smells and historically ambivalent spaces. The board was placed at the centre of the table where father ritually cut the *polenta* into slices with a long piece of cotton thread, coiled like a wreath around one of the handles. As a child in Friuli, I had often watched my grandmother unwind the thread, kiss it, recite a prayer and then make a sign of the cross on the *polenta* before slicing it into pieces by sliding the thread under the bread-like form and working from the bottom up. Only after this ritual was performed were we allowed to speak and grab for food. And any *polenta* crusts that were left over were meticulously boiled in milk the day after for our morning breakfast. Maybe that was one of the reasons why cornflakes and hot milk became my favourite Canadian substitute.

Even the importance of cheese in a Friulian diet cannot be undervalued, especially in the farming communities where cooked Montasio cheese had always accompanied *polenta*. Historically this cheese had been produced in Friuli since the 13th century by the monks of the Abbey of Moggio Udinese and later took the name of the plateau on which the Abbey stood: the plateau of Montasio. To-day most of north-eastern Friuli still produces Montasio with the same simple recipe underlining the characteristic salty hard yellow texture and hazelnut aftertaste.

Unfortunately, Friulian Montasio cheese was not imported to Canada until many years later. I still remember my mother's first attempts at making *frico* with pieces of aged Canadian cheddar cheese and potatoes, but somehow these ingredients just never worked. Instead of being moist and soft, the cooked cheese and potatoes became dry and hard. This was a good ten years before the arrival of my aunt Rose from Italy, who like a magician spread a thin layer of a variety of grated cheeses onto a non-stick frying pan, tossing and turning the mixture with two forks as she moulded and created little cup-shaped baskets. Mother finally learned to make an excellent light and crispy fried cheese *frico*, this time without potatoes but which was artistically shaped and filled with soft polenta to accompany her stewed-meat dishes full of thick spicy sauce.

There were also moments of disappointment. Maybe it was the fact that later, when I was a teenager, I was embarrassed by the "exotic" food presented to my mock-faced Canadian girlfriends who stayed over for dinner: "What's this smell? What's that yellow stuff? I can't eat that muck!" And I would try to explain that it was only cheese and cornmeal bread, both cooked over a wood fire rather than in an oven, the way my mother used to in the old days.

Naturally those days have passed, and its association with poverty and peasant culture is no longer a problem, especially since *polenta* and *frico* with its many regional Italian and world-wide variations has become the favourite recipe of a large number of international chefs. I consider my mother one of them. Her *polenta* is now fried, baked, grilled, integrated and enriched with numerous alternative ingredi-ents, my favourite being *polente cuinçàde* where soft cornmeal is spooned out into a terracotta baking pan and layered with grated smoked ricotta cheese, foaming hot browned butter and cinnamon. It's more like a dessert than a dinner.

Over the years, however, the cultural significance of this dish has changed with futile arguments focussed on texture and colour and whether white corn flour is not a more refined ingredient than yellow corn flour, which in Italy is often considered coarse animal stodge. Traditionally though, polenta has always been the consoling colour of gold, and today is reproduced in every "Fogolâr Furlan" around the world as evinced by the Polenta fest held in Windsor in September 2011, where the Friulian community prepared an enormously huge cauldron weighing over 6,500 pounds thus beating the previous Guinness world record held in Feltre, Belluno the year before. In Windsor, the Polenta fest brought together Friulani from all over Canada, Italy and the United States, symbolically uniting and bonding families and friends of all ages and backgrounds, thus performing in macrocosm what it had always done within the microcosm of my immediate family.

In retrospect, I guess I was pretty lucky to have had a Friulian mother, Tilde, who emigrated from Northern Italy when she was only 26, bringing with her a culinary baggage that was quite uncommon in predominantly Anglo-Saxon Toronto in the early 1950s. I still have fond memories of our *polenta* dinners, with their rituals and festivities, their values and beliefs and why not, even their moments of discord because they were always occasions of importance in our family life.

As a final consideration, when I think of *polenta* today, a very moving narrative poem always comes to mind, written by Canadian poet of Friulian origins, Dôre Michelut, after the painful death of her mother. In the poem, the author's meticulous re-enactment of her mother's preparation of rabbit and *polenta,* to be ceremoniously served to friends, permits Michelut to mediate between the pain of loss and love itself:

Overnight, I soaked the meat
to drain the wild taste that rabbits
sometimes have.
Then I cooked it: first, I browned it well
so it would dry; then I added garlic,
rosemary, salt, pepper and three full glasses
of good white wine.
I invited friends.
As I made *polenta,* I told
them the story of you and the rabbit.
Then, we feasted.[1]

In this case the *polenta* becomes the metaphorical threshold of a window opening out to the psychological dynamics of family life and its painful interactions. In the same manner, *polenta* and *frico* will always be with me, reminding me of my mother, our family reunions and our early life in Canada.

1. Dôre Michelut, "The Earth: In memory of Dirce, my mother," *Ouroboros: The Book That Ate Me.* Laval: Éditions Trois. 1990, pp. 79-80.

The Food of Love in All Seasons

LORETTA GATTO-WHITE

I TRIM THE roses, tease down the tangle of sweet pea vines from the trellis, turn the compost and scrape up the apple leaves into a tidy pile. As I rest on my rake to consider the last flush of windfalls, I think of my father whose favourite time of year this was; the reckoning season, a time when things are weighed and tallied, the outcome being either something gained or something lost.

And my father loved all the seasons, claiming he could never be a "snowbird," because he would miss the change of seasons in Canada. It wasn't just the wonder of nature's cycles that gladdened him, it was the food which each season brought for him to forage, make and share. It was the sharing which was the most important part of each seasonal tradition.

Spring found him up north netting smelts with his Uncle Roger to be dredged in flour and pan-fried in the old cast iron pan until crisp and golden, to be eaten bones and all, the tiniest sprats, dug into the garden for fertilizer. Then later, foraging for the bitter *cicoria* as he called it, from his jealously guarded patch in Earl Bales' Park, so secret he never let me accompany him, too many other competitive *paesans* following the trail.

He cleaned and trimmed each bunch and parcelled them out according to the recipient's need: his daughters, then his brother Graddy's gang (being the largest), then Aunt Carm's, etc., all the way down the line to Dolly Bianchi, proprietor of Toronto's oldest French restaurant, La Chaumière; hers in exchange for empty wine bottles. The *cicoria* was our spring tonic, but it was more to my father as it gave him occasion to "make the rounds" as he called his ritual, seeing how everyone was after the winter hibernation and passing-on the news to whomever was the next recipient.

Midsummer brought corn, peaches and cream, straight from the farmers' fields outside Huntsville which he distributed on his bi-weekly return to the city, to again make the rounds of friends and family with the offering of the best of summer's sweet golden treasure.

Late-summer was the time for the deep garnet Bing cherries he chose, just at, but never beyond their peak of perfect ripeness to preserve in brandy, which he shared amongst family and friends as the perfect, potent little Christmas *cichetto*.

But fall was the best of all. My father's absolute favourite season. It wasn't only the beautiful display that fall's burnished brush created on the sugar maples, birch and tamarack that drew him 'up north' — it was above all pepper season! Big bushels of bright red shepherd peppers made their way along the 400 in the trunk of his old Buick to be transformed into smoky wood-roasted peppers, this ritual bringing his numerous nephews, 'the cowboys' as he christened them, and his best *compares*, Strano and Terziano, together for the weeks-long enterprise, the unbroken tradition to each cottage-closing season.

Later, back in Toronto in his tiny apartment kitchen, he set about carefully slicing, brining and bottling the eggplant for his pickled *melanzane*, another offering to see his friends and loved-ones through the deprivation of winter's barren months.

Then there was the wine. When we were young, the deep fruity smell of ripe carignano grapes permeated the house as well as the infestation of attendant fruit flies. The "must" or grape-pressings being fermented on a stove-top still into the deceptively innocent-looking grappa — pure, clear "dragon's breath." Years later, he and his *compare*, Rino, made their potent brew from "uva," fermenting in demi-johns, instead of the old oak barrels. Still later, under the influence of "the cowboys," dad's vintner efforts progressed from old school D.I.Y. tradition into "we brew for you" enterprises, the carignano being replaced with the upscale merlot and ruby cabernet or *carbenet* as he always mispronounced it.

Finally, Christmas brought on the production of prodigious amounts of carefully fried potato croquettes — but not too much garlic ("Everybody loves that garlic!") and lots of cheese — but only pecorino, never, parmesan ("over-used and too trendy"). Rolled in paper towels to absorb the oil, then in waxed paper, they were eagerly awaited by us all. "What, dad, only this little bit? There's not enough here to freeze for later!" Okay! And a week later, they would appear, like some savoury magic, which I ate far too much of ... yum ...

For every season there was a food, an occasion for my father to celebrate what he loved about Canada, his hometown, our cottage, his friends and family with which to share its seasonal bounty. He truly was a father, grandfather, uncle and friend with the gift of the food of love for us, in all seasons.

My Mother's Bread

SALVATORE ALA

WHEN I EAT my mother's bread
I taste my mother's breast.
My mouth fills with strong milk.
I am an infant again.

What I can't remember
Is still in my flesh.
Kitchen heat, the odour of yeast,
White dough rising, flour on her face,
Breasts swollen with milk,
The warm bread of her hands
On my face and lips.
Sleep coming over me.

Arancine

MARCO LO VERSO

POOR LONELY J. Alfred Prufrock in T.S. Eliot's poem measured out his life in coffee spoons. For him the social event is a moment of crisis; the coffee spoon is a symbol of alienation. I, luckily, come from a family of eaters and talkers. Food binds us together—and none quite as well as *arancine*. I like to think that I have measured out my life in *arancine*.

Some readers might ask, what are *arancine*? *Arancine* (pronounced "Ah-rahn-CHEE-neh") is plural for *arancina* (little orange). The *arancina* is a deep-fried rice ball stuffed with ground meat, peas, and sometimes cheese and other ingredients. To my mind it's the best thing that's ever happened to a bowl of cooked rice, and it's the perfect symbol of sociability and family cohesion.

The *arancina* is a classic of Sicilian cooking and, like the orange, which is almost emblematic of Sicily itself, can be found all over the island in slightly different forms. In Palermo, where I'm from, it's round and feminine because it's shaped like a small orange (*arancia* is a feminine noun). In eastern Sicily, the same dish is more conical in shape, and—maybe because of its more protuberant shape, I don't know—it's known by the masculine form of the noun: *arancino* in the singular, *arancini* in the plural.

Anyone who cares about linguistic accuracy will see how ridiculous this masculinization is. In Italian, the names of fruits are usually feminine, while the names of fruit trees are masculine: So apple is *mela* and apple tree is *melo*; pear is *pera* and pear tree is *pero*; orange is *arancia* and orange tree is *arancio*. Clearly, the rice cones of eastern Sicily look nothing like a little orange tree (*arancino*); they look like a little orange (*arancina*) with a fat nose. But I'm not here to quibble. If some people want to deform their *arancine*—and their language—that's their business.

As I was saying, I have measured out my life in *arancine*. In my family, we have a tradition of making *arancine* for festive occasions. When I was growing up we would make them at Christmas or for birthdays. And now that we do not all live in the same city (or country), whenever we happen to be together, we form a kind of assembly line, with my mother serving as team captain, and we make *arancine*.

The last time we did it was for my birthday, when my mother was visiting. We started by cooking about one and one half pounds of Arborio rice in salted water. While that was going on, I (who fancy myself good with a knife) chopped a small onion and a celery rib, while my wife (who actually knows what she's doing in the kitchen), heated some olive oil in a pan, sautéed my chopped offerings in the oil, and then added about half a pound of ground beef and browned it. She then stirred in a dollop of tomato paste, some wine, salt, and pepper. (Ingredients are added *ad occhio*—"by eye," depending more on traditional knowledge and feel than precise measurements.) She let the sauce simmer for about 20 minutes, and towards the end my mother added one cup of peas plus two ingredients that make this recipe unique to our family but very Sicilian nonetheless: a fistful each of pine nuts and raisins. When the rice was cooked and drained, my mother added two beaten eggs and about half a cup of grated parmigiano cheese, plus some salt and pepper. We then set both the rice mixture and the meat sauce, or *ragù*, aside to cool.

During this whole process, my daughters would ask my mother to tell them stories of our relatives in Sicily and about me as a little boy. The central narrative, the one that my mother routinely repeats every year on my birthday, was the story of my birth, which took place in a villa in Sferracavallo, a fishing village/resort just outside of Palermo. I was born at home, with the assistance of a midwife. My mother is always proud to point out that the whole experience was natural and went splendidly well. Except for one shocking fact: when I slithered into the world, my head was not round, but elongated. "Come un uovo!" ("Like an egg!"). My mother laughs when she tells this story. She could just as easily have said that my head was shaped like an *arancino* from Messina. But, being a mother, her thoughts run more to symbols of fertility and new life. Besides, the midwife quickly assured her that babies' heads are very soft and that the elongation was just the effect of the pressure of the birth canal. My mother happily ends her story by pointing out that my conical feature lasted only a few weeks and that my head eventually assumed the perfect rotundity that it enjoys today. Which is great, but in recent years I've come to suspect that my dislike of the shape and name of the eastern-Sicilian *arancini* might have something to do with this birth trauma. (I also have an almost Poe-like fear of confined spaces). But I'll leave it to my analyst to figure that one out.

When the rice was cool enough to handle, the *arancine*-making process resumed. For each *arancina*, my mother took enough rice in her left hand to cover her palm. She pressed in the centre of the rice with her right hand to form a hollow, and my daughters took turns spooning about a tablespoon of *ragù* into the hollow. Finally, my mother took enough rice to cover the *ragù* and to form a sealed ball of rice the size and shape of a small orange. (*Nota bene*: It is much easier and more natural, given the shape of cupped human hands, to form spherical balls rather than anything looking like a cone or, heaven forbid, an orange tree!)

While the *arancine* were being formed and placed on dishes, my wife and I prepared a bowl of flour, a bowl with four beaten eggs, a bowl of breadcrumbs, and a bowl of warm water. My mother started by handing each *arancina* to my wife, who rolled it in the flour and passed it on to daughter #1, who immersed it in the beaten eggs and passed it on to daughter #2, who rolled it in the bread crumbs and placed it on sheets of waxed paper to dry. From time to time, my daughters dipped their hands into the bowl of water to rinse off the sticky mess building up on their fingers. (A professional chef might tell you that you can avoid this sticky mess by using gloves or a slotted spoon at each stage, but a professional chef is used to working alone and is probably measuring out his life in coffee spoons. For us, making *arancine* is a family affair, and getting messy is part of the fun.)

I then heated vegetable oil in a pot big enough to accommodate and completely immerse three *arancine* at a time. Once the oil was very hot (a test bit of bread should sizzle like a soul in hell), I slipped the *arancine* into the oil with a slotted spoon, fried them to a golden brown, and then placed them on absorbent paper to cool. This might sound like the most solitary part of the process, but actually the rest of the family supervised my every move, making sure that I had enough oil, that it was the right temperature, that I did not crowd the *arancine*, and that I didn't either undercook or overcook them. The pressure was tremendous!

The reward to all this effort is in the satisfaction of having worked together and, of course, the pleasure in the eating. If *arancine* are done properly they are not at all greasy; very little cooking oil is absorbed by the breadcrumb mixture. The outer layer will be firm but still tender. The first bite combines in your mouth the savoury, slight crispiness of the fried batter with the creamy softness of the egg-and-cheese-infused rice. Another bite adds the richness of the pea-filled ragù with the crunch of the pine nuts and the soft sweetness of the raisins.

To really appreciate *arancine*, they should be shared on the day that they're cooked while they're still warm. They will keep in the fridge for a few days, but they should be heated slightly to bring out the full flavour. But the sharing part should never be forgotten. If any family member were to feel that he or she has not been apportioned an equitable number of the *arancine*, there is the potential for a disruption to the harmony and cohesion that the *arancine*-making created in the first place.

We experienced an instance of this danger many years ago when my wife was expecting our first-born. We had a full house of relatives who had come to Canada from Sicily for a wedding, and we had made a batch of *arancine* for everyone. My wife, being pregnant, had a heightened craving for these treats. But she couldn't eat them right away when we made them because she was having medical tests the next day and wasn't allowed to eat dairy products. So, while the rest of the family was enjoying the still-warm *arancine* and feeling harmonious and cohesive, she was on the sidelines, a forced smile on her face, her fingers drumming a martial tap on her growing belly. But she made the best of an irritating situation: she set two *arancine* aside in a separate dish for herself in the fridge.

"I'll eat them tomorrow after my tests," she said.

"Yes, yes," we all agreed, licking our fingers. "Eat them tomorrow after your tests." And we continued to eat and feel harmonious and cohesive.

The next day, after all of the other *arancine* had been consumed, my father came upon the dish with the two *arancine* in the fridge during one of his peckish moments. Apparently he forgot that they were my wife's *arancine* (or so he claimed afterwards). And since he did not want to see them go stale, he warmed them up and dispatched them.

Shortly thereafter, when my wife, who had by this point had her medical tests and was hungry for *arancine*, went to the fridge to satisfy her craving, she found a space where the dish of *arancine* had been. She looked around in panicky surprise and then saw on the counter an empty dish with a few crumbs on it — crumbs that looked suspiciously like the remnants of something deep-fried and round. Her mind clamped on the truth with the force and swiftness of a falcon's talon and set her off on what amounted to an only semi-controlled cry of indignation aimed at me.

"Not only have I been cleaning and cooking for a household of YOUR relatives for days and days, but now someone has gone and eaten MY *arancine*!" she ranted — audibly.

And my father heard her. He was surprised. He was probably embarrassed, but he hid it by growing indignant himself.

"What's she going on about?" he said. "She's from the North. I didn't think she cared about *arancine*!"

This was the wrong thing to say. Quasi-murderous thoughts were entertained. And a cloud of resentment hung over the household. Only with time did the resentment pass — but even then, not completely. If I mention the event today — more than thirty years after the incident — my wife still remembers being deprived of her *arancine*. It's a subject better left untouched.

All of which serves to prove that *arancine* have power. They encourage cooperation and conviviality. They provide extreme pleasure and nourishment. They represent the flavour, warmth, and roundness of a fulfilling life. But if they are misused in any way, they can be like the forbidden fruit.

They must be respected and shared. All of us must get our fair portion — especially our spouses. I have learned a profound lesson: if I measure out the *arancine* to my wife, I can measure out my life in *arancine*.

Banana Man

JIM ZUCCHERO

It's January and minus 20 degrees outside my window
I'm sitting at my desk, at work, my lunch bag in front of me
I have a treat today—strawberries!
I raise one to my lips
Pause
consider its wilted stem and cardinal redness
breath in its surprisingly strawberry smell
and suddenly, unexpectedly, I am transported

the potent aroma triggers an olfactory sensation
a lightning bolt to my work-numbed brain

I am standing on the loading docks of the Ontario Food Terminal
a scrawny boy of 10
exhaust fumes waft up from the few rumbling trucks
perched below the concrete decks with the blunt steel edges
the hum and drone of electric fork lifts whizzing by
dragging skids of crates of oranges and beans piled high
swaying, shifting, but never jarred enough to tumble off

at every stall—door for door—hustlers hawk
the same goods, chiselling a quarter off the price
of a case of cantaloupes, or a buck on a lot of twenty cases
trying to move railroad cars of produce
before the next shipment arrives

"Johnny, c'mere! ... where you goin'?
My grapes are better than his. He's got crap! ... c'mere
OK, who's goin' for coffee?"

Chinese store owners holler and jump as they toss coins
against the wall in their favourite ancient gambling games

farther down the dock somebody is flogging tickets
for tonight's Leafs game against the Habs
and the price is going up

hulking truck drivers with names like No-Neck and Pee Wee
snatch receipts from checkers at the door and trudge off grumbling
to make their next delivery

the potato packing room at Ontario Produce has the best girlie
    calendars
but you have to pretend not to notice them
or the packers will make fun of you
(aaaaa — look at the woody!)

the Carmelite Sisters huddle close together
and waddle down the dock going door-to-door
collecting contributions for their cause
foul-mouthed men cringe and smile awkwardly
when the good sisters slip past them
within earshot of their barrages of curses and expletives

a roast beef sandwich or a fried egg at Bill's coffee shop
before we check the load and head for home

weary banana men have done a day's work here
before the sun is up
before they even tote their precious cargo back to their stores
to display it

they feed Toronto
but most of their customers have no idea
what a circus their produce comes from

I'm glad my dad was a banana man
I know

Olivo Secolare

BRUNA DI GIUSEPPE-BERTONI

(Oliveto nella Ciociaria. Macchione, Villa Santo Stefano)

Albero di frutta
vigoroso.
Simbolo di pace.
Sbiego da secoli
Coltivato da loro,
mio nonno, suo nonno.
Parlami di loro.

Old Olive Tree

(An olive grove in Ciociaria Italy)

Vigorous fruit tree.
Symbol of peace.
Curved for centuries
Cultivated by my
grandfather, his grandfather.
Tell me about them.

Abandoned Rituals

DELIA DE SANTIS

In 1958
when we were new immigrants
picking dandelions was
a good thing to do
survival had not yet
taught us shame
then slowly we began to shop
in supermarkets
and things that grew in ditches
were forgotten
until today
when I walked along
a country road again
my eyes searching
for tender shoots
to bring home ...
and see my mother's face
blushing through sheets
of steam
as she stands by the stove
tending to a cauldron
of good old fashioned
sustenance

Cicoria

DARLENE MADOTT

COME SPRING, MY father would tell of the time, during World War II, training in Courtney, on the west coast of Canada, he and about eleven other Italians from the Sault St. Marie and Sudbury Regiment, saw these hardy weeds with their tight fisted buds poking from the spring earth, gave each other the look of recognition, and began picking them deftly with the bayonets on their rifles. Later that night, at a long table in the mess hall, they sat down to dinner, when their Provo Captain interrupted the feast of weeds, garnished with salt, olive oil, and kitchen vinegar. They convinced the Provo, on medicinal grounds, that this was an Italian ritual, to eat this *insalata*, rich in iron from the spring earth, to re-invigorate the blood. On medicinal grounds, wanting a landing force in battle readiness for beaches the likes of Dieppe, an exception was made, rules bent, to allow the WOPs to eat their weeds in the mess hall, after hours.

"Did he taste with you?"

"We offered, but he refused. The rest of the camp heard about it, though, and the other Italians who'd missed out were all drooling at the chops."

"My favourite part is the unopened flower. I love that bud, the texture and the burst of flavour—the best are the ones left at the bottom of the salad bowl, soaked in the balsamic."

"Wasn't balsamic, just kitchen vinegar, but it did the job, nature did the rest."

We are at the hospital, while we exchange this dialogue. My father is ninety-three. He is dying. His false teeth no longer fit. But this weekend, I have picked the weeds from my garden, and I have made him *cicoria*, and he is gumming away at a single paddy. This act of will and deliberation is taking an hour of minutes divided by seconds.

⊗ Other memories of cicoria:

The raising of the walls atop the walkout basement in Muskoka, when finally my father could afford to build. We had lived in the basement and slept on bunk beds in a small cabin off to one side, for five summers. That night, we drank champagne and ate cicoria paddies in celebration around a camp fire, down near the lake. While the walls and roof were being raised, my sisters and I had picked the cicoria in the three acres of farmer's field. The process of cleaning the root of sand, rinsing in pails of water pulled from the lake, and then individually again, in fresh water brought from the city, was arduous, and my mother had initially said "no" to the idea. But the act of making the cicoria paddies undertaken in the Muskoka sun to the sound of hammering and dreams, as each wall went up, was a celebration.

⊗ In Rome:

I see cicoria on the menu. It comes blanched with sea salt, then sautéed in garlic and oil. I am waiting for my man to join me. He is flying from Norway, and I am filled with anxiety as to when he will arrive, whether he will find me. The converted monastery where we will be staying is just up the street, and I have left a note in our key cubby. Sunday in Rome. It is 4:00 in the afternoon, and I alone remain in the garden restaurant, as near the entrance the restaurant owners pick tablecloth fabric. There is a commotion. I look up, to see him standing, with his massive arms folded, leaning against the frame of the door, just looking at me. The taste of his first sweet kiss after long absence becomes wedded to the bitter taste of cicoria.

⊗ Father, every springtime that remains of my life, I will pick cicoria and see you again, working away with your mouth, chewing without teeth, with that inward look that tries to suck life from a weed, trying so hard just to live.

A Special Day

DELIA DE SANTIS

I AM HAVING coffee and toast. The window of our dinette is tall and wide. I am glad I can look outside.

What I see is good. A lot of space, yet somewhat restricted too, confined. Our back yard, then an open field, it's distance broken by a thick line of trees.

My husband planted the trees, evergreens — it's our property. I helped him.

My parents also came to help. Filling buckets from the barrels on the truck they carried water into the rows. They were eager, excited. They know so much about the soil and what it takes to make things grow, the nutrients. Before emigrating to Canada they lived off the land. It means a lot to them to give plants a good start.

Our two boys were there too, pretending to labour — too little for real work.

The trees are tall and bushy now. Our sons over twenty — my parents old.

Yesterday, my niece's baby was baptized. Afterwards, there was a big dinner. My parents were very proud. The child is their great granddaughter.

Mama and Papa are very lucky — they're already blessed with four great grandchildren.

The reception was held at the Italian-Canadian club, where they serve seven course meals, with all the trimmings. Liqueur, *espresso* coffee.

The hall is on the second floor of the building, and there's no elevator for people to get upstairs. My mother, who still loves to wear high heels, is starting to accept my hand on her arm when walking up or down steps.

Mama has always been a proud woman, independent. And I am saddened by this weakening in her spirit. Her fear of tripping, falling. Mama who used to climb trees to pick cherries, back home. Agile and quick all her life, now even putting on some pounds. Just a few extra, to weigh her down. A slowing down of her body, her mind somewhat angry over this incapacity. Snapping at her children, at us the younger ones.

Papa is good. Leaning, bent, but still doing fine. Never complaining about his aches and pains. Refusing to wear his hearing aid, but all eyes, alert. Missing nothing. But thankfully relenting a little on the observance of old country traditions. Not as rigid as he used to be.

It seems that, with the coming of the great grandchildren, he has finally started to accept the new generation, including some of the ways of the new world. Perhaps he has seen that, even with a certain breaking away from the formality and the stiff "old country" ways, nothing terrible has happened. No wrath of God, no crumbling of the world, but just beautiful, healthy children, born to his own children, and now to his grandchildren.

Maria Benedetta. Born to Adriana and John. She's the fourth of Mama and Papa's great-grandchildren, after Julia, Anthony and Joseph ...

A miracle baby. We like to think that ... both sides of the family waiting for this birth. People praying, then crying. Relief—everything okay.

A beautiful baby. The mother thirty-five—there was fear. The first child ... a hard time conceiving. Infertility clinics. A difficult pregnancy.

Maria Benedetta. The name Maria after her paternal grandmother, a gentle and kind woman who passed away several years ago; Benedetta, after Benedetto, the paternal grandfather recently gone to his rest.

But also Benedetta with other meanings ...

Ave Maria ... tu sei benedetta fra le donne ... Hail Mary ... blessed art thou among women ...

Blessed.

Soon, the day is over and most of the guests are leaving. Family members start gathering things from the hall, to take back to their cars. Leftover cake, baking ... big bows and centrepieces, the bassinet ... and I am so pleased my niece, who is also my godchild, asked me to hold Maria, while the cleaning up is being done.

Maria is still sleeping, as she has done most of the day. So pure and sweet in her white baptismal gown. The satin headband, with a small flower on the forehead.

Someday I'll be a grandmother, too. My son got married last year — the older one. He and his wife have not left the hall yet; they're still in the lobby, where I am now sitting with Maria in my arms. I can tell they're waiting for a chance to hold her, too. So after a little while I carefully hand the baby over to my daughter-in-law. Standing beside his wife, my son smiles.

About a month ago, Maria Benedetta's maternal great-grandmother died. At the party, I kept picturing her as though she were still alive, sitting at one of the tables, with her family.

I know how much she was missed at this celebration. But no one spoke her name, her death too recent. Memories too painful. Her husband dabbing at his eyes often with his white handkerchief ...

I too have tears in my eyes now. So much to think about. My uncle, my mother's brother, has lost so much weight. There were seven children in my mother's family, now there's only two left.

I sigh and lift my mug. It's empty — I need more coffee. But I don't want to get up yet. I don't want to leave my windowpane of memories ... but I know I must.

I stare at my back yard. Around the patio, white clematis, and roses in a variety of colours. So many buds. And *i fior di gelsomino* ... with their white blossoms so perfumed, the fallen petals scattered on the ground, as though at some ceremonial event in the country we still call "home."

Suddenly I decide to unwrap the *bomboniera*, the "favour" the baby's parents had given to the families who had accepted their invitation and come to give them honour. A little white angel on his knees ... with shiny wings, and a tiny basket by his side. Inside the basket, the *confetti*, held together in a tiny pouch of white netting. I cut the narrow ribbon around the frilly net and take away the tiny sprig of dried flowers used as decoration. The thank you card, tiny, folded, has the baby's name and christening date on it. I will not throw it away — I'll keep it between the pages of my bible, for future memories.

I hold the candies in my hand, the *confetti*, white ones for purity and pink for the gender ... sugar for the sweetness in life and almonds for the bitterness.

I put one of the *confetti* in my mouth and place the remaining four in a little crystal bowl on the counter, for the rest of my family to sample. But I'll keep the angel. I'll put it somewhere where I can see it ... for remembrance of a special day. For Maria Benedetta. For me ... for all of us ... for all the generations to come.

Food Companion Wanted

ELIZABETH CINELLO

THE PARK SITS in a deep dip on Caledonia Road just before the street climbs a steep hill, probably the steepest in the city. It's morning and nobody's around. The grass glistens in the spring sunlight. She is sitting on a bench near the playground where they agreed to meet.

Nina gives the old guy a once over. She came an hour early so she could watch him arrive. He is early too, but she was earlier. He had spotted her dark coat from around the corner and watched her for a while. She looks like a black rock in a sea of green. He walks slowly across the field from Caledonia Road. He leaves a curving trail of flattened grass where he steps. He smiles when he is close enough for her to see his face. He has a kind face, open and relaxed. Hers is plump with few wrinkles. Finally, he is standing by the bench. He lifts his hat. They both notice he has more hair on his head than she does.

"Signora Crocetti? Alberto Di Rota, a pleasure to meet you."

"The pleasure is mine."

They shake hands. They are both wearing wedding rings. After an hour on the bench, the tip of her nose is a little red. The tips of his leather shoes are wet from walking across the moist field.

"May I sit down?"

"Of course."

To avoid awkwardness when he arrived, Nina sat at one end of the park bench leaving him enough space to place himself comfortably beside her but not too close. Alberto takes the hint.

"I wasn't sure you would show up," he says.

"Why not? I said I would."

"It's unusual, don't you think, for people like us to meet like this?"

"I met my poor husband like this. I walked off the plane and there he was. I was 23 years old. We were married by proxy. I was in Italy, he was here. His cousin showed me his passport picture. I liked his eyes. There, now you know everything about me."

Nina and Alberto had spoken on the phone before setting up the meeting. He placed an ad in the local Italian Canadian paper:

> *I am an older gentleman, healthy, clean, retired. I live by myself. I am a widower.*

The call for help in the paper's back section caught Nina's eye. "*Interessante,*" she thought, "a widower, not a bachelor. That means he knows how to be with a woman." Nina answered the ad.

"Where are you from?" His accent said *Abruzzi.*

"*Torre dei Passeri.* You said you were from *Sora.*"

"That's right."

"I bet your *matriciana* is delicious."

"You would win the bet. Do you live around here?"

"Within walking distance, if you like to walk."

"We lived near here in the early years. Is your place near a bus stop?"

"I live closer to Rogers Road than I do to the park."

"That's good. Do you have a dog?"

"No, no dog. Just a canary."

"I'm not interested in cleaning up after you or your canary."

"I have a cleaning lady who comes every week."

> *I'm looking for a live-in cook, a food companion who knows what real food tastes like and how to cook it. Cannelloni, lasagne, ravioli, and gnocchi. If you have knowledge of traditional Italian cuisine, if this food means anything to you, call me. I will provide room and board and a stipend. No funny business.*

Nina lives in a cavernous house in a subdivision of twisting curving streets that don't lead anywhere. After her husband died, her daughter convinced Nina to sell her house and move in with her and contribute to expenses.

In her daughter's house the big screen television is on all day and it makes Nina nauseous. The kids are on their iPads all the time. The dog soils the dining room carpet almost every day. Her daughter is on a no-carbohydrate diet to lose weight. Her granddaughter is a vegetarian going gluten-free.

"So, you want to eat cannelloni?"

"Like I said on the phone, my wife died a few years ago. I haven't eaten a good meal since."

"I'm not interested in replacing your wife, do we understand each other?"

"Absolutely. I'm not looking for a wife, I'm looking for someone who knows food. I want to eat again."

"You don't have children?"

"No. My son died when he was three years old. Meningitis. We didn't have other children after that."

"*Mi dispiace.*"

Alberto's shoulders scrunch up and slouch down as if to say: "That's life and it's awful." In the distance the Caledonia bus breaks the silence with a roar as it starts to lumber up the hill.

"Do you eat everything?" Nina asks.

"*Tutto.* Every single thing."

Nina clicks open the clasp of her big, black purse. She reaches in and gives Alberto a hand-written list—a compilation of dishes known to all who have come from the land that should have been shaped like a fork.

"Here's what I can make for you ..."

> *Pappardelle alla lepre* (pappardelle with rabbit sauce)
> *bigoli grossi con l'oca e porcini* (thick bigoli pasta with goose and porcini mushroom sauce)
> *quaglie all'uva* (quail with grapes)
> *trota ai porri con polenta* (trout with leeks and polenta)
> *stracciatella*
> *osso buco*
> *scaloppine al marsala* (veal cutlets in marsala wine)
> *risotto alle capesante* (risotto with scallops)
> *calamari ripieni* (stuffed squid)

abbacchio alla romana (roast lamb Roman style with rosemary and anchovies) ...

"Of course I prepare all the typical dishes of central Italy, some dishes from the north, and some from Sicily."

Alberto digs into his coat pocket for his list.

"These are the dishes I must have. No negotiation on this list. I'm open to innovation, to new things, but these classics have to be there."

Nina raises an eyebrow and looks up from the list.

"Tripe in tomato sauce?"

"Why not?"

"Sautéed kidneys with *peperoncino?*"

"I can handle it."

"Here's a surprise, stuffed capon."

"For special occasions."

"I debone it and stuff it with two kinds of meat. You'll love it. How do you like your ravioli? I can make for you ravioli stuffed with pumpkin, with crushed amaretti soaked in milk."

"Can you make ravioli with spinach and ricotta cheese?"

Nina nods as if to say "obviously."

"I make sausages with nutmeg, red wine and fennel seed. I learned that from a neighbour. But I don't use pepper in anything. You want pepper you add it in yourself."

"You make sausages?"

"I've got a sausage machine."

"I've got one too."

They pore over the lists in silence commenting with facial gestures — an approving nod, a head tilt of reluctant acceptance, pursed lips, a smile, a glance of unexpected delight. Alberto puts the sheet down on his lap. He turns to Nina and looks at her straight on.

"Let's talk about *lasagne.*"

"Okay. Talk."

"There are so many kinds. I'm impressed with your list."

"I make everything from scratch for you. I have my own pasta machine, by the way.

"*Benissimo.* But tell me about your sauce. I want to know about your sauce."

"The secret to a good sauce is the meat. I use veal, pork sausages, and lamb. And I stew the meat slowly, very slow, for hours. I start early in the morning. By noon, when the house smells delicious, it's done. When the sauce is on the *lasagne*, it is thick enough to hold the bits of meat floating in it, but clings to the pasta for only a second or two, then it trickles off, so that in the time it takes you to bring a forkful to your mouth, the sauce is just about to drip from the pasta, but doesn't. It slips into your mouth where it becomes a flavourful saucy bed. That is my sauce."

Alberto stares into Nina's eyes as if she is a big hunk of steaming *lasagne* right out of the oven.

"Ingredients," she whispers. "You'll pay for the ingredients."

"I will do whatever you want. I'll give you the money. You do the shopping."

Nina fixes his eyes.

"We're going to write this in a contract. Know that I don't skimp on quality when it comes to ingredients. I don't believe you have to spend a lot to get good results. I'm a frugal shopper, but a good piece of Romano cheese is important. I mean it. I'm serious about cheese."

"Agreed. Cheese is important."

"At the grocery store I see what's fresh, what looks good, that's how I decide what to cook."

"Yes, yes. But ... I do want an item from my list at least three times a week."

"*Va bene.* Is it three meals a day you want?"

"No, I'll take care of breakfast. I get up very early, before the sun. You take care of lunch and dinner, with dinner being the main meal except on Sundays. On Sundays lunch is the main meal. I like to eat with a tablecloth and a cloth napkin. Of course we will eat together. Food doesn't taste the same when you eat alone."

"How do you feel about leftovers?"

Nina adjusts the silk scarf around her neck. Alberto senses the answer to this question could make or break the interview. People can be funny about leftovers.

"Sometimes ... I believe ... leftovers taste better than freshly cooked."

Nina looks out across the grass.

"Olive oil?"

"Extra virgin."

"Bread and wine?"

"With every meal."

"Do you have a vegetable garden in your backyard?"

"Of course. I have fruit trees and a vine of concord grapes."

"I like the dark grapes. They're sweet. I'll need garden fresh herbs—rosemary, basil, sage, parsley, and oregano. And I like to use garden fresh onions, celery ..."

"Yes, yes, of course. I have garlic too."

"And dessert?"

"I don't care about dessert but I'll eat it, if you make it."

Nina reaches into her purse and pulls out a fork rolled up in a white cloth napkin. She offers it to Alberto. Without saying a word he removes the fork and places the white napkin across his right knee. She reaches in again and pulls out a small sealed aluminium tray swaddled in a clean, white dish cloth, decorated with a floral motif. It's still warm. She unwraps it, releasing a sweet aroma. Alberto knows he is about to go to heaven. Six cannelloni are lined up side by side. They fill the container completely. The red, meaty sauce clings to the curve of the pasta and rests snugly between the valleys formed by the plump tubes lying side by side.

"*Buon appetito.*"

He is speechless for the next few minutes—the time it takes him to eat. He mumbles through his mouthfuls ...

"*Madonna mia, mamma mia.*"

When he's done, he wipes his mouth, and then brings the tips of his five fingers to his pursed lips. He blows a kiss. Nina smiles.

"Well then, let's draw up the contract. I can start right away."

"With pleasure, Signora Crocetti."

"My name is Nina."

She reaches into her purse once more and pulls out a bundle of aluminium foil. She unwraps it for him. In it, wrapped a second time in parchment paper, are two gooey, honey-soaked, spiral-shaped *caragnoli* (fried dough). Alberto reaches out for the sweet sticky treat.

"*A presto,* Signora Nina."

"*A presto.*"

Nina goes home to pack.

a tavola

Joseph Anthony Farina

sunday mornings
were not for sleeping late
on water street

mothers early in their kitchens
they and daughters
cutting chicken, lemons and potatoes
sautéing pork and veal for their ragù
prepared in the aroma of rosemary, sage
secret spices and espresso coffee
their weekly sunday pranzo

fathers and sons in their back yard gardens
picking climbing beans, peppers, plum tomatoes
rapini, arugula and romaine lettuce
their morning harvest for the sunday salads

my cousins and i
quickly washed and dressed
in our sunday best
readying for early mass
clutching sunday missals
hungry for God's bread and Wine
and mommas and poppas after,
we walked to Our Lady of Mercy church
her carillon sounding the first blessing

of this day and for the feast
awaiting our return

after mass our families would gather
into a crowded cacophonous sea
of hungry cousins, aunts and uncles
our plywood tables heavy with food
made by my aunts and mother
who, aproned were still cooking
in their never ending kitchen dance

never believing the dance would end
the ritual of homemade food and bread
became lost, gatherings dispersed
in our quest to be Canadian
leaving only silence and the constant
hunger for the delicious past

I Remember My Days

M A R I A   L U I S A   I E R F I N O - A D O R N A T O

Tavola di Nonna

I DREAM OF the sweet taste of honey and of loved ones by night, then remember my "dolce" grandmother (paralyzed from the waist down) singing to us from her bed, *"Tu Scendi dalle Stelle,"* whenever we called her in Italy over Christmas. Softly over the phone, she managed to carry the tune:

> *Tu scendi dalle stelle,*
> *O Re del Cielo,*
> *e vieni in una grotta*
> *al freddo al gelo.*
> *O Bambino mio Divino,*
> *io ti vedo qui a tremar.*
> *O Dio Beato!*

Nonna always sent us *mustazzuoli* for Natale. These compact, chewy honey-based cookies were shaped as sirens, fish or doves and decorated with small triangular pieces of metallic red or green paper, and were impossible to replicate. They were made of rye flour, orange essence, aromatic spices like ground cumin, anise, nutmeg, cloves, bay leaves, usually *vino cotto* or unfermented grape juice and generous amounts of honey.

Nonna's mind was sharper than Parmigiano Reggiano, her generosity was legendary, and her words were sweeter than marmalade. *"Tu scendi dalle stele … O Re del Cielo,"* she would sing merrily, bestowing benedictions on every member of our large family; reciting names, anniversaries and birthdays like mighty mantras. Nonna would pray each day, with rosary beads in hand and with careful whispers. My mother told me one day that Nonna had visions of Padre Pio and that he would often pray by her side. I believed her in my heart.

Sunday was the day of the Lord and it was a day of celebration and my mother recounted to me how Nonna Rosina enjoyed cooking and caring for her family. She described her bucatini pasta made from the finest whole wheat as light and heavenly. Each piece of dough was rolled around *cannicci di palude or junchi* in dialect … long and sturdy marsh reeds, to form the long strands of pasta.

My mother watched and learned her secrets as Nonna added a blush of red pepper paste to *la salsa di pomodori*, adding vibrant basil and hot round cherry peppers; it was a Calabrese symphony of red white and green that Nonna conducted with pride. There were *melanzane ripiene, carne di capretto* and sautéed Swiss chard cooked with garlic in the cold pressed, extra virgin olive oil that they processed from their very own olive trees. *La pizzata* was the golden cornmeal bread she baked. Desserts consisted of citrus fruits, figs, prickly pears, roasted chestnuts and almonds. There was abundance from the land she cultivated and revered. The rich soil that was hers from generation to generation proved to be strong, sultry and sustainable. Nonna's family was never hungry with their *cucina povera*!

But, the fondest I have of all the stories of Nonna is of her visits to needy families from the village every Sunday, before going back home to serve her own family lunch. My mother never knew which families had received the bountiful food basket from Nonna. In Mammola, she had created her own ritual and legend.

Tavola di Mamma

I remember my mother telling us about the Greek Gods and their myths. My parents, grandparents and even my husband were born in Mammola, Reggio Calabria, a medieval town not far from the Strait of Messina, and an historic land known as Magna Grecia, as it was built by the ancient Greeks.

My mother would warn us about the "evil eye," how not to tempt fate or the Gods. Offering gifts of food to appease the Gods was strongly recommended. A curse, *mu ti fai comu Reggio e Messina* in the local dialect, to self-destruct like Reggio and Messina, was the most horrible saying that mother recalled from her childhood. This was a region devastated by many earthquakes and the last one about one hundred years ago nearly wiped out the twin cities. This remained a region of mystery and mysticism despite the natural disasters or possibly because of them.

I was born in Montreal, an island between two banks of a mighty river. It is autumn and I am daydreaming about the Medusa as well as Scylla and Charybdis. In Greek mythology Scylla was once a beautiful nymph that would turn into a monster upon entering the Mediterranean Sea. Scylla lived on one side of a narrow channel of water opposite its counterpart Charybdis. Homer taught us that Odysseus successfully sailed his ship past Scylla and Charybdis but not without Scylla capturing six of his men, devouring them alive with her gargantuan appetite. Manoeuvring between Reggio (Scylla) and Messina (Charybdis) was a losing battle as depicted in the modern-day expression "caught between a rock and a hard place." I have now meandered too far and the Medusa entices me back home. I am practically famished.

It is the feast day of San Nicodemo, Patron Saint of Mammola, which we religiously commemorate on the first Sunday in September. On the menu at my parents' place in Montreal North, besides high spirits and good cheer, are the classic Mammolese dishes. The legendary *pasta di manu* or literally, the hand-made pasta which is simply mixed with durum-semolina, flour, "holy water" and then cooked al dente with Mother's blessings. The best part of the home-made specialty was not only the ladling of fresh seasonal tomato sauce over it, but also grating the rich, luxuriant *ricotta affumicata* on top of the hot pasta, which melted slowly to a real creamy consistency. Whenever we visited Mammola, my grandmother and great aunts reserved this special cheese for us.

The smoke-flavoured cheese is our culinary heritage. The artisan process requires at least 24 hours of smoking over a dense and aromatic smoke created from the burning branches of chestnut trees and heather. This aromatic goat cheese is typically shaped as a phallic symbol, denoting fertility and produced only between the months of June and December each year.

Another dish, *melanzane ripiene*, a vegetarian delicacy, is made with baby eggplants in season, boiled and halved, the pulp scooped-out and squeezed. The stuffing is made by adding a mixture of eggs, goat cheese, garlic, basil and *peperoncino* to the pulp then brushing it with egg whites to create a golden crust when fried in olive oil. Fresh pecorino romano or parmigiano appear on top like snow, thanks to Dad's grating wizardry. My dad, called "Nick" after the Patron Saint and his nonno Nicodemo, whistles merrily and sings sentimental songs like *Mamma* as he graciously helps my mother in the kitchen.

We delighted in consuming these tasty dishes and in hearing about the origin of the feast day and the procession in Mammola. Mom would oblige and remind us why we were celebrating the holy day. This was our opportunity to get together as a family and to strengthen our bonds. It was a time to share vintage village stories and a time to be grateful for a bountiful harvest and for all we possessed. It was a time to remember.

The Patron Saint of Mammola, San Nicodemo, was a Byzantine monk who lived over 1000 years ago. He was a pious man who built a monastery in pre-historic La Limina in Reggio Calabria to protect his fellow monks from invaders. This ascetic hermit subsisted, Mom told us, on practically nothing!

He fasted most of the time and his daily meal, contrary to ours, consisted of boiled chestnuts for which he thanked the Lord as though it was the finest brew. "The chestnut gave him all the nourishment he needed!" Mom cried out emphatically. Then she lavishly served us sweet, ripened figs and her fabled cheesecake, a favourite Canadian recipe, followed by black espresso laced with anise liqueur. On the next day we would surely plan to fast.

Tavola Mia

I dream of a late autumn night's stroll with my daughter and my husband in Rosemere, brisk smoke-filled air and the promise of a glowing fireplace, all beckon us back home for a *spuntino* and for more intimate conversation.

Together we gather our ingredients from the carefully stocked Italian larder and busy ourselves with creating antipasto master-pieces, drinking fine Barolo wine and reminiscing about last year's trip to Italy. Arias uplift us, nostalgia awakens us and we pretend to dance under the kitchen lights that appear like flickering stars.

We are thankful for this calm Sunday evening together and for the superlative *spuntino* that nourishes our bodies and revives our spirits. We tend to think like the characters in *Waiting for Godot* that there will be a grand "momentous" occasion to define us, to move us and to save us ... yet we repeatedly forget that each and every mo-ment is the one to hunger for, the one to savour, the one to relish, and yes, the one to swoon over!

We sit very quietly in front of the fireplace and each flame seems to offer me a different message. One flame promises time travel and another fuels my imagination. I warmly weave nostalgic stories in my mind, jot down a few lines and then create my personal myth-ologies just as my mother and grandmother did before me. I fondly watch my family unwind, as this "down time" is the dessert or the true tiramisu. My husband is reading his favourite book and written all over his countenance is the sweetest hint of satisfaction and con-tentment.

We play our favourite songs by Sting and the magical words float in the air. I allow myself to relax and am happily in "theta," in between the dream state and the waking state. In slow motion I vividly observe every minute detail in the room and I suddenly real-ize that this is the moment to appreciate, to relish, and to love. We are constantly searching for meaning and it is dreamily here, here in this comfortable den, in this mundane scene and in our daily bread.

The lyrics by Sting continue to transport me.

> Let me watch by the fire and remember my days
> And it may be a trick of the firelight
> But the flickering pages that trouble my sight
> Is a book I'm afraid to write
> — THE BOOK OF MY LIFE, STING

I proudly glance at my daughter who appears to smile here and there in her virtual world, as she swiftly communicates back and forth with her friends, using her Blackberry. I named her Aviva, Hebrew for eternal spring, and now she creates her own mythologies and writes about them on Facebook.

Aviva serenely glances back at me. I hope that she too will remember these days and dream of loved ones by night.

The Essential Italian-Canadian Larder

Extra Virgin Olive Oil for overall golden health
Aged Reggiano Parmigiano for sharp good taste
Perfect Pasta for sacred substance and noble tradition
Fresh tomatoes with basil for colour and youthful vitality
God's nectar (wine & balsamic vinegar) for eternal exuberance
Strong espresso coffee for energy and character
Family and an autumn harvest of love ...

These are the delectable staples for the (www) whole wide world!

Fifth Course:
Dolce

Snail Recipe

SALVATORE ALA

As a boy I dreamt snails,
Dreamt my mother was mother of snails
Who nursed them with milk and honey,
Cooked pastina, sage, and basil,
To cleanse and sweeten the flesh.
I dreamt snails and cringed.
At dinner, I slowly picked snails from their shells,
Savouring dark morsels, eating my dream.

Fever Food

DARLENE MADOTT

My older sister had moaned for days with diarrhea and vomiting. These were the days doctors still made house calls, and people avoided emergency wards and hospitals, where their loved ones went only to die. My mother was told to try to make my sister drink tea with honey, and to force her to eat dry toast. Finally, on the fifth day, the fever broke, and my sister slept.

At eleven-thirty that night, although I was only ten years of age, I was allowed to eat a midnight-snack with my parents, and to drink wine. My mother broke out a tin of sardines and made *sarde salada*. I watched as she sliced the Spanish onion fine, and chopped in the ripe red tomatoes into a large bowl, de-boned and skinned the sardines, draining them on paper towels. She added black sweet olives from a Unico tin, and a fennel bulb, sliced fine that had been soaked first in salted water, then rinsed and patted dry, then some capers, and dressed the colourful salad with salt, her best olive oil and a thick balsamic vinegar.

She gave me the bowl and tongs and asked me to *gonza l'insalada*. During the process of combining the salad with its dressing, a stale loaf of bread was sliced, blessed with water from the tips of my mother's fingers, wrapped in tin foil, and heated in the oven.

My father uncorked a bottle of red wine. Silently, we took our places at the kitchen table. My mother lit a candle. We listened for sounds of moaning from my sister's bedroom, but heard only the gentle sound of regular and peaceful breathing. With a collective sigh, we clinked glasses and gave thanks, and dug into the salad — the bowl placed communally between us. I was invited to dip my bread, now crusted on the outside, but warm and soft as cake on the inside, down to the bottom of the bowl — to *soppa* the dressing. Over and over again, I dipped my bread. Olives and onions slopped off my fingers, and I spooned these pieces with my free hand back onto the bread again, or scooped the droppings from our wood table.

By the third glass of wine, my mother and father were giddy. They laughed, that night, about nothing. I basked in the candlelight and warmth of our table, and helped myself to more wine, undiluted by ginger ale which I typically had to use on our Sunday dinners, and seemingly unnoticed by my parents, who drank relief from each other's eyes.

The night my sister's fever broke became a feast day, and ever after, *sarde salada* has been synonymous with the lifting of fear, the celebration of some malady overcome. Since leaving my parents' home, I have made this peasant ambrosia on the occasion of escaping an abusive lover, the relief of rain after a summer of drought, the first meal with which to break fast — such as the midnight snack on Good Friday. And now, in a talismanic way — to ward off a pending crisis pre-emptively, holding my sopping bread plate on high, with two fingers on either side, as if to say, *do this as you did for the breaking of my sister's fever; be as if nothing — all you pending fevers to come!*

mamma corleone

DOMENICO CAPILONGO

MARIO AND FRANCIS got it wrong. vito corleone, the godfather, didn't run the family. it was his wife. she sat in shadows. spoke to him with her eyes. sent messages through food. the amount of salt in pasta sauce. the configuration of pizza toppings. the strength of his espresso. all held meaning.

to her he listened. could not refuse the warm touch of her smile. soft whispering voice in his ear. *they must show you respect. they must fear you.*

she knew the weight of his mind from the way he sighed as his body sank next to hers.
the way his heart beat beneath the palm of her hand. she told him what to do and he would do it.

Life is Theatre
Or
O To be Italian in Toronto Drinking Cappuccino on Bloor Street at Bersani & Carlevale's

MARY DI MICHELE

BACK THEN YOU couldn't have imagined yourself
openly savouring a cappuccino,
you were too ashamed that your dinners
were in a language you couldn't share
with your friends: their pot roasts,
their turnips, their recipes for Kraft
dinner you glimpsed in TV commercials —
the mysteries of macaroni with marshmallows.
You needed an illustrated dictionary
to translate your meals,
looking to the glossy pages of vegetables
melanzane became eggplant,
African, with the dark sensuality of liver.
But for them even eggplants were exotic or unknown,
their purple skins from outer space.

Through the glass oven door
you would watch it bubbling in Pyrex,
layered with tomato sauce and cheese,
melanzane alla parmigiana,
the other-worldliness viewed as if
through a microscope
like photosynthesis in a leaf.

◈ Educated in a largely Jewish high school
you were Catholic.
Among doctors' daughters,
the child of a fruit vendor.
You became known as Miraculous Mary,
announced with jokes about virgin mothers.

You were as popular as pork on Passover.
You discovered insomnia, migraine headaches,
menstruation that betrayal of the self
to the species. You discovered despair.
Only children of the middle class are consolable.
You were afraid of the millionth part difference
in yourself which might just be character.
What you had was rare
and seemed to weigh you down
as if it were made of plutonium.
What you wanted was to be like everybody else.
What you wanted was to be liked.
You were in love with that Polish boy
with yellow hair everybody thought
looked like Paul Newman.
All the girls wanted to marry him.
There was not much hope
for a fat girl with good grades.

◈ But tonight you are sitting in an Italian café
with a man you dated a few times,
faked love, then passed into the less doubtful
relationship of coffee and conversation.

He insists he remembers you as vividly
as Joan Crawford upstaging Garbo in *Grand Hotel*.
You are so melodramatic, he said.
*Marriage to you would be like
living in an Italian opera!*

Being in love with someone who doesn't love you
is like being nominated for an Oscar and losing,
a truly great performance gone to waste.
Still you balanced your espresso expertly
throughout a heated speech,
and then left without drinking it.
For you Italians, after all, he shouted after you,
life is theatre.

feathers

DOMENICO CAPILONGO

THE SOUND OF my *nonna*. my mother's mother leaning into the sink. the shape of her short body hidden in her dress. the movement of her elbow. the calisthenics recalled from a long ago sicilian town. from a time of war when her husband would lend their scale to the butcher meat. the sound of rhythmic ripping. thicker than tearing paper. the crunch of evening snow under my boots on after dinner walks with my sons brings this moment back.

my little-boy-feet approaching *nonna* at the sink. where did my father go? did he buy chickens at the grocery store? she turns. a look as wet as blood in her eye. caught in the act of some crime of passion. like killing her dead husband's lover in the corner pew of that forgotten church. the white of snow-like feathers everywhere.

the constant pump of her plump elbows tearing and stripping the chicken. its neck limp in the sink like a wet dishcloth. in half whispered pants. short of breath. she tells me to go. let her work. protecting me from some devil that's taken her over. will she dance with the head around my bed as I sleep? the sound still ringing in my ears.

A Passion for Fravioli

VENERA FAZIO

THE DAY BEFORE his scheduled surgery, Dad asked Mom to make him *fravioli*, his favourite Sicilian pastries. These delectable, crescent-shaped ricotta turnovers, although not difficult, take several hours to prepare. Mom later told me that, although she felt tired that day, she complied. She had a premonition he would not be coming back home from the hospital. The memories of her act of kindness and of Dad enjoying his favourite food would later help console her.

My father, Rosario Fazio, was born in 1914 in Bafia, Sicily, a village burrowed like a bird's nest in the Peloritani Mountains. Dad's mother, *Nonna* Venera, made *fravioli* frequently. Ricotta cheese made from sheep's milk was, and is, a staple in Bafia, as many of the villagers own strips of pasture in the nearby hills and raise sheep.

Zia Carmela, Dad's sister, delighted in reciting the following story of my father's passion for ricotta turnovers. Whenever *Nonna* served *fravioli*, my father, one of six siblings, without waiting his turn, would reach for the largest turnover on the plate. One day, *Zia* and her mother decided to teach him a lesson. They fried a batch of pastries and made one crescent noticeably larger than the others. This larger pastry, they filled with ricotta mixed with salt, rather than the usual sugar and cinnamon. When Rosario bit into the salty turnover, the family enjoyed a good laugh. *Zia* was quick to add that my father joined in the merriment. He had an impish personality and loved to laugh as well as make others laugh.

Dad came to Canada in 1950 to join his sister and two of his brothers. When he had earned enough money for our voyage, he sent for my mother, brother Domenic and me. Dad did not feel at ease in his new environment. Whenever he encountered an English speaking neighbour, I heard the knots in his voice and saw him stiffen. He acquired a passive knowledge of English, able to understand many words, but spoke only Sicilian, even when English became the preferred language of his children. He also seemed to have lost his sense of humour.

I believe my father's light-hearted nature reasserted itself in my brother, Jackie (Giacomo), born after our arrival in Canada. The two of them had an affinity for each other. Dad smiled his ear to ear smile at Jackie's antics. Jackie loved to entertain us with silly "Knock! Knock!" jokes:

> *Knock! Knock!*
> *Who's there?*
> *Luke*
> *Luke who?*
> *Look out here and you will soon find out!*

My brother would also amuse us by singing along to the songs on the radio. Whenever the radio station played the Kingston Trio song *Hang Down Your Head, Tom Dooley*, Jackie would grab a wooden spoon to use as a microphone and belt out a dramatic version. He wanted to be a singer when he grew up, he said. But on a foggy evening, while riding his bike, Jackie was struck down by a car and died.

My father turned inward and never regained his sense of humour. And with his depression, came physical illnesses too.

I make *fravioli* three or four times a year. Occasionally I serve them to guests when I want to share a dessert from my culture of origin. My daughter loves them and insists our family eat them on special occasions and for holidays such as Christmas and Easter. But mainly, I will fry a batch of turnovers whenever I want to honour the memory of my father.

I miss him still and enjoying his favourite food helps me feel close to him. Now that I am also a parent, I understand his grief of losing a child. *Fravioli* also anchors me to my father's sense of humour and helps me keep a balanced perspective of his personality. When I bite into the delicate pastry and savour the comforting burst of cinnamon, I remember Dad as a joyful person.

A Bouquet of Rapini

MARY DI MICHELE

(Eating is touch carried to the bitter end.)

i

The vegetable is bitter green
                        and full of *vite*
amens, the iron I
            need, my blood
tired from a hole
            lotta loveless
ness and it's nicely
            wrapped as if it were a
gift and it is
            my trophy, it has real weight
this bouquet, but the
            man, the wished-for

end to a long line of men
offers me something fresh, something nourishing
he fills me up with much more than the daily
recommended ferrous sulphate and folic acid.

ii

You know romance is roses
but perhaps the pattern on the paper
is not
           what's inside.

iii

No, it's not
            flowers he brings me
what I need
            his body, his bloody
                        rapini, the scent of rain in tin

cans is better for my health and he's so
good to me I'm surprised when he won't
stay to dine because his taste is for
alone, doesn't need my company, just breathing

room and the men —

iv

u's planned for one,
                  he's gone
for good this time.
                  O woman starved,
O woman buy your own
                        (it's not so dear)

rapini for $2.50 a small bunch
at *le Faubourg.* But when he pays
no price
            is too high.

I'm good

v

Steam rapini or drop into a few inches of salted, rapidly boiling water until tender. They turn neon green. Heat olive oil, extra virgin, cold pressed, gently in a frying pan. Sliver cloves of garlic, many, and cook until golden, along with some red dried chili peppers. Drop the steamed rapini into the oil and stir fry. May be served as a side dish or on top of pasta along with some ricotta cheese you simply warm in the pan with the rapini for a minute or two.

vi

                                        at pumping irony.
Away from his this strength is new, I lie

Alone in bed and like it.
Observe these arms are winter
                        white and the biceps

are taut, are lone
                lean and feline. The lynx,
before it devours the inner child,
                        as it crouches to spring

or settles to sleep
                curled under snow.

Where the Lemon Trees Bloom

LORETTA GATTO-WHITE

IT WAS FROM two famous mountains in the ancient Mediterranean world that we acquired the vital and conflicting elements of fire and ice, forces crucial to our social evolution. From Zeus' Olympus, Prometheus gave us fire and ironically, from Vulcan's fiery Etna, or in Sicilian, *Mongibeddu*, we took ice.

Fire was necessary to warm our homes, cook our food and later, as steam to power our engines. An expedient force that, once tamed, is unremarkable. No one was ever shocked to see a brazier glow in the heat of July but was certainly grateful for its heat in the cold depths of January. However, the appearance of ice and snow in the stifling heat of August is magic. The Mongols, Incans and Persians knew it; the Romans and Sicilians knew it too.

The magic that is wrought by conserving ice in ice houses, adding all manner of exotic flavours to it, then forming it in whimsical shapes has held an enduring fascination for Sicilians who learned the art from the Arabs who made *scherbet* (sweet snow) called *sorbetto* by the Sicilians.

Perhaps what inspires these flights of fantasy is our visceral and psychological relationship to ice. For instance, we cannot consume fire unless we are consumed by it. Thus it is an element that serves us, but is never fully under our power. Our relationship is an uneasy one as it always holds the potential for danger as those living near Vulcan's lair know.

But ice, especially in the form of gelato, delights, mollifies and refreshes us as with Promethean satisfaction we can languorously lick our ice-cream cones in August, having summoned what nature tells us properly belongs in one season to our service in another.

Fantasy and invention are hallmarks of the Sicilian confectionary arts. In this they are distinct from their peninsular cousins, especially the Florentines who adore gelato, indulge in it with gusto but purvey it with characteristic restraint.

Sicilian gelato takes many forms: sweet and icy *granite* which are shaved-ice flavoured with fruit syrups, spices, coffee or chocolate; elaborately formed *semi-freddi* composed of a sponge-cake moistened with liqueur and filled with successive layers of variously flavoured gelati, preserved fruits, nuts or *tortoni;* the whimsical *tartufi* which are shaped like truffles, either white (vanilla), or black (chocolate) and often served *con panna*, with cream. Finally, the classic dish of *gelato* (which is simply the Italian word for frozen) is more of an ice milk than an ice cream. Being lighter than the French custard-based version, it hasn't any eggs, and instead is thickened with a *rinforzata* of cornstarch and cream, rendering it light, smooth and slightly icy.

The Sicilians make their ice creams in a delicious spectrum of flavours from the sweet chocolate to the savoury chestnut and rosemary. But my favourite is the tangy and intensely lemony gelato flavoured with the syrup of sun-ripened lemons and elegantly presented in the halved hollowed-out fruit of the tree which is so emblematic of this southern island.

The lemon tree has its botanical roots in either South Central China or Northern India, and was likely brought to Sicily from Alexandria, via the Romans. That the Romans cultivated lemon trees is without question. A fresco circa 38 BC in the Villa Livia at Prima Porta features a lemon tree, an exotic plant which only the wealthy could afford as its cultivation is labour-intensive and precarious in all but the warmest climates. Its tender fruit is destroyed if the temperature drops to a mere -1 degree Celsius.

It is the stubborn and perverse nature of humankind which provokes us to desire ice in summer and propagate lemon trees in Northern climes. And to suffer the undertaking of the elaborate construction in the *cinquencento* of the fabled lemon pavilions of Lake Garda, like Prometheus' stolen treasure, the sight in the cool north of the lemon trees' promising sunny golden orbs and the sensation of their profoundly bitter-sweet taste is at the very heart of life's experience.

In 1747, the tonic of a Sicilian sojourn eased the melancholic, Teutonic temperament of Goethe who was moved to invoke the seductive powers of the south in his romantic lines:

> *Knowst thou the land where the lemon trees bloom?*
> *Where the gold orange glows in the deep thicket's gloom*
> *Where a wind ever soft from the blue heaven blows*
> *And the groves are of laurel and myrtle and rose?*

Alas, the opening lines Goethe penned were destined to become the canon of the cad who, wishing to seduce a gullible virgin, promises to take her away to "where the lemon trees bloom," a euphemism for the sybarite and exotic life (but really just for his bedchamber).

Seduction between the sexes is only possible if they are allowed the opportunity to "strut their stuff," flash their eyes, flirt, giggle and finally, mingle. It was left to a Sicilian, Procopio dei Coltelli, to remedy the dearth of opportunities afforded young, romantic middle and upper class women in 17th century Paris to mix and mingle with young, romantic gentlemen in a respectable, upper-class public venue. Before the opening of *Café Procope*, there were only bars, bistros and music halls, places where a gentlewoman wouldn't dare to venture.

Signor Procopio dei Coltelli or *Procope* as the French called him and as his establishment became known, was a Sicilian émigré from either Palermo or Aci Trezza whose grandfather, Francesco, invented an ice cream machine that made a product superior to any other. Procopio took the invention to Paris and became a *limonadier*. So synonymous was the connection between lemon juice, extracts and lemon by-products and the libations of cafes, that the café owners were known and licensed as *limonadiers*.

Seeing his opportunity in 1686, Procopio opened the elegantly appointed *Café Procope*, whose décor became the standard for Parisian and Italian cafés ever since. It was so successful he moved to a larger place across from La Comedie Française, on what is now Rue de L'Ancienne Comedie. The ambience of his café and the quality of his *granite*, *gelati* and *sorbetti* were famous, earning him a royal patent and drawing such patrons as Voltaire, George Sand, Victor Hugo and Napoleon. We can only guess whether Josephine deigned to join him, or if she preferred to indulge alone.

So it was that, in a brilliant stroke of engineering and marketing, Procopio raised the quality of Sicilian gelato, and democratized its availability to the *hoi polloi*, while providing gentlewomen with an appropriate, respectable place where they could participate independently in public, social life and yes, meet cute guys.

Later, in 1804, other transplanted Italians followed suit. The Signori Velloni and Tortoni, after whom the eponymous dessert was to be named, opened the Pavillion du Hanovre, where they held fireworks' displays, concerts, and balls but where unaccompanied women were only allowed to sit outside on the patio to enjoy their ice creams. However, we surmise that their public position on the patio in no way diminished the enjoyment of their dessert, as Italians understand that "going out for ice cream" is a social ritual in which the consumption of an icy confection is somewhat beside the point.

Going out for gelato is central to Italian and Sicilian social discourse. The enjoyment of this cultural ritual escaped Toronto's city council when confronted with an application to license an outdoor patio on St. Clair. They declared that no one would want to eat outside. Fortunately, alderman Piccininni convinced them otherwise and, in 1963, La Sem Patisserie and Café on the Corso Italia became Toronto's first licensed outdoor café.

From then on, summer transformed the Corso Italia's sidewalks and curbs into a village piazza where old and young congregated to see and be seen, especially the youth who would go for a *passeggiatta*, a courting ritual performed in one's Sunday best.

As a young girl, I was fascinated by those who I came to think of as "the Boys of Summer." It was under their watchful eyes that the Sunday peacock pageant progressed. They'd give a low, slow whistle and purr: "Ciao Bella," "Che Bella," "Ah, Bellissima!" I marvelled at their naked appreciation of beauty, whether of the low, sweeping lines of a Trans Am or the silhouette of a pretty girl. Not even a cool bite of a tangy lemon gelato could chill the deep brown warmth of their sloe-eyed gaze.

It was as if by some magic they were conjured like a mirage from the heat waves dancing up from the scorching summer sidewalk, only to disappear with the first sweep of fall's brazen brush or the slight tickle of its cool breeze. Like young urban Vulcans, they'd retreat, vaporous beneath their concrete vault, to languish, sealed in slumber, waiting for July's rising mercury to ascend.

Works Cited

Goethe, Johann Wolfgang von. From *Wilhelm Meister's Apprenticeship*, Book 3, Chapter 1. Quoted in *Sayings of Goethe Translated; the Maxims and Reflections of Goethe*. Trans. Bailey Saunders. New York: Macmillan & Co., 1893.

Almond Wine and Fertility

LICIA CANTON

THE EXCURSION TO Sicily was not planned. We had a late lunch in Taormina, then drove up the winding road to Castelmola, a quaint village located on Mount Tauro.

The afternoon was cloudy and wet. We walked around while the rain subsided. When it began raining again, we sought refuge in Bar Turrisi at Piazza Pio IX. Bar Turrisi inhabits four floors of a tall, narrow building which dates back to 1812.

The first floor was dark and sombre, filled with people. We took the steep, tiny staircase to the second floor. There was no one there. The tables at the back were cluttered with some big objects. We sat on the small covered terrace which looked down on the empty wet piazza, with Taormina and the ocean in the distance.

There were only two tiny round tables on the terrace.

"This is the perfect spot," I said.

I turned slightly to look around at the inside. It was dark and gloomy.

"What's that on the table ... at the back?" I asked my husband.

"That ... That looks like ... "

I got up and took a few steps towards the back to get a closer look.

"It's a ... ," I muttered.

"Yes, that's what I thought it was."

I was glad we hadn't chosen the table in the dark corner.

"Who would want to sit there?" I asked.

As I looked around more closely, I saw that erotic statues and sculptures were in every corner, some even on the larger tables. A newspaper article which was framed on the wall caught my attention. I walked over to read it.

"It seems that the decor is a commemoration to the male sexual organ," I said as I sat down again.

"It's called a penis," my husband said with an amused expression.

"I was quoting the article," I specified.

"Does it make you feel uncomfortable?" he asked.

"Well, I wouldn't sit there," I answered.

People began streaming onto the second floor, choosing between lava-stone and chestnut-wood tables. A group of young people sat at the table with the oversized wooden penis.

The waiter came to take our order. He brought us complimentary glasses of a golden drink.

"It's *vino alla mandorla*," he said. "The elixir of love and fertility."

We had never tasted anything like it. It was deliciously sweet and velvety.

As we savoured the almond wine, we talked about the two children we had left behind in Montreal.

"What do you think they're doing right now?" I asked.

"I don't know, but I'm sure they're very happy with their grandmothers. Are you worried about them?"

"No, not at all," I said smiling.

It was the first time we'd left the children behind for longer than a weekend.

"Well, maybe just a little ... But I'm really enjoying being alone with you!" I said.

"Me, too!" He smiled and took my hand.

We were oblivious to the others in the bar, which was crowded now. It was like being on our first date again. We had known each other for years, but we were taking the time to rediscover one another. We weren't in a bar in Sicily anymore, we were in a time and space of our own.

"Would you like to have another ... ?" The waiter's question startled us, bringing us back from our reverie.

"So how about it?" he asked, when the waiter had moved away.

"How about what?" I asked. I had an idea of what he was referring to.

"Would you like to have another ... ?" He looked at me playfully but with an intent look which I knew well.

"I'm not sure," I answered truthfully. "I'm just starting to feel like I can catch my breath. Your life wouldn't change much, but mine would."

I didn't need to go on. He had heard it before.

"We don't need to decide now," he said gently.

We drove back tired and wet along the road which coasted the beach. The sun was setting as the ferry left Messina. There wasn't much time for sleep that night. We caught an early morning flight as the sun rose onto another day, a day which would go on without us.

Two years later, we count the days to the arrival of our third child, the child we talked about in Bar Turrisi as we sipped almond wine ... amid symbols of fertility.

Our Love Affair

DELIA DE SANTIS

OUR LOVE AFFAIR
is a delicious apple
you take the flesh
and I the peelings ...
and we scatter the seeds

Pizza and KFC

DELIA DE SANTIS

MY DAUGHTER COMES to see me Tuesdays and Fridays. She touches my hand when she comes. When she leaves, she kisses my cheek, but never when she arrives. That's okay. My daughter is not real Italian anymore. She was very young when she came to Canada, when we brought her here. She's more of this country now than over there where she was born.

I am always happy to see her ... but sometimes she's a big pain you know where. Every time she comes she makes me tell her stories about my past. She says it's for my mind, to exercise my mind. I say she's the one who forgets and that is why she wants me to tell her things over and over again.

"Mom, how did you get that first job working in the restaurant, do you remember?" she asked me yesterday. She is sitting at the end of my bed and me in a straight chair in the corner of the room, my walker right in front of me ready for when I want to get up — I don't always use the wheelchair.

"Of course I remember. What do you think!" I say, gripping tighter the handles of the walker.

She runs her fingers through her bleached blond hair. Probably white like mine if she would let it go natural. "Mom, I know you told me before, but sometimes you change the story ..."

"I don't change the story. Why would I do that?"

"I don't know. Maybe you don't change it that much. But you need to tell it exactly the way it was. I didn't mention this before, but I have been giving a lot of thought to writing down your stories of when you first came to Canada. I was thinking of making a book, one just for the family."

"You could make three books on the stuff I went through. But best not think about that. I only like to tell the happy stories now; the sad stuff I want to forget. So don't bother asking."

"Well, your first job is a happy story."

"It is a good story, but it didn't start that way. It started with tears ..."

"But then it was good. You were happy after that, as I remember you telling me. What year was it? Late fifties?"

"It was 1956 ... and I might as well tell you how it happened ... or you will never leave me alone. But shouldn't you have brought pen and paper if you wanted to write it down?"

"You're right, I didn't think."

"Who forgets, me or you? But never mind. Are you sure you want to hear it again? I must have told it before."

"Of course I do. Besides ... I know you like to tell it."

"Well, okay if you say so ... It happened that first summer in Canada. One day I was sitting on the steps of the front porch of that old house we had rented when we first arrived ... I was feeling really sad, missing everyone we had left in Italy, I was crying. And just as I was crying, an Italian lady happened to go by — I knew she lived down the street. I used to see her walk by all the time — but I had never talked to her before. She stopped and came to sit beside me. She asked why I was crying. I managed to stop the tears and tell her my story. I said to her: 'What am I doing in this country? I can't speak English ... I can't work, I can't do anything. I am useless ...'

She waited for me to finish drying my eyes and then she said: 'Tomorrow morning, when I come by, you be ready. I'll take you with me to talk to my boss. They need someone to wash dishes — the young boy who was there just quit. And don't worry, you won't be washing dishes for long. In no time I'm sure they'll have you cooking.'

"I put my tear-soaked handkerchief away and I told her: '*Dio ti benedica*, may God bless you ... but how can I cook in a restaurant when I've never done it before?' 'Oh,' the woman said, 'just try to learn some English words, the cooking will be no trouble. Every good Italian mother gives her daughter the training she needs in the kitchen, I am sure that was the case with you too. You wouldn't have found a husband if you couldn't cook.' She told me her name was

Nunziata, but at work they called her Nancy, then reminding me to be ready, she turned and left.

"*Husband*, I thought. There is a bit of a problem there. My husband didn't want me to work — that was your father, you know."

"Mom, I know your husband was my father. Do you think I forgot?"

"You didn't forget, but you didn't know how stubborn he used to be. By the time you came along, he had mellowed. He didn't want me to work. But I didn't tell him anything. In the morning I went with Nunziata. He had already gone to work; he didn't know that I was going. That day I came home ten minutes before he got back, and he wondered why his supper wasn't ready. I made up an excuse and didn't tell him anything about going to the restaurant with Nunziata. I told him the next morning. He got really angry, but he was going to be late for work and had to go. Through the day some of his anger went away, thank God ... and then, when I brought home the first pay cheque, that took care of any anger that was left."

"You worked there quite a while, seven years?"

"I was there until I got that job at the hospital. I hated to go — it was only because of benefits. But it wasn't the same. Not the same at all. Getting that first job was like a dream. I got hired on the spot. Johnson's was the first restaurant in town to make pizza. Another Italian lady had started making it, and she showed the other two Canadian cooks how to make it. And, just like Nunziata had told me, I didn't have to wash dishes for very long. Soon they started giving me shifts making pizza, too."

"They did deliveries, too, didn't they?"

"Yes, a lot of pizzas went out at night, about fifty."

"That was a lot in those days, for a small town."

"Yes, and it got even busier when Mr. Johnson bought the Kentucky Fried Chicken franchise. Then I had to make the fried chicken, too. Colonel Sanders came to train us, to show us how to use the pressure fryer."

"So you met the Colonel. What was he like?"

"Nice man. Polite. Never got upset with us once. He trained us for three days. He looked just like we used to see him on TV. The same."

"Pizza and KFC, two novelties in this with-nothing-to-do town. That must have kept the cash register ringing."

"Mr. Johnson made a lot of money alright. People went crazy for pizza and Kentucky Fried Chicken, I tell you. And the pizza was good in those days, not like the garbage they make now."

"Mom, come on. It's not garbage, it's just different. They put different things on it. People like different toppings."

"Uh, they're crazy — it's garbage. Just like the food in this place."

"Oh there we go. No matter what I do or say, I can't take your mind off this *food* thing for more than ten minutes. You're getting paranoid. Maybe you should tell me another story, that would keep your mind occupied."

"Never mind another story. I just finished telling you a story ... and then we always end up arguing. I am done for today. You go home and feed your husband."

"I think I will do exactly that. I will see you in a couple of days. But look, I am going to give you a kiss anyway."

Did I tell her she couldn't? Silly woman, my daughter.

"Mom, are you eating well ... are you going for all your meals? I hope this *thing* about the food is not making you skip meals."

"I go, I go. I pay enough money in this place. They take my three pensions and a lot more. I make sure I go for meals alright. If you can call them meals. I don't know where they learned to cook, the people who work here. I should be in that kitchen, I'd show them."

"I know you would, Mom."

"Yesterday they served us soup — they said it was Italian soup. The other lady at our table asked me if that was the soup I used to make at home. I said to her: You crazy!"

"Well, Mom, you've always been somewhat critical. Maybe it wasn't that bad. And I bet you didn't even bother trying it."

"Then why didn't the other two at our table eat it either? One lady is Greek and the other Canadian?"

"You're a bad influence on them, that's why. You must have told them it wasn't good and they believed you."

One thing about Mary, she can always read my mind. Sure I told them the soup was no good. I told them it was awful. I don't care what my daughter thinks. She's not the one eating the food they make here day in and day out, is she?

"What about the other person ... there's four of you at the table, isn't there? There's a man ..."

"Oh, him. He never speaks, except for two words. He ate a few spoonfuls and left the table. Never came back, not even for dessert."

"And what did he say—the two words?"

"He said the same thing he always says."

"I know, Mom. But what is it? What does he say?"

"Stupid words. He says, *Infinite Possibilities.*"

"Mom, they may not be stupid words at all."

"Well, if you know what they mean, you tell me."

"I don't know. But maybe it has something to do with the kind of work he used to do. Maybe he was a scientist who used to do experiments of sorts ... or maybe some book he read with those words in it, words that impressed him."

"Well, they don't impress anybody here."

"Mom, you're in a bad mood today. I should get you to tell me another story, like you did the other day ... that's the only time you're happy. You're a born story teller, did you know that? Anyway, the poor man, he probably had a stroke or something, that's why he can't talk and can't remember."

"I had a stroke and I am not like that."

"Really Mom, sometimes you're impossible. You just had a mini stroke ... and you're in here only because you broke your hip, nothing to do with brain function. You're a bit forgetful, but at your age, what do you expect?"

There, she's getting impatient with me. I hope she doesn't start harping about old people saying too much of what's on their mind. What else should a person say? What's on someone else's mind? Ridiculous!

"Okay, you went to university for seven years, you tell *me* what those words mean, because I'd like to know, since I am the one who's going to have to listen to them until my last day on earth— unless he dies first."

"Five years, not seven, and I didn't go to school to learn everything. And don't be nasty either, Mother. But you know what ... it could mean that possibilities are endless."

"That's not possible, everything ends. And when it ends, possibilities end too."

"If you're referring to dying, you're wrong. And as a Catholic maybe you shouldn't be speaking like that. Think of what you could do in Heaven—and don't give me that dirty look."

And who am I supposed to give dirty looks to? She tells me to be nice to the nurses, the doctor, the therapist—not to mention the cleaning lady. I even have to be nice to that dog they bring here on a leash that I don't know what for. Well, at least I don't have to be nice to the squirrels out at the back, and the cute little chipmunks. They're always running up into the trees when they see me. But that's because I never give them peanuts. And really, I would give them peanuts if someone in the family would bring me some peanuts. But no, they all bring me chocolates. I swear they have a chocolate factory hidden somewhere. Oh, shut your brains up, old lady.

"Well, Mary," I say, sighing, "maybe they'll have a restaurant in heaven, if I ever get there. Then I can be a cook again ... Or maybe St. Peter will have a nice big kitchen waiting, for old people in wheelchairs. Yeah, I can sit and mix dough, fry things on the stove. Make zucchini fritters, battered cauliflower, red peppers that I could put between two nice slices of crusty home made bread ... never mind being careful with my dentures. Some stuffed artichokes, a nice frittata with potatoes, some focaccia with anchovies, some pasta e faggioli ... No polenta though, and no corn bread. I would stick with wheat flour. Only the poor in Italy used to make corn bread ... though it was good dunked in milk for breakfast. Then I would make all kinds of biscotti, especially the ones with the roasted hazelnuts, and the pretzels with white wine. And then, some, some ... some ... never mind. Just never mind."

Mary didn't say anything. She just pushed her hair to one side. Then combed it with her fingers back into place. Bad habit. I used to tell her not to do that when she was a young girl, but the more I told her and the more she did it.

"Well well."

"Well what?"

"Oh, nothing. You just made me hungry, Mom. You did. But can I ask you ... if you could be in their kitchen today, here at the nursing home, what would you cook?"

"I'll tell you what I would cook. I would cook food that has flavour ... food that isn't hidden underneath ridiculous sauces that I have to scrape off with my fork to eat. I would cook the same food I raised you on. Food we were used to. Food your father used to like. Food your husband likes. Food I always cooked for your kids in the summer when you were working and I babysat them — after I retired. Have you forgotten? That kind of food!"

"Oh Mom ... I know it isn't the best in here. That's why I like to take you to our house on weekends as much as I can, so that you can have some good home cooked meals. Of course, they're not the kind of meals you used to make ... not home made ravioli ... not home made lasagna — remember how fine your lasagna noodles used to be ... smooth like silk ..."

She can be sweet when she wants to be, my daughter. She's okay. I must be thankful. I must not be so cantankerous.

"And the tiny meatballs I used to make to put in the lasagna. It used to take hours to make," I say, remembering. "Now they just throw in the ground beef. Like throwing it to the dogs. Lumps. Everything is thrown together these days."

"I know. But life is different now. We don't have the time, the health, whatever, anymore. I am not as strong as you were, Mom."

Yes, I must be nice to my daughter. Must. I don't think I'd want their fast paced life. Everything nowadays is a whirlwind. It's crazy.

"I know, *figlia*. I know. But you make good dinners, too. Lots of nice vegetables. Nice pasta, nice soups. I always eat lots when I come to your place. And it doesn't make me sick eating so much. I come back here and sleep good. Sleep all night without waking up once. My stomach knows good food. I know, even though times have changed, you still make good food. I never thought you'd be making your own bread — by hand."

"Neither did I. But everyone loves my bread, Mom, you should see ... I only make it once in a while now, but come winter I'll make it more often. But I will mix whole wheat flour in with the white. I know you like white bread, but we must think about our health. Cholesterol, all those things."

"Yes, whole wheat is good. You must eat what is best for you. Maybe not as many fried foods. Less salt — I know salt gives flavour. But it isn't good. You know what's best for you and your family."

My daughter, my only daughter, she smiles, a large smile. Then she kisses my cheek.

"And live as long as you, Mom, uh?"

I laugh, something I don't do very often these days.

"And then come to a nursing home to live," I say, "and complain as much as I do?"

"Like mother like daughter," Mary chuckles. "Nothing wrong with that."

She never comes Saturdays, but she's here today. Now she's bugging me about making friends.

"You've never been much for friends. Everything was always family with you. No outside people. You didn't need them because you had all of us — the family. But in here, I think you should try; it would help you pass the time away. You said yourself the days are long. A friend or two would be good for you. It might even take your mind away from ... from not liking the food."

"I suppose you're right," I say. I have to give in sometimes. I can't be miserable all the time.

"And really, the food is not that bad or you wouldn't be looking so good, so healthy. You look better now than when you were at home ... and that's because you're getting regular meals ... and all the nutrition you need ... I know you don't like me to say that, but it's true. So promise me you'll try to make friends with some of the other residents. Some of them are not that bad. Some still have a good mind. "

"Okay, okay, I'll make friends, *basta che ti stai zitta* ... as long as you keep quite, as long as you leave me alone. Anyway, weren't you supposed to go shopping? It's Saturday today."

"I know it's Saturday. But I worry about you — the stores are open 24 hours."

"Well, you don't want to go when it's dark."

"There's still three hours of daylight. But I know you want me to leave, so I'm going."

Meno male. Thank God she's going. She's like her father was. Just like him. Always worrying about something.

I lie on my bed, trying to take a little nap. I always need a little nap after Mary leaves. She tires me out. But this time I can't sleep; I'm too restless. No use wasting time on the bed if I can't close my eyes. So I get up, put my running shoes on and get in my wheelchair. I take the brakes off and wheel myself out to the TV room. There I park myself not far from the man who is always muttering those two silly words. I look at him. *A scientist?* Could my daughter be right. I manoeuvre myself closer to his wheelchair.

He stares.

"Are you a scientist?" I say.

He still stares, the way he always does; nothing different.

No, I guess he's not a scientist. Maybe I'll try something else. He's not a bad looking man. Not as good looking as my husband was, rest his soul; nevertheless he's a handsome old man. Clean looking — they keep him so clean here. They keep everyone clean. At least that they do.

"Do you like pizza?" I say.

"*Infinite possibilities ...*"

"Oh ... well ... I guess you don't like pizza. That settles it. But how about ravioli ... veal parmigiana? Polenta, maybe? No, you look too refined for polenta, for the real Italian polenta, with tomato sauce with sausages, spareribs, the sauce so perfumed the men could smell it from where they were working in the fields ..."

"*Infinite possibilities.*"

"Well, my good man, never mind about that now. Why don't you and me wheel ourselves to the front lobby instead? You know, where the piano is? No, don't get any ideas. I don't play music, nothing like that. But I could tell you stories if you would listen. Why not? If my daughter can listen, so can you. I could tell you stories about the war in Italy — the bombs ... No forget that. I could tell you about coming across the Atlantic and vomiting for eight days ... No, not that either. Well, I'll tell you about when my arm got burned from the pressure fryer ... It wasn't my fault; it was that dumb lady who never listened to what she was told to do. The boss was always telling her to be careful, but do you think she would learn? No. I still have the scar on my arm. I would show it to you if I didn't have these long sleeves. Oh, you could write a book with my stories ... No? You don't think you could? Well then, come on, let's go, let's make a little trip to the lobby, you and me. At least from there we can see the sunshine through the big windows."

I am half way down the hall when I sense he's right behind me. I stop. "Is that you there?" I say.

There is no answer, just a clearing of a man's throat. I know it's him. I have heard that same sound before. I don't know if he made that noise in answer to my question or just because he needed to clear his throat. Most likely because of his throat. It doesn't matter … he's there behind me. Close by. Suddenly, I feel tears in my eyes. I haven't cried since my husband died four years ago. But I don't want the nurses to see me crying … so I lower my head and slowly start to turn the wheels again, past the nurses' station … one wheelchair in front, the other right behind.

Infinite possibilities.

Our Mother's Kitchen

CARLINDA D'ALIMONTE

WHEN WE ENTER our mother's kitchen,
decorated with what is important, stories
of our lives, we know we are coveted.
We know to leave behind all sordid things —
deprecation, beatings, limitations,
violations, divisions — all manner of sin.

In our mother's kitchen she prepares to feed us
with bread and wine, and water.
We sit at the table and watch as she performs
these sacred duties with faith and joy
— each time is a new chance to sustain us.
In our mother's kitchen we eat.

In our mother's kitchen we talk
of small accomplishments,
to the eruption of accolades.
For the moment we believe we are
everything she says.

In our mother's kitchen
we eat more than we should,
as she applauds in a voice, loud
and vehement, our attempts
to ascend to great things,
though she would keep us tethered if she could.

In our mother's kitchen
we understand what she asks of us:
obedience,
good intentions,
the truth (as much as can be borne).
She asserts her condemnation
of crimes, of sins.
> (Our own shameful parts —
> those that need forgiving —
> have been whispered in her ear,
> washed away before we gather for the meal.)

In our mother's kitchen,
we know she is our one true virgin mother:
forever loving, committed, glad to be of service.

Maria's Feast: a Pascal Recipe in Six Stages

Loretta Gatto-White

First
Wrestle God from the Pharisee
Tuck him up into the warmth of your womb
Mystic golden halo of sanguineous glory
Fill it with this yeasty swelling
Raise it, punch it down, then let it rise again

Second
Transubstantiate your king from this leavening
To sit at his right hand
Tremble the legs off Herod's throne
Whisper moist in his waxen ear, "*Immanuel*,"
At Cana show him how to change water into wine
To keep the party going

Third
Suffer his limbs to be tortured
Nailed to a wooden peel
Bake and harden for seven long canonical hours
in the heat of the searing sun of Golgotha

Fourth
Take him down
Rest him in the ethereal blue of your voluminous sail
Remove the smouldering sacred heart,
Bleed its ambition with a crown of thorns
Reserve in a cold chalice

Fifth

Wrap him tightly in seamless linen, fairy spun
Anoint his eyelids with honey
Wash his feet with the milk of human kindness
On the tongue place bitter almonds
Pass your hands lightly over him and
Murmur strange incantations

Sixth

Tear staff of life into interminable pieces
Gather all up into your mantle-sail
Scatter evenly upon the sea of gaping hungry mouths
Carefully gather-up the crumbs
Moisten with holy water
Fashion between two cool palms, a host
staff of life everlasting,
Dip lightly in chalice of blood
Repeat, eternally

Our Contributors

Salvatore Ala (*My Mother's Bread, Snail Recipe*)
Savatore Ala was born in Windsor, Ontario in 1959. He has published
three books of poetry: *Clay of the Maker, Straight Razor* and *Lost Luggage*.

Michelle Alfano (Excerpt from *Made Up of Arias*)
Michelle Alfano is a Co-Editor with *Descant* and co-organizer of the
(Not So) Nice Italian Girls & Friends Reading Series. Her novella
Made Up of Arias (Blaurock Press) won the 2010 Bressani Prize for
Short Fiction. Her short story "Opera" was a finalist for a Journey
Prize anthology. She is featured in the documentary, *Saturnia* on
OMNI-TV in 201, and is currently at work on a new novel entitled
Vita's Prospects.

Licia Canton (*Almond Wine and Fertility*)
Born in Cavarzere (Venezia), Montrealer Licia Canton is the author
of *Almond Wine and Fertility* (2008), short stories for women and
their men. She is also a literary translator and critic, and editor-in-
chief of *Accenti Magazine*. She is (co)editor of five anthologies on
Italian Canadian and multiethnic writing. A member of the Writers'
Union of Canada, she has served on the board of the Quebec Writers'
Federation. She holds a Ph.D. from Université de Montréal.

Domenico Capilongo (*tomatoes, muskoka pasta, al dente, mamma
corleone, feathers*)
Domenico Capilongo is a high school teacher from Toronto, Ontario.
His first poetry collection, *i thought elvis was italian,* was published in

2008. His poetry has appeared in many literary magazines and he was short-listed for the *gritLIT* 2009 Poetry Contest. Quattro Books published his new jazz-inspired collection, *hold the note*, in 2011. Guernica published his short story collection, *Subtitles*, in 2012.

Glenn Carley (*Caravaggio's Light, Lezioni and Leftovers, On Cucina Casalinga and the Mobius Life*)
Glenn Carley is the author of *Polenta at Midnight: Tales of Gusto and Enchantment in North York* (Vehicle Press, 2007). A Chief Social Worker with a school board in the Greater Toronto area, Glenn resides in Bolton, Ontario, with his wife and their two children. He recently completed a second novel.

Anna Foschi Ciampolini (*The Tortellini Connection*)
Anna was born in Florence and now lives in Vancouver. An award-winning short story writer, journalist and translator, she co-edited the anthologies *Emigrante* (1985), *Writers in Transition* (1990) and *Strange Peregrinations: Italian Canadian Literary Landscapes* (2007). Her writing has been published in anthologies and literary magazines in Canada, Italy and Costa Rica. She is cofounder of the Association of Italian Canadian Writers and the F.G. Bressani Literary Prize.

Elizabeth Cinello (*Food Companion Wanted*)
Elizabeth Cinello lives in Toronto, Canada. She writes, performs, and produces multidisciplinary events. Her writing projects include short stories, video documentaries, and travel articles. She is a co-founder of Art Starts, an organization committed to arts-based community development.

Dosolina Cotroneo (*The Birth and Rebirth of Biscotti*)
Dosolina Cotroneo was born and raised in Ottawa's Little Italy. The youngest daughter of first-generation Italian immigrants, Cotroneo's passion for writing was evident from a young age. After compiling many short stories based on her large, close-knit Italian family, Cotroneo approached her local newspaper and was soon to become a widely-read weekly columnist, reporter, and photographer. Cotroneo's love of family, traditions, and fine Italian leathers, tend

to be at the centre of her column writing. She is the author of *The Secret Diary of an Italian Girl*.

Carlinda D'Alimonte (*The Kitchen Table, Our Mother's Kitchen*)
Carlinda D'Alimonte (B.A., B.Ed., M.A., OCT) has authored two books of poetry published by Black Moss Press — *Now That We Know Who We Are* (2004), and *Other Living Things* (2009). Her works have appeared in several anthologies and literary magazines. She teaches English and Creative Writing at an arts-based high school in Windsor, Ontario where she is Department Head of English. She regularly organizes readings and clinics given by visiting writers and has co-authored several online English courses for the Ontario Ministry of Education. She holds both Canadian and Italian citizenship and lives in Tecumseh, Ontario.

Marisa De Franceschi (*Plump Eggplant, International Cuisine*)
Marisa De Franceschi is the author of *Surface Tension* (Guernica, 1994), the short story collection *Family Matters* (Guernica, 2001) and editor of the anthology *Pillars of Lace* (Guernica, 1998). Her short stories, articles and book reviews have appeared in a variety of publications including, *Canadian Author & Bookman, Pure Fiction* and *Accenti Magazine. Random Thoughts,* a collection of poetry and prose sketches, was recently published by Longbridge Books, Montreal.

Giulia De Gasperi (*From Tomatoes to Potatoes:* La Bella Marca *on Cape Breton Island*)
Giulia De Gasperi is a post-doctoral fellow in Ethnology at the University of Edinburgh. For the past two years she has conducted fieldwork among members of the Italian-Canadian community of Dominion, in Cape Breton Island. She also researches traditions and customs of Venetian farming life. She has presented her research at academic conferences and has published articles and essays in magazines and journals both in North America and Europe.

Alberto Mario DeLogu (*Once Upon a Time in Italy's Fine Cuisine*)
Alberto Mario De Logu was born in 1961 in Sardinia, but for twenty years he has been dividing his time between Europe and North

America. Currently he lives in Montreal, Canada, where he is an international broker. He has written several papers and technical and scientific articles and in 1993 he was co-author of *The World Cashew Economy.* He was one of the founders of the Compagnia of Teatro Stabile "La Botte e il Cilindro." He acted for the "Pirandello Theatre Society" of Toronto. He was editor of the magazine *Trentagiorni.com* and he contributes *to Italia a Tavola, AboutFood.com, Altravoce.net, Accenti* and others. He is a member of the Editorial Board of the Italian-Canadian Writers Association. He has just published *Sardignolo*, a new book of poetry all Sardinians living abroad should find interesting and should consider a must-read.

Anna Pia DeLuca (*Polenta* and *Frico*)
Anna Pia DeLuca received degrees from the University of Toronto and Trieste and now teaches English language and literature at the University of Udine where she is Director of the Centre for Canadian Culture and Director of the Centro Linguistico e Audiovisivi. Her main fields of interest include contemporary Canadian migrant literature and in particular Italian-Canadian female writing. Her recent publications include the volumes, *Itinerranze e Transcodificazioni: Scrittori migranti dal Friuli Venezia Giulia al Canada* (co-editor Ferraro, Forum 2008) and *Investigating Canadian Identities* (editor, Forum 2010).

Delia De Santis (*Pizza and KFC, Our Love Affair, A Special Day*)
Delia De Santis' short stories have appeared in literary magazines in Canada, United States, England, and Italy, and in several antholo-gies. She is co-editor of the anthologies *Sweet Lemons* (Legas, 2004), *Writing Beyond History* (Cusmano, 2006), *Strange Peregrinations* (The Frank Iacobucci Centre for Italian Canadian Studies, 2007), and *Sweet Lemons 2* (Legas, 2010). She is the author of the collection *Fast Forward and Other Stories* (Longbridge Books, 2008).

Bruna Di Giuseppe-Bertoni (*Olivo Secolare/Old Olive Tree*)
Bruna Di Giuseppe-Bertoni was born in Italy and immigrated with her family to Canada in 1964. Her passions are painting and writing and she has won a number of literary awards for her poetry. She has published in Italian, the poetry collection *Sentieri D'Italia.* Her writing

appears in a number of anthologies, including *Writing Beyond History, Reflections on Culture,* and *Sweet Lemons 2.*

Mary di Michele (*Life is Theatre, A Bouquet of Rapini*)
Mary di Michele was born in 1949 in Lanciano, Italy. In 1955 she and her family emigrated to Canada. In 1972 she received her B.A. in English Literature from the University of Toronto and, in 1974, she received her Master's in English and creative writing from the University of Windsor. She has done freelance writing work for *Toronto Life, Poetry Toronto* and the *Toronto Star,* and is the author of a number of published works, including two novels and many books of poetry. She has won a number of awards for her work, and currently teaches creative writing at Concordia University in Montreal.

Sonia Di Placido (*Zuppolone*)
Sonia Di Placido is a poet, writer, performer and artist currently enrolled in the Creative Writing Optional Residency MFA Program with the University of British Columbia. She graduated from the Ryerson University Theatre School in 1996. In 2000, Sonia began to focus on publicity and promotions in the publishing industry while engaging in poetry and completing an Honours BA Humanities, York University, 2006. She is a member of the Association of Italian Canadian Writers. Sonia has published creative non-fiction and poetry in literary journals and various anthologies. Her first book of poetry, *Exaltation in Cadmium Red*, was published in 2012 by Guernica Editions.

Loretta Di Vita (*An Extra Helping, Coffee Envy*)
Loretta Di Vita (B.F.A., M.A.) runs Decorum Consultation Incorporated, a consulting service established in 2000, helping individuals and corporate groups reinforce the ideals of civility in their personal and professional lives. Based in Montreal, Loretta enjoys a happily dynamic life with husband, Antonio. Besides her beloved family and friends, some of her favourite must-haves are abstract art; mid-century furniture; jumbo cocktail rings; Woody Allen films; *Mad Men*; Dostoevsky novels; and unfussy homemade Italian food. Her musings on etiquette, fashion, art and lifestyle have

appeared in *Accenti* (first-prize winner of 2010 writing contest), *Cucina Etc*, *Montreal Gazette*, *Panoramitalia*.

Caterina Edwards (*Arrangiarsi or Zucchini Blossom Blues*)
Caterina has published a novel, a book of novellas, a collection of short stories, a play, and a memoir, *Finding Rosa*. She has also co-edited two books of life writing, twice been a writer-in-residence, and written a radio drama. She cooks, usually Italian, every night; her pasta dishes are good, her soups superb.

Joseph Anthony Farina (*A Tavola, A Colour Called Family*)
Joseph Anthony Farina practices law in Sarnia, Ontario. Born in Sicily, he immigrated to Canada with his family in 1950. He has been published in many poetry journals in Canada, the United States and Europe. He is the author of two books of poetry, *The Cancer Chronicles* and *Ghosts of Water Street* (Serengeti Press, Ontario).

Venera Fazio (*A Passion for Fravioli, My Mother's Tomato Sauce*)
Venera Fazio is co-editor of the anthologies *Sweet Lemons: Writings with a Sicilian Accent* (2004), *Writing Beyond History* (2006), *Strange Peregrinations: Italian Canadian Literary Landscapes* (2007), *Reflections on Culture: An Anthology of Creative and Critical Writing* (2010), and *Sweet Lemons 2: International Writings with a Sicilian Accent* (2010). Her poetry and prose have appeared in literary magazines in Canada, the United Sates and Italy.

Loretta Gatto-White (*Taking Back the Meatball, Giant Rabbits and the Best Way to Barbeque, Maria's Feast, The Food of Love in All Seasons, Pasta is Magic, Where the Lemon Trees Bloom, Zucchini and the Contadini: an apocryphal tale?*)
Loretta Gatto-White holds an Honors B.A. in Visual Arts (U.W.O.) and a Bachelor of Education (U. of T.). She was a food columnist for four years, winning second place for Best Specialty Column in the 2010 Atlantic Community Newspaper Awards. Loretta is now a freelance journalist whose work appears in Panoram Italia and Accenti magazine and online in her food journal, at www.saveurfaire.

net. Her writing has been short-listed by the Ottawa Valley Writers' Guild for the Turner Award for non-fiction and her essays and poetry have appeared in the anthologies *Sweet Lemons 2: International Writings with a Sicilian Accent, Behind Barbed Wire* and in *Christmas Chaos*.

Genni Gunn (*Crostoli, Intrigoni, Bugie*)
Genni Gunn's nine books include three novels: *Solitaria* (long-listed for the Giller Prize), *Tracing Iris* and *Thrice Upon a Time*; two story collections: *Hungers* and *On the Road*; two poetry collections: *Faceless* and *Mating in Captivity*; and two poetry collections by Dacia Maraini in translation *Devour Me Too*, and *Travelling in the Gait of a Fox*. Her opera *Alternate Visions* (music by John Oliver) was produced in Montreal in 2007. Her works have been translated into several languages, and have been finalists for the Commonwealth Prize, the Gerald Lampert Poetry Award, the John Glassco Translation award, and the Premio Internazionale Diego Valeri for Translation. She lives in Vancouver.

Maria Luisa Ierfino-Adornato (*Mammola's Slow Food, I Remember My Days*)
Maria Luisa Ierfino-Adornato, author of *High Spirits*, has enjoyed creative writing since the age of sixteen. A professional Montrealer, she appreciates the fine arts, noetic sciences, travel and gourmet cooking. She is the proud mother of Aviva, her Muse, and devoted wife to architect Nick Adornato. Maria holds a Master of Arts degree in English Literature as well as an Executive MBA. Her MA thesis focused on the scatological dimension in the poetry of Irving Layton. It was published when her daughter was born, and the poet praised her "for producing two masterpieces in the same year." Maria recently published an historical novel, *McCord's Quiet Rebellion*, with Chronicler Publishing.

Angela Long (*This is Sunday Lunch*)
Angela Long is an award-winning writer whose work has appeared in numerous Canadian and international publications including *The Globe and Mail, Utne Reader* and *Poetry Ireland Review. Libros Libertad*

released her first collection of poems, *Observations from Off the Grid*, in 2010. She lives with her Sicilian husband and tortoiseshell cat in a log cabin on Haida Gwaii, British Columbia.

Marco Lo Verso (*Arancine*)
Marco LoVerso was born in Sicily and grew up in California, two places that taught him the value of fresh produce and lots of sunshine. He has lived most of his adult life in Edmonton, Alberta, a winter city for six months out of the year, which has taught him the value of greenhouses and a sense of humour. He bakes bread twice a week, makes a decent pizza from time to time, and has a hard time keeping his wine cooler full.

Darlene Madott (*Fever Food, Cicoria, Making Olives and Other Family Secrets, excerpt*)
Darlene Madott is a Toronto lawyer and writer. Prior to law, she worked at *Saturday Night* and *Toronto Life* magazines. Her published works include: *Bottled Roses* (Oberon, 1985); film script, *Mazilli's Shoes* (Guernica, 1997); *Joy, Joy, Why Do I Sing?* (Women's Press/ Scholar's Press, 2004). Included in that collection was "Vivi's Florentine Scarf," which won the 2002 Paolucci Prize of the Italian American Writers' Association. The title story of *Making Olives and Other Family Secrets,* (Longbridge Books, spring, 2008) won the Bressani Literary Award, 2008. She has been widely anthologized, most recently in *Sweet Lemons 2*, (Legas, 2010). Forthcoming: *Stations of the Heart*, a collection of linked short-stories, about the journey, rather than destinations! A mother of one son, she continues to write and practice, primarily in the area of matrimonial law.

Carmelo Militano (*The Creation of a New Grape*)
Carmelo Militano holds a B.A.Honours in English Literature from the University of Manitoba, a Master's degree in History and Political Studies from the University of Winnipeg and a Certificate in Education from the University of Manitoba. Carmelo has also done graduate work at Oxford University (Exeter College), U.K., and the Italian University for Foreigners, Perugia, Italy. He has worked as a freelance journalist and broadcaster for CBC Radio. In 2002 he

won the San Bernardo Literary Prize (Italy) for poetry from Italian authors abroad. His poetry collection *Ariadne's Thread* won the F.G. Bressani Award for poetry in 2004. Selected publications: *Ariadne's Thread* (Olive Press, 2004), *The Minotaur's Keys* (Olive Press, 2005), and *Special People in a Special Place* (H.J.M. Press, 1990), editor. He is currently working on his third collection of poems and a family memoir. Carmelo Militano works as a high school English and History teacher. He lives in Winnipeg with his family.

Caroline Morgan Di Giovanni (*Learning to Cook with Dante and My Suocera*)
Caroline Morgan Di Giovanni grew up in suburban Philadelphia. She came to Toronto in 1966 to attend St. Michael's College in the University of Toronto where she currently resides, serving as a school board trustee, then a municipal councillor, and a community volunteer. A writer, editor, and occasional speaker on Italian Canadian writing, she edited two volumes of the anthology *Italian Canadian Voices*, first in 1984, and a revised version in 2006: *Italian Canadian Voices: A Literary Anthology, 1946-2004* (Mosaic Press, 2004). Extensive travel in Italy and the works of art found everywhere in that country inspired the poems in her first book, *Looking at Renaissance Paintings and Other Poems* (Quattro Books: 2008). Born in 1947, Caroline Morgan Di Giovanni is an authentic "baby boomer" who chose to live in Canada and contribute wholeheartedly to the cultural life of this wonderful country.

Emma Pivato (*The Pro-turkey Resistance Movement: Part Two*)
Emma Pivato has worked as a psychologist in the Edmonton Public School Board, the Toronto Separate School Board, Alberta Hospital, Edmonton and Catholic Social Services, Edmonton, as well as in private practice. She has worked as an advocate for people with severe disabilities and as a result published the book, *Different Hopes, Different Dreams* (1984 & 1990). Since 2004 she has been teaching graduate-level psychology courses part-time in MA-IS program at Athabasca University. She recently completed a novel which is being considered for publication. She was born Emma Wyoma Hatchard in Elk Point, Alberta and earned a Ph.D. from the University of Alberta.

Joseph Pivato (*Turkey War: part one*)
Joseph Pivato, professor of Literary Studies at Athabasca University (Edmonton), has focused his research and writing on Italian-Canadian writing. His publications include: *Contrasts: Comparative Essays on Italian-Canadian Writing* (1985 & 1991), *Echo: Essays on Other Literatures* (1994 & 2003), *The Anthology of Italian-Canadian Writing* (Guernica, 1998), *F.G. Paci: Essays on His Works* (2003), *Caterina Edwards: Essays on Her Works* (2000), *Literatures of Lesser Diffusion* (1990), *Mary di Michele: Essays on Her Works* (2007), *Pier Giorgio Di Cicco: Essays on His Works* (2011), and Africadian Atlantic: Essays on George Elliott Clarke (2012). He was born in Italy, lived in Toronto, and has a Ph.D. from the University of Alberta.

Joseph Ranallo (*Summer and Figs*)
Joseph Ranallo was born in Vinchiaturo, Molise. In 1952, he immigrated to British Columbia, Canada. He has earned a BA (Honor's English) from the University of Victoria and an MA (English) from Washington State University. He has taught and has been an administrator at the elementary, secondary, college and university levels. His work has been published in Canada, the US, Italy, and China. In 2001, he was licensed as acupuncturist in BC. Currently, he is working on a novel.

Laura Sanchini (*Pizze Fittte e Baccalà: A Narrative of Christmas Foods Past and Present*)
Laura Sanchini is a Ph.D. candidate in folklore at Memorial University of Newfoundland. Her research interests include Italian Canadian identity, foodways, and folk art. A Montreal native, she moved to St. John's in 2007 for graduate school and fell in love with the city's distinct flair. She has published works in *Ethnologies* and *Material Culture Review*, and is the current French Editor for the journal *Culture & Tradition*. She lives in St. John's with her husband Ian and their two spoiled calico cats Tigerlily and Lulu.

Carmine Starnino (*The Wine Press*)
Carmine Starnino was born in Montreal, Quebec. His first poetry collection *The New World* (1997) was nominated for the 1997 A.M.

Klein Prize for Poetry and the 1997 Gerald Lampert Award. His second collection *Credo* (2000) won the 2001 Canadian Authors Associate Prize for Poetry and the 2001 David McKeen Award for Poetry. He has also written *A Lover's Quarrel* (2004), a book of essays on Canadian poetry, and *With English Subtitles* (2004), a third collection of poems. Starnino's fourth collection, *This Way Out* (2009), was nominated for a Governor General's Literary Award in Poetry. He is the editor of Signal Editions, and editor-in-chief of *Maisonneuve*.

Debby Waldman (*My Authentic Italian Cooking Experience: in Edmonton*)
Debby Waldman grew up in a food-obsessed Jewish family in central New York. Two uncles were kosher butchers. Another hunted and built a smokehouse. His smoked turkey spoiled Debby for life. Her grandmother made her own bread, and an aunt was a professional food service manager. Her mother, a fearless, adventurous cook, is a continual inspiration. When Debby isn't cooking, eating, or looking after her husband and two children in Edmonton, she writes. Her articles have been published in *People, Parents, Sports Illustrated and Glamour.* She is the author of three picture books, a juvenile novel, and two parenting books.

Jim Zucchero (*Banana Man, Grocery Stories*)
Jim Zucchero grew up in Toronto. He now lives in London, Ontario with his wife and two children where he works as an academic counsellor at King's University College, UWO. He also teaches courses in writing and Canadian studies there. He has published creative non-fiction and essays on the Canadian National War Memorial and Italian-Canadian writers. In 2010 he co-edited *Reflections on Culture* (with Licia Canton and Venera Fazio). He spends his spare time walking Caesar the dog, cooking Italian dishes, and playing loud music in garage bands with his friends.

About The Book

Food is much like a John Coltrane or Eric Dolphy free jazz piece that goes "out there" over generations and then returns to a few bars of recognizable themes to punctuate, bring the listener back to ground and rest-on-the-familiar before going off into the stratosphere again. The evolution of Italian food in Canada is like that to an enchanted foreign palate. So much of my experience of South-Central (second wave, ancient order) Italian-Canadian life is rhythmic and cyclical; but speaking more celestially, *filled with mobius motion* ... the invisible twistings and turnings of fertility; of gender complementarities and rigidity; of evaporation and condensation; of a sun rising triumphantly then setting in soft indigo light; of one ancient man and one ancient woman's myriad *sisteme* in the garden ... Food then, becomes, in the spontaneous "free" compositions of life, the melodic reference point, the diatonic reliever of chordal tensions, the quiet magnificent within the cacophony and greater magnificences of a living opera that is unique to each Italian-Canadian family. — Glenn Carley on *Cucina Casalinga and the Mobius Life*

If literature can be delicious take a taste from this smorgasbord of treats, words and food, that will entice you to the entire feast. But be prepared, *Italian Canadians At Table* is not the literary equivalent of fast food grabbed at the drive-though, pulled into the car and gobbled behind the wheel. The reader of this fare needs to sit and leisurely enjoy. It is food for the mind, full of simple, essential philosophical, spiritual, historical and social truths. It is serious writing about real food but it will often make you quietly laugh the way tasty food makes you smile. Read this book to increase your vocabulary, whet your appetite and awaken your creative juices. —Sheldon Currie (author of *The Glace Bay Miners' Museum* and *Down The Coaltown Road*)

Italian Canadians at Table: A Narrative Feast in Five Courses is a love letter to Italian food culture at its most authentic. The poems, stories, and recollections included in *Italian Canadians at Table* are an accurate and elegant portrayal of the distinctive place that food holds for all cultures, but particularly for Italians. Food occupies a unique position as something both universal and culturally specific; we all have to eat, even if we don't go about it in the same way. For Italians, there is a special emphasis on food, on the need to demonstrate generosity, to offer extra servings, to always have something on hand for guests and family alike. For immigrant families, food also serves as an important reminder of the country left behind, as well as the trials of making a home in a new country. Through the generations, the struggles of poverty have turned into the art of simplicity. A family's entire history can be told through a dish cooked from the heart, with an emphasis on local, seasonal, and quality ingredients. These stories capture that language of food, both from outside of Italian culture and from within it, and convey a range of emotions, disparate and nuanced. Anyone who has been jolted back to childhood memories by a whiff of sautéing garlic will find themselves adding their own associations to the contributors', sharing in the special magic of food and memory.

Above all, *Italian Canadians at Table* offers something that is too often forgotten in an age when cookbooks are being replaced by Google searches: heart. The stories and poems selected for the collection, like each recipe selected for a cookbook, have been chosen for their importance to the author, a specific feeling or memory, the most important ingredient in any authentic, home-cooked meal. This collection is sure to be a treat for anyone who has felt the profound connection in passing down a recipe through the family, who has longed to find a place at the table, or even anyone who appreciates the simple perfection of preserving red peppers on an autumn afternoon. —Maria Filice (Author, Food Stylist, Publisher, Food and Fate Publishing)

Credits

Salvatore Ala: "My Mother's Bread" copyright © 2004 by Salvatore Ala. Previously published in *Straight Razor*, Biblioasis, Emeryville, ON, 2004. Used by permission of the author.

Salvatore Ala: "Snail Recipe" copyright © by Green Alley Press, 2011. Used by permission of Green Alley Press.

Michelle Alfano: Excerpt from *Made Up of Arias*. Pages 43-55. Excerpted from *Made Up of Arias* by Michelle Alfano. Copyright © 2008 by Blaurock Press. Reprinted by permission of Blaurock Press. All rights reserved.

Licia Canton: "Almond Wine and Fertility" copyright © 2002 by Licia Canton. Previously published in *Sweet Lemons*, edited by Venera Fazio and Delia De Santis, Legas, New York & Ottawa, 2004, and in *Bibliosofia, Letteratura Canadese e Altre Culture*, 2007, and in *Almond Wine and Fertility*, Longbridge Books, Montreal, 2008. Used by permission of the author.

Domenico Capilongo: "mamma corleone" copyright © 2005 by Domenico Capilongo. Previously published in *Grimm Magazine*, Spring 2005, and in *Sweet Lemons 2: International Writings with a Sicilian Accent*, edited by Venera Fazio and Delia De Santis, Legas, Mineola, New York, 2010, and in *hold the note*, Quattro Books Inc., Toronto, Ontario, 2010. Used by permission of the author.

MIX
Paper from
responsible sources
FSC® C100212

Printed in December 2013
by Gauvin Press,
Gatineau, Québec